JAN TURK PETRIE

TOO MANY HEROES

Printed in the United Kingdom

First Printing, 2019

Pintail Press
Pintailpress.com

Author's website: JanTurkPetrie.com

28TH JUNE 1942

Over the Dutch coast they pick up more flak. At the rear, squeezed into his turret, Frank scans the sky for any night fighters that might be on their tail. The plane reels with every new shockwave. Through the worst of it, he hums that stupid song they sing in the mess hall to the tune of Waltzing Matilda.

Ops in a Wimpey
Ops in a Wimpey

'Shit,' Ferguson says. 'Shit that was too effing close.'

Who'll come on ops in a Wimpey with me? And I sang as the ack-ack –

'We've been hit.' Doc tells them on the intercom, like they hadn't all heard the explosion, felt the splinters running the length of her. At his back, a hard clang on the door seals him in.

They're trailing flames – lit up like a ruddy beacon for a second or two. Doc's trying to sound calm, 'Fire's out but we've lost the starboard engine.' Then, 'Dammit – prop won't feather.'

She slews to the starboard. 'We need to lighten her. You know the drill, ditch all non-essentials.' Frank posts his thermos flask through the gap between the guns. There's nothing else.

She's straightening up. Good old Doc.

'Door's jammed,' Ferguson shouts out from behind. It's no

surprise. 'No good, can't get the damn thing open. 'Fraid you'll have to stay put till we're down, Frankie-boy.'

'Okay, I hear you,' he shouts over his shoulder. He's long since made his peace with the hazards of being tail-end-Charlie.

Shells like starbursts all along the length of the coastline they've left behind, like there's a celebration going on. 'It's getting harder to turn the turret,' he tells them.

'Got a bit of a leak in the hydraulics.' Doc again. 'Just a few pinholes – nothing too serious.'

More reports of damage all over the shop.

Dark expanse of the North Sea directly below.

Even if he could get out, he wouldn't want to ditch now. Last quarter moon must be picking them out nicely.

'Two thousand feet.'

So much quieter with just the port engine.

'Everybody's gone silent back there. Look chaps, there's no need to panic,' Doc's telling them if they'll listen. 'Luck of the devil, no one was hit.'

Matthews isn't having it: 'What about my ruddy thigh?'

Ferguson's laugh. 'Leave it out will ya – I've had worse cuts shavin'.'

'We've still got one engine. Fuel situation's okay for a bit,' Doc tells them. 'Electrics seem to be holding up.'

Frank thinks of Clara, how she'll still be asleep; her long hair spread out over the empty pillow on his side. '*Of course I'm missing you less now it's warmer,*' she said in her last letter. '*In fact, I'm enjoying all the extra space in the bed.*' He can picture the smile that might have been playing on her lips as she wrote the words, her way of telling him not to worry about her.

'Fifteen hundred feet. I can see the coast. We're back in Blighty, lads. Not far to go now.'

He's the last to see the line of white waves breaking against the shore. 'Bale out, for Christ's sake,' Frank shouts at them. 'Go on, piss off out of here you lot while you've still got the chance.'

Doc comes back at him. 'You know the drill, Whitby. Like the musketeers: all for one and one for all.'

'For fuck's sake will you all just get out of here.'

'Hold it together back there, Whitby. We've made it home when it's been worse than this.'

'A thousand feet.'

'Will you look at that. There's a flare path up ahead. They've laid out the red carpet for us. Oh yes, that'll do very bloody nicely.'

'This is goin' to be hairy.' (Smithy now.) 'Brown trousers time, lads.'

She's trying to lurch to the starboard, but Doc keeps bringing her back again. 'Five hundred feet.'

Frank can smell escaped oil.

'Here we go, chaps.'

CHAPTER ONE

Thursday May 15th 1952.

Frank opens his eyes. The space above his head is weighed down in deep, grey silence. Heart racing, he's caught between imaginings and reality, trying to navigate. He can see nothing except for the soft band of light around the edges of the sack he'd fixed across the open window. The night's heat has made his body run with sweat. Eyes adjusting, he begins to make out the bulk of the overhead crossbeam that braces the roof timbers. Perhaps some nightmare woke him but, if so, already he's forgotten. Why this sense – no, this growing conviction – he's facing some kind of threat?

He sits up by increments, alert for any movement within the space around him. The air inside the barn is stifling and tainted with an odd, musty sort of smell. The soft glow from the window tells him it's a clear night, the moon almost full.

Must be really early, the birds aren't even singing. Ah yes, the small hours – how they have a habit of looming large.

Several minutes pass before he shakes his head and tries to dismiss the fear, putting it down to old instincts that, even after ten years, are dying hard. Though he lies down and closes his eyes, his senses remain alert – those old habits again. He needs more rest, or he'll regret it later – they've still got the best part of the flock to finish.

He's adjusting his pillow when there's a sound like someone breathing. There it is again – barely audible and yet there alright.

Frank sits bolt upright, his body readying, a new vigour pumping into his muscles. It's a short reach to grasp the metal-shafted torch on the floor beside the bed.

He's ready to strike but no figure comes lurching at him. He hears only the deep stillness.

Ha – he's just being bloody soft. How could anyone have traced him here? Probably only a mouse, possibly a rat weaving through the remains of the straw on the other side of the wall; he'd noticed the other day those smoothed-out hollows marking a new network of runs. Frank exhales. Yes, that'll be it for sure – nothing unknown, nothing untoward.

A scream rips the still air.

The shock of it jolts his whole body before he has time to register that the sound was not the anguished cry of a person but the shriek of a barn owl – and coming from directly above his head.

He swings the torch beam across the rafters until it picks out the bird's clamped-on talons. The two black eyes in that ghost-like face are trained directly on him.

Outside an eerie call answers.

Blinking against the intrusion of the light, the owl bends to issue a long, accusing hiss. He wonders if the bird is about to swoop down upon him but in the next instant the owl's wings open to launch it into the air; a twist midflight and it glides out through the gap between the sacking and the window frame.

He stumbles across the room to pull aside the curtain and follow the bird's flight. Under the starry lid of the sky, he can see nothing except the outline of the far ridge and a few shards of moonlight on the surface of the dewpond.

Frank's about to turn away when he sees a flicker of light

up in Hathaway's wood. Another, stronger beam winks out through trees some distance away from the first. At this hour, it can only mean one thing.

Sunlight is streaming in through every crack in the barn when he wakes for the second time. Out of bed, his bare foot steps on something soft and damp. He picks it up. It's not a dead mouse, as he'd first thought, but an owl's pellet. He spreads the contents out in his palm and examines the mass of regurgitated hair, feathers and tiny bleached bones – a detailed record of his visitor's recent kills. Feels like some sort of omen.

Dew wets his boots as he goes to draw a kettle of water from the standpipe. The sun hasn't yet burnt off the thin mist clinging to the valley bottom. He may be used to it, but it's still not easy shaving with a tin mug full of water and a tiny mirror nailed to the outside wall. The blade he's using was too cheap and, after only three shaves, it's leaving tramlines across his face. Finishing off, he nicks the skin under his chin and has to hold a finger to the spot to stem the flow of blood.

While Frank waits for the bleeding to stop, he examines his reflection. The hot weather has tanned his skin and bleached the ends of his hair to straw on top. Fine white lines fan out from the creases around his eyes – not exactly laughter lines, more the result of too much squinting into the sun.

He turns his head to check his profile and then back again reassuring himself (though of course he'd deny it if someone was watching) that he's not a bad looking man and, despite being thirty-three years old, still in his prime.

The rays of the sun are already warming his back. He boils up the kettle for his last twist of tea then stirs more hot water into a bowl of oats to make porridge. Once it's thickened, he adds the creamy top from the small jug of milk Ma Jenkins had given him on the QT. It's already a tad sour.

A single shot rings out; birds take to the air in every

direction. Another three shots – each one amplified against the hills. The blunt crack of shotgun fire – definitely not a rifle – is coming from the direction of the Hathaway Estate though the gaming season is some four months away.

It all goes quiet again, but Frank is up on his feet jittery and alert as he finishes his breakfast. The mist has retreated to give him a wider field of vision. Above him, the sky has cleared to unbroken china blue.

The early morning quiet is invaded by the cries of harried sheep. A wet spring delayed the shearing; with this hot, dry spell the fleeces have started to lift at long last. They need to get them shorn while this fine weather holds. Last night's forecast warned of breaking storms.

He walks over towards the farmhouse with its huddle of outbuildings and straight into the din of fretting sheep. This lot have been rounded up by Jenkins and his dogs and brought down into the home field where they're milling and bleating inside a large pen. Some of them look ragged, already beginning to shed the burden of their winter-stained fleeces.

It's hot work; he's soon stripped to the waist to be plagued by swarms of midges. Thanks to his night visitor, Frank's mind remains fogged though he does his best to concentrate on the job in hand.

Sam calls across, 'Aye, Frank,' droplets of sweat already running from his jaw, 'How many you've done so far?'

'Not sure.' He takes a quick breather. 'Ten – eleven tops.'

'Fancy a bit of a bet – see who can manage the most? Course it's hardly fair with you being a southpaw, you can't help being a bit cack-handed.'

More than ten years his junior, Sam's a cocky bugger right enough. The lad runs a hand through his short, fiery hair, his pale eyes full of challenge. 'Go on, Frankie – just for a bit of fun.'

'Aye, okay you're on; as long as you don't leave the poor animals with too many cuts.'

'As if I would.' The lad gives him a toothy grin. 'Anyroad, winner buys the first pint tonight. That alright wi' you?'

From the outset Frank knows he's not going to win this wager. Whenever Sam aims a wry look his way, he tries to stick a smile on his face so he doesn't look like a sore loser.

Around midday they stop for a break, dowsing their heads in cold water before they flop down in the shade of the old elm and wait for their bait.

Ma Jenkins soon waddles out with a basket of bread and some decent looking cheese along with a jar of her notorious pickle. In the old days there would have been a flagon of cider to wash that lot down but all they get now is a flask of stewed, not-very-sweet tea. A musty, cabbage smell hits Frank's nose as he opens the pickle and, after another confirming sniff, he gives it a miss.

The peace of their meal is fractured by another volley of shots. The lad touches his arm. 'No need to jump like that, Frankie,' he says. 'That'll only be old Kirkwood taking pot-shots.'

'I saw lights up in the wood last night,' Frank tells him, trying to still the tremors in his hands. 'Them lampers need to watch their step,' he says, 'someone could get hurt with that trigger-happy old bugger out and about.'

'I wonder why they bother. He's already caged up the hens.' Sam takes a last swig of tea then wipes his mouth with the back of his hand. 'What's the name of that magistrate – bloke who's great mates with Lord Hathaway?'

'Ah – you mean Sir William Frith-Hatton.'

'That's the one. I hear he's got a bee in his bonnet about poachers. Can't be worth the risk of getting had up by him – not for a brace or two of old cocks.'

Smirking, Frank gets to his feet. 'They say an old cock can be a powerful attraction to some.'

The lad's laugh is unbridled. 'Dare say you'd know more about that than I would.'

By mid-afternoon, they've moved on to the Oxford Downs – strong, barrel-shaped animals that are easily the heaviest sheep on the farm. Sid Jenkins is gradually replacing these larger breeds with the hardier Swalesdales that are smaller and easier to manhandle. It's a shame to see only these couple of dozen Oxfords left and a disappointing lot of lambs beside them.

Frank wrestles the first of the big ewes down until its backside is on the board. The wool is tight and hard to grab onto with his hands already slick from the grease that waterproofs their fleeces. Trapped outside the hurdles, her distraught twins cry out their shared anxiety, making a racket not dissimilar to tearful human babies.

Once his shearing clippers begin to work a pathway down the centre of her chest, the ewe stops struggling and goes limp against his legs. His right hand makes sure her skin is taut as he works his way round, taking care to keep the whole fleece intact.

All done he releases the dazed animal and she scrambles back to her feet. He picks up the heavy fleece, tucks the ragged edges under and rolls the whole thing up into a neat bundle, which he places on the ground alongside all the others. Without looking, he knows Sam's line will be longer.

It's much easier to catch the next ewe and Frank's thankful this one's more docile. As he works, just like a tongue keeps going back to that mouth ulcer, his mind keeps running over the fear that overcame him in the night. Perhaps all his fretting over a damn bird boils down to the superstition sown in his mind by that Yank Staff Sergeant – chap by the name of Todd Walters.

A deep rumble had drawn everyone's attention up into the clouds to watch what he soon identified as an AAF Flying Fortress coming straight towards the base and trailing black smoke. She almost overshot the runway, coming to a grinding stop only yards short of where the ground fell away into a deep gulley – known by everyone on the base as Shitter's Ditch.

He was amongst the crowd running across the airfield. Her ten-man crew emerged pretty damn fast. Lucky bastards were shaken to bits but otherwise okay. Even after they'd been given fags and tea with a drop of something stronger, they kept trembling and checking – literally pinching themselves – to be sure they weren't already dead and dreaming this part. They'd been on their way from Prestwick to East Anglia when the one of the engines caught fire. Seemed like none of them could get over the fact they were back on solid ground in the middle of the Lincolnshire countryside.

It took the best part of a week to get the new engine in-stalled and their kite all patched up and ready to fly off. For the duration of his stay, Todd Walters had bunked in the empty one above Frank. Todd was built like a jockey – ideal for a ball gunner. He hadn't yet seen enemy action.

One night they'd both been lying there awake chatting as they listened to the tawny owls calling in the oak tree opposite and Todd told him how the Apaches reckoned that if you dream of an owl it's a sure sign that death is on its way. Didn't seem to know if that meant your own death or someone else's. Must have been sometime in May '42 – months before his own crash-landing. Shame he couldn't have been more specific.

After that, Frank willed himself never to dwell on those damn hooting owls when he was drifting off. Back then su-perstition ruled the roost. You kept to the exact same routine before and after every op; repeated all the little rituals to ensure your luck held. They all did it – all of them believing or pretending to, that such things could make a difference.

It's gone eight o'clock when the two of them set off for the pub. Frank can feel the ache of the day's labour in every muscle especially his shoulders and arms. The sun's now dropped behind red streaks of clouds just above the horizon; its warmth continues to radiate from every surface.

Sam nods towards the sky. 'Shepherd's delight, eh?'

'Aye, with a bit of luck, it'll be another fine one tomorrow and we can get it all done.'

It's a good twenty minutes' walk. The most direct route takes them through the Hathaway Estate where they detour off the main track; scrambling over the ridge and flushing up a pair of squawking cock pheasants before they rejoin the footpath.

A short distance on, they enter a clearing overlooking open pasture. The barbed wire fence running between the two is hung down with a row of small corpses all impaled by the neck. The stench of decomposition catches in Frank's throat.

It's easy to identify the flyblown remains of assorted buzzards, magpies, jays and even a few stoats.

Sam shakes his head, 'For the life of me, I don't understand why they go in for all this malarkey.'

'Some reckon seeing these dead'uns hanging up deters the others from raiding nests.' Frank averts his gaze, keeps on walking, not wanting to acknowledge the degrading fate of these animals.

'D'you think it really does put the other birds off?'

'Why would a small creature learn from such a thing when we humans never seem to?'

Not content with shooting, he's seen how Kirkwood, the keeper, likes to lay gin traps on the top of perching posts to crush the legs of any hapless bird of prey that lands on them. Franks shakes his head. 'Reckon it's more a case of that idle gamekeeper wanting to show off how busy he's been protecting his lordship's precious birds.' The practice is meant to be illegal these days but he doubts the local coppers would be willing to pursue the matter with the high and mighty Lord Hathaway. Each time he come across one of the wretched things – usually with the feathers of its previous victims still stuck to its metal teeth – Frank yanks the chain from its tether and buries it under a rock to be sure nothing will dig it up.

The sun is beginning to set as they reach the Saracen's Head. What with the fine weather and the place being so packed, customers have spilled out into the road and the dwindling daylight. Just as they arrive, the streetlight above the crowd winks twice then floods the drinkers in its amber glow.

Sam decides to stay outside in the cooler air while Frank steps into a concentration of heat and smoke. Someone is plonking out a sentimental tune on the piano. He makes his way towards the bar, taking care not to acknowledge the piqued interest of three young women standing just inside the door.

Halfway to the counter, a dart player's elbow comes back to jab him sharp in the chest. The chap barely glances round; his apology is more perfunctory than it ought to be. In the past Frank might have pointed this out but these days he prefers to keep his head down and avoid a scrap if he can. Rubbing at the sore spot, he ploughs on, his mouth already tasting the relief of that sweet bitter.

Frank emerges from the pub balancing two brimming pints. He's looking around for Sam when one of the young girls – a bottle-blonde in a blouse that's fighting to contain her ample breasts – deliberately knocks his arm.

His curse is not quite under his breath. He looks past the distraction of the girl's flushed cleavage to the lines of precious liquid now staining his trouser leg. The level in both glasses has dropped by more than an inch.

'Oh dear, I'm ever so sorry about that.' Her pouting mouth is unnaturally red. She steps closer to him, smelling of rose-sweetened sweat. 'Hope I haven't gone and ruined them trousers of yours.'

Was there a note of sarcasm in that? He'd washed up a bit before they'd left and put on a cleaner shirt, but his trousers are in dire need of a good scrubbing.

'Forget it,' he tells her. Up this close, all that makeup and sprayed hair can't disguise the fact that this little trio are younger than they appear to be.

The blonde leans in. (He gives the girl full marks for perseverance.) 'My parents are out tonight so, if you want, you could come back to our house for a nightcap.'

Her friends are giggling behind their hands. Undeterred, the blonde girl runs her tongue around the inside of her top lip in a way he imagines her practicing in front of a mirror. 'You could take 'em off and I could give 'em a quick seeing to.' To the guffaws of her mates she adds, 'A good wash, that is. They'd dry in two ticks in all this heat. It'd be no trouble, would it Marcy?'

Unable to contain her sniggering, her fatter, prettier friend can only nod.

Frank wonders if this is a dare. 'No thanks.' His smile is brisk. 'Ta all the same.' He moves away toward the edge of the crowd as their laughter explodes, concentrating only on steadying the beer glasses.

Sam walks out of the shadows, drops his glowing fag butt and grinds it under his boot. He hands over the boy's beer, their wager settled. 'Ta very much. Cheers!' Sam clinks his glass against his. Under the lamplight, Frank can see how the sunshine's caused the freckles on the boy's face to merge into larger rafts that might soon join up.

'I'd hardly call that a full pint, but I'll let you off.' Sam takes a long swig. 'Ah – the sweet taste of victory.'

He allows him that one, concentrates instead on those first long mouthfuls.

'Looked like you were in there with one of those three.' The lad wipes his wet chin with the back of his hand. 'Don't look now, but they're still eyeing us up. What say we saunter over in a minute or two for a bit of a chat and that?'

'You've got to be ruddy joking. Best you leave those young lasses well alone; that's if you want to stay out of trouble. I doubt any one of them is older than fifteen.'

'I'll grant they're way too young for *you*, Frankie.' Sam adjusts his stance, pulls his skinny frame upright to look past him towards the girls. 'I wouldn't mind having a shot at that little redhead. She's smiling this way – seems pretty friendly to me.'

'Then you go right ahead, son.' Raising his beer, he gestures the lad away. 'You'd best get on over there. But mind you don't come running to me afterwards – that's all I'm saying on the matter.'

Feeling more annoyed than he should, Frank walks away. The three girls turn their heads as he strolls on past them. On his way to the bar, he checks the change from his pocket and finds only a couple of sixpenny bits and three pennies.

He's thankful the piano player's moved on to a more upbeat number about baking a cake. With drunken gusto, various voices join in with the chorus. They sing out all around him, eyes shining with affability as they repeat the same stupid words to one another.

Norman Kirkwood is sitting on one of the barstools, his elbow resting on the copper counter. He's encountered the gamekeeper on Hathaway land several times when he's been on the legal footpath and dodged round him many more times when he's been trespassing off it. Kirkwood looks older without that cap; his short, greying hair oiled into its proper place. Despite the heat, the man's wearing a tweed jacket; his face more flushed than usual. Looking down at the keeper's arm, he half expects to see that broken shotgun lying across it. He catches his appraising stare and this forces Frank to mutter: 'Evening, Norman.'

The keeper's confused for a moment; it's obvious he can't quite place him. Along with a slight tip of his head, he returns a toneless 'Evening' in Frank's
general direction.

'So now – what can I get you, sir?' Frank turns towards the speaker. He's not seen this young barman in here before.

'Pint of Linley's bitter and a packet of crisps, if you please.' He's careful not to count out his money; instead he slaps it down on the counter like he's getting rid of a bit of spare change. 'Oh, and you can drop the *sir* – I've not been knighted, lad.'

As this is to be his last pint, he intends to savour the full taste of the ale. It might be a ha'penny dearer than some of the pubs in the centre of town but the beer is always well kept.

'Seems you're not a member of the aristocracy then,' Kirkwood says. 'Now there's a surprise; if you hadn't said, I'd have taken you for a proper toff in all that finery of yours.' The keeper looks around hoping to share the joke.

Frank's free hand curls into a fist. Moving closer, he stares the man straight in the eye and, without a word, laughs right in his face.

Kirkwood's expression doesn't give an inch. 'Don't think I don't know who you are. You've been staying on the Jenkins' farm. I've spotted you mooching about in my woods where you've no right to be. Just this morning I found a whole lot of pheasant feathers under the ashes up on Windy Ridge. Poaching's a serious offence round here and we know how to deal with it. I've more than a mind to have a word with Sergeant Roberts about you.'

At first Frank's mirth is forced but then the funny side of the situation becomes so apparent his eyes moisten with genuine amusement. 'Ah, Norman, don't you sometimes think to yourself of an evening how it's a poor sort of an occupation for a grown man – killing free birds and little animals that are only following their nature and all of it just so a bunch of rich fools can take potshots at the pheasants and partridges you've gone and fattened so much the buggers can't take off without being frightened half to death?'

'Oh aye!' Kirkwood rises from his stool so abruptly it falls back with a loud crash.

The noise silences the voices around them in one beat. 'And

what the hell makes you so flamin' superior, boyo?' Kirkwood thrusts his forehead close to Frank's eyes. 'Look at you – a bloody down-and-out standing there smelling like a rancid fox without so much as a pot to piss in.'

Frank's about to take a good swing at the keeper's jaw when a hand grabs his upper arm. Before he can shake it free, his other elbow is pinned back slopping his bitter in every direction.

With no one singing, the pianist stops playing. Vic, the landlord, appears in front of them, two still-to-be-thrown darts clenched in his meaty right hand. 'Now then, gentlemen – I'll have none of that behaviour; not in my pub. Understand?' He aims the twin points at each of them in turn before settling on Frank: 'Best you get off home and cool off a bit. And don't come back here till you're ready to behave in a civilised way.'

'Civilised, eh?' The keeper's crowing now: 'I'm not sure this young commie knows what that means. Look at him – the man's not fit for shagging shit.'

The landlord's face boils. 'Let me remind you there are ladies present, Norman.' He bends into the man. 'Watch your language, d'you hear me, or you'll be following him out of that door.'

The big man looks from one to the other before he nods for the two holding Frank's arms to release him. 'Off you go now, sunshine.'

With no choice but to oblige, Frank downs what's left of the beer he's clung to and slams the empty glass down on the nearest table. He adjusts his shirt and picks up his crisps, careful to take his time as he walks through the murmurs of the parting crowd.

CHAPTER TWO

Without a word to the lad, Frank strides away into the gathering darkness. He's thankful it's still light enough to see his way through the woods without using his torch. All around him the night air is redolent with wild garlic – the smell strongest where it's been crushed underfoot.

He's damned if he's going to stick to the path. Reaching the top of the ridge he lingers amongst the beech trees looking for lights but there are none. Once he's out of the woods it's an easy downhill tramp. The liquid song of a nightingale does nothing to soothe his mind; as he nears the farmyard his fury hasn't begun to subside.

Back in his bunk, anger won't let him rest. He keeps changing position unable to settle things into a shape that offers him any kind of comfort. He's forgotten to pull the makeshift curtain across the open window and so a sliver of moonlight is illuminating the wall beside his head like a spotlight.

Frank's mind keeps running back over that threat. He'd only wanted to be left alone to enjoy a couple of pints at the end of a hard, working day. The sheer injustice of being ordered out makes him want to go back and tear the damned pub apart. Kirkwood and his master are well in with the law; a quiet word in the sergeant's ear would be the spark that could light a fire.

From a long way off he hears a dog's incessant barking.

Nearer, a worried lamb voices its concern in plaintive cries before it stops abruptly.

Frank's sigh is long and drawn out. Looked at another way, perhaps this evening's been the spur he needed to move on. Though the fresh air and honest work suits him well enough, it's not like he's living in the lap of luxury. In any event, he'll need to find better shelter come the colder weather. Why not push off now? There's nothing much keeping him here but familiarity; maybe it's high time he let that go. In the next breath, he changes his mind again. Won't he be giving in? He's done nothing wrong. The last thing he wants to give that bloody keeper is the satisfaction of thinking he's run him out of the village.

Frank's finally beginning to drift off, when a shriek rouses him back to full consciousness – that ruddy barn owl seems determined to disturb his sleep. Judging by the volume, the bird is perching right outside. He should get up and shut the window to stop it flying another recce in here; he certainly doesn't want to be dumped upon from a height – not twice in one night. But then a welcome breeze steals in bringing with it the earthy resonance of sun-hardened fields.

Turning onto his side, he tries to settle his body at least. Outside the owl calls twice more and it reminds him of old Bart Cockle and what he used to say about owls. Frank can picture as clear as day the old man's bent frame and weath-er-hardened features; the way he was forever pulling at that sparse white beard. On a fine evening, the old bugger liked to sit on a wooden seat outside his cottage in Cove Road smoking a skinny roll-up. Bart had many a tall story and old sayings he was willing to share if the kids pestered him for long enough. They'd sit themselves down in a disorderly circle at his feet and listen to his tales with serious faces – only to laugh like drains behind his back. More than once Bart had claimed, in all seriousness, that if you kept walking round and round a tree beneath where an owl is perched, the bird will continue to follow your every move with its eyes until, by and by, it wrings its own neck.

Poor old Bart, along with all his damned silly ideas, he must be long dead by now. Frank's sigh turns into a yawn. All that had been another lifetime ago. At sixteen, he'd matriculated near the top of his class but, with nothing left to keep him in Yorkshire, he'd moved south looking for work. When the war started, he'd been a general hand on Pascoe's farm for a few years. Though he was in a reserved occupation, he'd volunteered straight away – so ruddy eager to *do his bit* for his country. At the time, joining the RAF seemed the most glamourous option – how chuffed he'd been when they accepted him. God only knows why he'd been so determined to *play his part* as they used to say – like they were all actors and the fighting wasn't real.

A stronger wind seems to be getting up and with it the temperature in the barn begins to drop a little – a signal the weather might be getting ready to break at last.

Before long the tin roof above him is creaking; a groaning wind tugging at the edges of the corrugated sheets. Although he's tired out, Frank fights his need for sleep – he has no intention of resting until he's worked out what to do next. Any minute he expects to hear rain beating down on the tin roof, but it never comes.

Monday, May 19th

With everything settled and his wages bulging the wallet in his pocket, Frank boards the eight-thirty train to London.

For the journey he's dressed in his best clothes – clean trousers and shirt with a proper tie and jacket. Though itchy, he knows the stubble on his face will soon thicken into a beard. His new haircut is making his bare neck feel too exposed.

Everything he owns is contained in the small, battered case he stows in the rack above his head. Before the train sets off, heavy rain begins to streak the windows, washing away the fine weather's accumulated dust.

Once they've pulled away from the platform, Frank stands up to peer out of the top window; mesmerised by the changing countryside, the way the hills they're leaving behind become obscured by clouds of steam and smoke. He's enjoying the swaying motion, the fleeting glimpses of houses and then the factories – each presenting momentary pictures of the myriad small worlds where other people's lives go on.

Unwilling to sit down, he leaves the carriage to stalk the length of the corridor, excited to be off somewhere different and leaving behind the gruelling daily routine he's grown used to.

And yet a part of his mind remains troubled. Without intending to, he revisits the awkwardness of his leave-taking. Jenkins was disappointed enough to be losing a hard grafter but didn't express much surprise. As good as his word, he even agreed to cough up every last penny of the overtime pay Frank was owed.

'Be sure to look after theself, lad,' Ma Jenkins had said. Her sudden motherly hug had stirred too many memories.

Sam's reaction was different. 'But I don't understand,' the lad wailed at him. 'I mean, I know you had some sort of argument with that bloody keeper in the pub, but I thought –' He turned away then, his face screwed up in a manner that suggested he was close to blubbing.

Frank touched his shoulder unsure whether to pat or squeeze and settling on an awkward mix of the two. 'Look on the bright side, lad – we've finished all the shearing now and the flock's in fine fettle.' He soon let his hand drop away. 'Things will be easy enough for you and your dad to manage here till August and then them factory lads will be along as usual to help out with the haymaking and that.'

'But that's not the flaming point, is it? I thought we were mates; that we were a team you and me. Why the hell do you want to go and up sticks just because you've had a bit of a run-in with old Kirkwood?'

'It's not about that, lad,' Frank said, with a careful nonchalance. 'I could do with a penny for every little argy-bargy I've had with some bugger in a pub after a few pints – I'd be a rich man by now.'

He allowed his smile to falter then. 'Look, Sam, the honest truth is that I've stayed here longer than I meant to. It's high time I was moving on to pastures new and all that.'

Eyes gleaming with tears and pain, Sam looked straight at him. 'Then I'm coming with you.'

The train's long, mournful whistle shakes him from his reverie. In any case, it's better he doesn't dwell on the rest of it – how at the end the lad had practically begged to be taken along. He was embarrassed by Sam's strength of feeling, the way he clung onto his shirtsleeve more like a woman he was spurning than a grown man.

Shaking his head at the memory, Frank re-enters the empty carriage and sits down next to the window.

After the next stop, a dapper looking chap comes in. 'Good morning to you,' he says, taking off his hat and placing it on one of the empty seats. Before he sits down, he's careful to pull his well-pressed trousers up at the knees.

'Morning,' Frank says, averting his gaze to the window.

'Not much of a day out there, though I suppose the gardens have need of the water,' the man says. He fills and lights his pipe and then holds it clenched between his teeth. 'You off up to the big city, then; to *The Smoke*, as they like to call it?'

The man sucks hard on his pipe until he's satisfied with its outpourings and the small compartment is overwhelmed by the smell of burning tobacco. His unblinking brown eyes are upon Frank, poised for his answer.

'Something like that,' Frank mutters into the liquid windowpane.

Taking the hint at last, the man extracts a sharply folded newspaper from under his arm and spreads it out in front of him.

Frank can see it's the local rag. On the back page there's a report of the county cricket match between Worcestershire and Yorkshire. He leans forward to read the comments about the play so far. Before he can finish reading, the man turns the page, gives the whole thing a shake and then folds it in half. Next thing, he extracts a silver pen from his breast pocket and begins to fill in the answers to the crossword puzzle.

As the journey continues, the carriage starts to fill up with more passengers and is soon clouded with their smoke. Frank steps out into the corridor to enjoy its better ventilation and the views of the ever-retreating countryside.

They're now passing rows and rows of houses with narrow back gardens – all of them the same and yet each a little different. As the train slows, the dapper man pushes past him to alight at the next stop.

He returns to the carriage to check on his case. The dapper chap's left his spent newspaper on the seat. He's quick to retrieve it before someone else does.

The headlines are all about the local preparations for Coronation Day, even though it's a whole year away.

Frank turns to the inside pages. Halfway down, a headline draws his attention. **Gamekeeper Blinded by Own Shotgun.** Frank reads on, his heart beating faster.

> **Lord Hathaway has confirmed reports that the head gamekeeper on his estate,. Norman Kirkwood, 51, is lucky to be alive after an unfortunate accident involving the man's own gun left him badly injured and blinded in his right eye. Police investigators, called to the scene of the accident, have concluded**

that the barrel of the keeper's own gun must have become blocked by debris. This resulted in a build-up of pressure which led to the explosion that then shattered part of the upper barrel and propelled particles of shrapnel into the unfortunate man's face and upper body. His Lordship told our reporter, Peter Blackburn, "The speculation is, that Mr Kirkwood must have previously stumbled upon soft ground and this resulted in a small quantity of earth becoming lodged inside one of the barrels. Subsequently, Mr Kirkwood, having quite forgotten this earlier incident, discharged his gun whilst shooting at magpies without first checking that both its barrels were clear." Lord Hathaway went on to express his sincere regret that "a first-rate fellow who'd faithfully served the Hathaway family, man and boy, for 35 years has been forced to retire prematurely from the job he loved due to a moment's carelessness."

With trembling hands, Frank folds the newspaper in half and then in half again and again; each time flattening it with care until the whole thing's compact enough to fit inside his jacket pocket.

CHAPTER THREE

Friday June 13th 1952

Grace folds the envelope in two and stuffs it into her apron pocket. With the doctor about to call round any minute, there's no time to read what her husband might have to say for himself. Nerves frayed by thoughts of what he's written, she half jumps out of her skin when the doorbell rings.

The sun is glinting off his wire-framed spectacles, hiding the physician's eyes. He lifts his hat and, as always, she's struck by the pure soft white of his hair. A gull wheels overhead, filling the air with its cry; the stream of droppings it releases just misses the right shoulder of the man's jacket.

'I'm here to see Mrs Schmidt,' he tells her, like she might be the maid.

'Yes. She's expectin' you, Doctor; I'll take you on up.'

He deposits his hat on the hallstand before following on her heels. Grace can hear his laboured breathing behind her as they climb the steep stairs together. It reminds her of the phrase her father was fond of using: *Physician: heal thyself.*

She opens the bedroom door and then has to step aside so there's enough room for him to get around the bed. This house – her mother's house that's never been hers – is a segment of a building that's been cut too thin like a cake that won't quite go round.

'So, how are we today?' The old man is struggling to find his breath along with a space for his bag on the cluttered bedside chest.

'You tell me,' her mother says, putting on that weak voice. (Though she'd enough breath to shout her orders down not ten minutes ago.) When she sits up, the coughing begins again. This time it seems more for effect – what's expected if you call a busy doctor to your bedside.

Her mother's bony hands instinctively tidy her hair with its newly grey roots, pressing the curls into place and adding volume to the back where the pillows flattened it. He may be a medical man but he's still a man after all and it's clear that she's trying to look her best in front of him. Last week she'd hadn't cared one way or the other.

The doctor takes a thermometer from his bag and shakes it. Her mother opens her mouth like a baby bird. He unravels his stethoscope. Knowing the drill, her mother unbuttons her bed jacket and then the front buttons of her nightie.

He warms the chest-piece in the palm of his hand so that its touch doesn't shock her bare skin. 'Breathe in for me, Mrs Schmidt,' he says. 'That's right. Now out again. Slowly. That's grand. Now in again.' He repeats the same instructions several more times as he leans over to check her back as well. Next, he removes the thermometer and squints at it over the top of his glasses.

It's so quiet Grace can hear his breathing as the two of them await the verdict.

'Well now,' he begins, putting away his instruments with care. 'I'm pleased to say we appear to have turned a corner at last. There's been a marked response to the new medication; the infection in your lungs seems to have cleared up nicely.' He clips his bag shut. 'You're on the mend; though I suggest you continue to take things a little easier for the next few days or so.'

The doctor has to lean on the edge of the bed to stand.

'I expect you to make a complete recovery, Mrs Schmidt.' It takes him a while longer to fully straighten up.

'Please, Doctor, I prefer you to use the name *Smith*, if you wouldn't mind,' she reminds him.

'Quite so,' he says, giving no indication that he's taken any more notice than the last time she said it.

Her mother's fingers are wrestling with the closure of each button. From the expression on her face, you'd think the news was a disappointment.

Before he leaves the room, the doctor says, 'You know, with the weather as fine as it is, I think perhaps a short stroll outside and a dose of our famous sea air might do you the world of good, Mrs umm –' He fails to complete the sentence before he exits the room.

Her mother barely remembers to call out her thanks.

The doctor grips the shuddering handrail as he descends the stairs one step at a time. Grace follows behind, thanking him once again for all his trouble.

'I shouldn't need to visit again,' he tells her, putting his hat on. 'Tell your mother to come and see me at the surgery in a week's time.' He peers over his specs. 'I don't mind telling you now, I thought we were going to lose her a few weeks back; I'm pleased to see she's made of sterner stuff. Good day to you, miss.'

Just as she's closing the front door, her mother calls down: 'Gretchen!'

Before she's finished all the oxtail soup, her mother sinks back into the pillows and shuts her eyes. 'We need to get some fresh air in here,' Grace says. When she opens the casement window, a skein of gulls flies past crying out in a mournful chorus.

'That's too much, Gre – Grace; anybody would think you were doin' your best to finish me off.'

A breeze stirs the curtain. 'But you heard what Doctor

Kirkpatrick said – we need to get you up and out of this damn bed.'

'Those doctors don't know everything, you know.' The sides of her mother's mouth drop back into those twin frown lines.

'It's a beautiful day out there. I can help you get dressed; help you put on a bit of powder and some lipstick, if you'd like. The sky's as clear as a bell. D'you remember what Vati used to say about Brighton, before the war?' She decides not to add: before they locked him up.

'Your father said a lot of things.'

'Yes, but he used to say that if you squint your eyes up a bit when the sun's shining, Brighton seafront could be the Promenade des Anglais in Nice.'

'He must have been in his cups good an' proper to go saying such a daft thing.'

'Why don't we take a turn along it this afternoon? If we catch the bus down, we could be there in five minutes. It's a perfect day for a bit of a stroll along to the pier – you know how you love all that.'

When her mother's face brightens a little, Grace decides to keep going. 'They'll have the deckchairs out if you need to sit down. Eh, we could even treat ourselves to fish and chips a bit later.'

'Well, I suppose that would make a nice change from all that soft stuff you've bin givin' me recently.'

It's a good sign when her mother insists on dressing herself. While she's in the bath, Grace lays out her clean clothes on the bed – underwear, that smart grey skirt, the patterned blouse she's fond of and one of her thicker cardigans. A couple of weeks back she thought she might have to do something similar to dress her corpse.

Grace had been summoned here by Mrs Woodall's telegram:

COME AT ONCE STOP ELSIE IN A POOR WAY STOP.

For once her mother was delighted to see her. 'I told Kathy you'd come an' look after your old mum. She's bin doin' her best but she's got her Bill to see to. It's never the same as yer own flesh an' blood.'

Now she's so much better, the peace can't last. It's clear from what the doctor said that she'll be able to manage by herself soon enough. Up till these last few weeks, the two of them haven't managed to remain civil in each other's company for more than a couple of days.

By Monday, or possibly Tuesday, Elsie will be more than hinting that the place is too small for the two of them. Once she's re-dyed her hair and the signs of illness have faded from her face, she'll convince herself she looks a good ten years younger than she is. Having such a grown-up daughter was always an embarrassment she could do without.

While she listens out, Grace takes her mother's apron off. She fiddles with her wedding ring, turning it round and round. The envelope in the pocket crackles for attention. It doesn't weigh much – he must have felt he could say all that was necessary on a single sheet. (She'd need a whole flaming pad to say what was needed to that man.)

In truth, she's more than tempted not to open it. The gas ring's only an arm's length away – she could set fire to the damn thing unopened and be rid of it.

Another minute ticks by before her curiosity gets the better of her.

My dearest Grace, he begins, his slanting handwriting surprisingly neat for once. She scans through all the usual promises. With her gone, wouldn't you know he's seen the light and from now on she'll find him a changed man. *Come home soon. I've missed you more than words can express.* That last bit sounds like a line he might have got from a song. He signs off: *Your ever-loving husband, Dennis. xxxx*

The kettle whistles for her attention. Hmm; *your never-loving husband* would be more honest of the man. Oh, she knows he loves her after a fashion, but the sad fact is, not in the way a man should love his wife.

Through into the next room, that pile of bedding is mocking her from the end of the sofa. When all's said and done, how many more nights can she bear to spend half falling off that ruddy thing? No, she can't stay here indefinitely, that's for sure.

Her friend Dot is fond of reminding her how she's still young and how, with her looks, there's plenty of time for her to start again. 'Get yourself a decent one this time,' as she puts it.

A few months back, Dot even offered to have a chat on the QT with 'Our Reggie' – a cousin who'd now got a job as a solicitor's clerk. A week or so later, they met up in a café on the corner of West Lane. Dot wasn't her usual self – she was slow to sit down, took her time removing her headscarf and then fluffing up her dark hair. Before she uttered a word, the girl's face had said it all. Stirring her tea over and over, she'd told Grace: 'Our Reggie says getting a divorce ain't as easy as all that.' Leaning right over, she whispered: 'They'd have to make your case in the court and afterwards they report all the details – even the intimate ones – in the newspapers.'

From her handbag, Dot pulled out a scruffy piece of paper. 'I've written it all down for you. Reggie says you have to have–' She ran her finger under the words as she read them out. 'Cast iron proof of his *adultery* or his *cruelty*.'

Reading for herself upside down, Grace noticed how Dot had underlined the words adultery and cruelty.

'If you can't prove either of them, he has to *desert* you.' (Underlined.) She looked up. 'Not just for a night or two – he has to properly bugger off an' not come back.' Dot's finger travelled down the paper to the last sentence. 'Failing all of them, he'd have to be certified with *incurable madness*.' (For some reason she'd underlined incurable twice.)

The clock in her mother's kitchen strikes the half hour. They're going to have to get a move on if they're to catch the quarter to. Grace refolds her letter and puts it back in its torn envelope. Instead of the gas ring, she takes it over to the empty fireplace, holds it upright, strikes a match and sets the edge of it on fire.

Watching the fire's progress, she turns the letter onto its side to give the flames a better chance. They lick across the surface blackening her name care of her mother's address.

Though the heat becomes intense, she only lets go when the flames begin to scorch her fingertips.

CHAPTER FOUR

Friday 20th June

By a quarter to three, the stragglers have all left and Frank locks and bolts the outside doors in turn. Though you wouldn't know it from the gloom of the public bar, the sky outside is cloudless – another scorcher of a day.

Going from table to table, he collects the last of the empties and lines them up on the bar alongside the piled-up ashtrays. He takes a certain pride in washing the glasses and polishing them up with the drying cloth. Dealing with all those butt ends is the worst part of this job; however much he scrubs at his hands the reek of stale tobacco seems to linger on his skin. Perhaps he's already beginning to acquire the same ingrained smell as everything else in this pub.

Over the years smoke has stained the low ceiling the colour of dried dung. Sometimes, Frank thinks he must be the only man in London who doesn't smoke. Of course he's tried it more than a couple of times, especially during the war when every bugger seemed to find them such a comfort, but each time the bitter heat in his throat turned his stomach. Odd how some take offence by him shaking his head when they offer the packet round.

In these last few weeks, he's even losing his taste for beer now that it's free and plentiful; he's heard the same thing said about biscuit lovers working in the local biscuit factory. It's something to do with the smell of it always hanging in the air.

Frank's progressed to the bottling-up when a young woman walks out of the passageway that leads from the back. She simply stands there in the middle of the room with her hands on her hips, looking around the place like she owns it.

He straightens up with the necks of three bottles of stout in each hand. Right away he's struck by how pretty she is – brown hair just skimming her shoulders and eyes that seem to hold a provocative, teasing expression. Yes, she's a good-looking woman and she knows it right enough.

'Where the hell did you just spring from?' he demands, lining the bottles up in their rightful place before leaning across the counter opposite her. 'How did you get in?'

She doesn't answer him, just stands there on the spot, swaying her hips as if she can hear music somewhere. He wonders if she's admiring her own reflection in the long mirror behind him. The summer dress she's wearing is pinched in at her narrow waist. The colour of her eyes is hard to define. Advancing towards him, her full skirt whispers like secrets as it skims the polished sides of the bar. Despite his best intentions, his gaze is drawn to the way her close-fitting top sits snug against her full breasts.

Of course she's noticed his interest and now it's her turn to look him up and down; she even walks round to the open hatchway to get a better view of the rest of him like he might be a horse she's deciding whether to bet on or not.

Finally, her scarlet lips part: 'Who are you, exactly?'

'I could ask you the same question.'

She raises an eyebrow. 'You could, but I believe I asked you first.'

He can't help but smirk back. 'Should have thought you could deduce that I'm the barman here. My name's Frank.' He hesitates before adding, 'Frank Danby.'

'Well now *Frank Danby*, I suppose I should introduce myself: I'm *Mrs* Stevenson.' She holds up her left hand and waves it across his vision, the ring on it glimmering for attention. 'I assume my husband must have taken you on while I've bin away. Bin visiting my mum down in Brighton. She's not bin well for the last month – not that it's any of your business.'

Frank can't stop his mouth opening. He hasn't seen much of the landlord over these last few weeks and, though he'd somehow got the impression that Stevenson had a wife, he'd heard no mention of why she was out of the picture. He wouldn't have expected a man such as Dennis Stevenson could have possibly snared himself a woman like the lovely creature standing in front of him.

Twirling a strand of hair, the unlikely Mrs Stevenson saunters over to the far side of the room, peering at each freshly wiped table in turn before making a point of running her scarlet-tipped finger along the entire length of the lintel shelf above the fireplace, as if he's responsible for Bessie's work as well as his own.

She inspects the end of her finger then dusts her hands together in a single clap. 'Well you're quite a surprise, Frank Danby,' she walks towards him again, hands planted back on those swaying hips. 'You see, I wouldn't have thought we were in need of any extra staff. My Dennis usually manages well enough with young Jack to help him out on busy nights.'

It's clear old Dennis has been taking advantage of his wife's extended absence to go AWOL himself. What can he say? He doesn't want to lose this job, yet doesn't want to land the poor bloke in hot water with his missus. Frank's beginning to see the dull-as-ditchwater publican in a whole new light.

'A few weeks back there was a notice in the window asking for an experienced barman,' he says. 'Dennis – *Mr* Stevenson – was kind enough to take me on. It's been really busy; hectic more like, since I've been here; especially of an evening. Expect this hot weather has a lot to do with it – people getting thirsty and all that.'

He should stop talking, wait for her response; all too aware that sceptical look hasn't left her face for a second but instead he can't help but add: 'I'm a hard grafter, Mrs Stevenson, and I'm pleased to say that, so far, I've had no complaints. Far from it.'

'Is that a fact?' She seems amused and then she sighs in a way that could be good or bad. 'Well now, it would appear Dennis and I need to have a little chat about you, *Frank Danby*.'

She eyes him up and down one final time before turning away and walking to the end of the passage and through the door marked "*private – no entry*".

When he's finished clearing up, he leaves by the side door. His days here might be numbered but he's learnt the hard way that there's no point in him worrying about things before they happen. A glance at his watch tells him it's 3.40 already.

A hundred yards on, he leaves the shadows and the heat of the afternoon hits him. He takes off the jacket he's only just put on and rolls up his shirtsleeves. It's a grand day, right enough – hot sun blazing but with a breeze to take the edge off. On reaching the main road with its traffic fumes, he feels the familiar longing for green space and fresher air. The last thing he wants to do is head off back to his dreary bedsit. Besides, he's been finding that once he gets back there of an afternoon, there's only time for a quick nap before he has to leave again to get back in time to open up for the evening shift.

He walks along the pavement looking for a crossing point then dodges through behind a double-decker, getting a long honk from the driver of a black Rover. After that, it's a five-minute walk to Southwark Park. Once through the gates, he heads down towards the lake.

Halfway there, he spots two stout-bellied policemen strolling along side-by-side casting their curious eyes over the crowds. Frank loiters, pretends to be studying the sparrows pecking at some crumbs until they've passed on by.

Nearing the water, he watches the antics of some of the amateur boaters – all the shrieking and splashing going on for very little progress. Some youngsters are stretched out on the grass, sprawled on their backs as still as corpses.

Frank takes off his shoes just to feel something natural underneath his feet. He breathes in the smell of fresh mown grass. On the far side of the lake, a couple of bobbing swimmers are enjoying the water – taking a risk that the coppers or a patrolling parkie won't catch them at it.

The coast appears to be clear and he's tempted to wade in along with a group of lads doing just that, but he can't very well strip off without swimming trunks and he doesn't own a pair – until now there's been no need. He's seen a sign saying you can hire them at the lido if you've got the money and are patient enough for that snaking queue. On a day like today the pool will be packed out.

At least there's no regulation to stop him taking off his shirt and pushing the ends of his trousers up a bit. He spreads his jacket on the ground behind him, rolls his shirt into a pillow and lies back to stare at the sky.

At first, he wonders if he's imagining the sound of twin engines – the distinctive throb of an old Ox-box. No, there she is – definitely an Oxford – wings glinting in the sun and in no danger of coming under fire. With just a smattering of flat-bottomed cumulus humilis clouds breaking up an otherwise clear sky on a perfect training day.

The chimes of an ice cream van ring out. Before it's even stopped, children from all over the park begin to run towards it, hands clamped tight with those begged-for coins. Once the queue has gone down a bit, he might just treat himself to a cornet.

With his stomach rumbling more than usual, Frank calls into the chip shop on his way back. A fierce heat hits him and the smell has him drooling. 'I'll have a thrupenny portion,' he says searching his pockets for shrapnel.

'Give me ninepence and I'll throw in a nice piece of haddock – can't say fairer than that.' Eddie leans into Frank's ear. 'Mind you don't go telling any bugger else or they'll all be wanting the same.'

He finds a sixpence and two pennies and slaps them down on the counter. 'Go on, that'll do mate,' Eddie says. While appreciating his generosity, Frank's not certain he likes being the object of other people's charity. The man's deft hands splash on plenty of vinegar and a good dusting of salt before handing over the tightly wrapped package.

As he's leaving, a sharply dressed bloke pushes past him. 'Glad I've caught you, Eddie,' the fella says, lifting his hat. The chippie looks less than delighted.

Frank lingers on the threshold. Despite the heat, the man turns back to close the door on him and then continues to stare at him through the glass. Frank has no choice but to walk away.

Back in the street, he feels uneasy as he drapes his jacket over his shoulders, freeing both hands to unwrap those layers of damp and oily newspaper. He reminds himself it's none of his business. He should concentrate on his own problems – after all, come tomorrow, he might not even have a job. Though bar work doesn't pay much, it's always cash-in-hand and he's not bought a pint these last few weeks. With his wife now back, at least Dennis is more likely to show up tonight and along with that his wages. Not that the money will stay his for long: he needs to send a postal order to Annie and, once that's taken a chunk out of it, Mrs Harris, his landlady, will be impatient for her dues.

The tantalising aroma of fried fish is rising from within the warm bundle in his hands. Salivating in anticipation, Frank unwraps the newspaper and, blowing on a couple of too-hot chips, walks towards the pub in the golden light of the early evening sun.

Being well off the main drag down a side street, the Eight Bells attracts mostly local trade and Frank already knows a good many customers by name. Some even have their own tankards hanging from the beam above the mirror. The regulars expect him to remember what they like to drink though he always checks to be certain they haven't decided on something else. *'Pint of bitter is it, Charlie?'* he'll say, or *'Just your usual half of stout then, Mrs Norman?'*

The usual suspects come in as soon as he's drawn back the bolts. Wilf and Thin Harry practically fall into the place. Before he's finished pulling their first pints, Fat Harry saunters in.

The conversation predictably starts with them bemoaning the weather; where yesterday was pronounced miserable for a summer's day, it seems today's been too damned hot. Thin Harry works shifts down at the docks. 'Not a bit of shade to be had anywhere.' He fans his worryingly red face with his cap. Aside from the absence of overcoats, all three men are dressed like it could be winter.

For the umpteenth time Wilf bemoans the folly of 'them ruddy big-wigs who decided to get rid of our trams.'

'It's not like they were going to listen to the likes of you and me,' Fat Harry agrees. 'Always the same, en it, Frank?' And now the three of them are looking directly at him awaiting a response.

'Aye, it is,' Frank says. When it gets busier, the demands on him will mean he won't get drawn into these conversations.

Being payday, it's not long before they're coming in in droves all waving those crisp ten-bob notes in his direction. Without an extra pair of hands to help, Frank goes through to the other counter to serve the chaps in the saloon bar with their whiskies.

When he turns round, Mrs Stevenson is standing there, this time with an apron tied around her slim waste. 'Evening,' he says.

She gives a curt nod. Up close she smells of fresh soap and something more exotic, and is beaming at the customers like they're old friends. Still without a word to him, she takes hold of one of the empty glasses. 'Pint of black and mild is it, Bert?'

'That's right, darlin', you've not forgotten then.' The old man's face is alight with pleasure. 'I must say you're a sight for sore eyes, Grace Stevenson. What d'you reckon eh, Frank?'

Concentrating on the pint mug in his hand, Frank knows better than to be drawn into answering such a question. He places a brimming glass on the towel mat in front of a young student type. 'That'll be tenpence please,' he says, holding out his hand.

She continues to work alongside him. Within such a confined space, they have to move round each other one way and then the other; at times, it seems like they're involved in an elaborate dance.

The men in the bar are more animated than usual tonight. It's so noisy the customers are forced to shout their orders and lean right across the counter to be heard. At times Frank even has to lip-read.

His eyes are soon smarting from the cloud of blue haze enveloping the room; it's a wonder these city folks don't get more than enough ruddy smoke without adding their own to it.

'Could you go and prop those doors open?' Grace asks, though it's more an order than a question. 'We'll be fighting for breath before long if we don't get a bit of air in here.'

Frank lifts the flap and plunges into the midst of the increasingly raucous crowd. Through all the smoke and good-natured jostling, he manages to locate the collection of old flat irons they use to pin back the doors. As the night air flows in, he stands outside for a moment taking in blessed lungfuls of clear air.

Not daring to be idle for too long, he heads back inside. Behind the bar Mrs Stevenson is holding her own despite the clamour for service. The woman certainly knows her way around the bar; there's no denying she's more than pulling her weight.

With only one till between them, they inevitably brush up against each other. Several times their hands meet as they scrabble for change out of the open drawer. Frank keeps apologising. 'Sorry, after you, Mrs Stevenson.'

Finally, she holds up her free hand like a traffic policeman. 'Will you please stop saying sorry every five minutes, Frank – I can't stand that in a man. And for goodness' sake, just call me Grace.'

'I'm s– ' He bites his lip just in time. 'Right you are then, *Grace*.'

Despite being rushed off her feet, she keeps up with the to and fro of the conversations going on around them.

Wilf pushes his way through to lean on the damp and sticky counter. 'Blimey, there's a crush in here this evenin' and no mistake.'

While Grace is drawing his pint of mild, he says, 'Eh, darlin', did you know while you were away in Brighton, they decided to get rid of the last of our baa lambs?' He winks at her and then nods over towards Frank hoping to seed confusion.

'So I hear.' She puts his drink on the towelling mat. 'Although I must say, Wilf, I always preferred to catch an Uncle Gus anyway. What about you, Frank?' She turns to face him now and in her extraordinary eyes he sees the challenge.

'Me – well now let me see.' Frank's picked up a fair bit of rhyming slang though he makes them wait for his answer. 'I'd say, if I've got the necessary *Arthur*, I usually hail a *sherbet*.'

Amidst the general laughter, Thin Harry leans over to slap him on the back. 'Well done there, me ol' China. Nice to see you're a man who can give as good as he gets.' He slaps down a half crown. 'Give me twenty do-me-goods and a box of swans there, Frankie.'

Dennis pokes his head round the door. He has his jacket

over his arm and is turning his trilby in circles while he stands before his young wife. 'I *was* goin' to watch the television, like you said, but they've only gone and put a flaming ballet on. Load of people prancing around dressed like gypsies; I ask you – on a Friday night. Practically drives a man out. So I thought I might just pop down to the –'

'I thought we agreed.' Grace gives him a long look and then glances down at the watch encircling her slender arm. 'That Jimmy Jewel's on the wireless in a couple of minutes – you like him, don't you?'

Dennis's face clouds over. It seems he's been given his orders.

Thin Harry nudges Frank's elbow and nods in their direction. 'Comes to somethin', don't it?' he whispers, 'when a man's own trouble and strife won't let him put a bet on a nag or two.'

'Oh. Right then,' Dennis tells her. 'If you're sure you and Frank can handle things here, I'll go back up. Give me a shout if you want any help.'

'Don't you worry, the two of us are managing just fine between us, aren't we, Frank?' Grace says above the racket. 'There's no room for the three of us behind here.'

Mopping his sweating forehead with his hanky, Dennis heads for their private quarters. His wife's raised voice pursues him: 'And don't forget the man will need paying in full before he leaves here tonight.'

CHAPTER FIVE

A brief lull in demand gives Grace a chance to turn to the big mirror and pin back some strands of hair that have been getting in her eyes. Despite how hard she's been working and the way her mascara seems to have melted away in the heat, she's pleased with how lively she looks tonight.

From her apron pocket she removes her lipstick (Red Flame by Coty) and reapplies it with care, pressing her lips together afterwards to make sure of an even spread.

Though nothing about the pub appears to have changed, there's a different feel to the place. As she re-ties the back of her pinny, she takes a minute to check around her for anything that might have been altered in her absence. In front of her the three beers on the pumps are exactly as before; the usual bottles are on the shelves or under the counter, and even the spirits lined up next to the hatch for the saloon bar – all of them are in precisely the same order they were in when she left here last month and pretty much exactly as they were when she first began working here as a girl of seventeen.

Looking down, there might be a few extra scuffmarks on the walls but nothing to speak of. Certainly those ruddy floor tiles on this side of the bar are cracked in exactly the same places as before. (How long has she been on at Dennis to lay some new ones so they can clean the floor properly?) That familiar old galvanised bucket is sticking out from its normal place beneath the bottom shelf to the left, whilst its tangled mop is propped up, as always, next to the broom at the end.

No, not one solitary thing seems to have altered in this place – so why does it feel like it's changed?

She doesn't have to look far to her left to find her answer – Frank.

He's a sizeable man, tall and well built – takes up a fair amount of space, that's for sure. Ignoring his more obvious attractions – and you'd have to be half dead not to notice that handsome face of his – there's something about his physical presence that seems to have affected the atmosphere in the pub.

He reaches up for a bottle of pearl barley and she glimpses bare skin where the buttons on his shirt end. Unlike most of the men in this city, the man's suntan clearly extends further than his neck and lower arms. On his way over to the till just now, he'd brushed so close she could smell him. This night's work has made him sweat, for sure (hadn't she felt her own back running with it) and, studying him now, she can see the darker patches staining his blue shirt to prove it. There's certainly no denying that by the end of the night the man will benefit from a bath but, that said, the aroma he's giving off doesn't seem stale. Despite all the smoke and spilt beer surrounding them, Frank Danby smells of something different, something fresher that's very far from unpleasant.

By the next run of orders, they're in the swing of things, working together as a team and not getting in each other's way like they had been earlier on. Grace remembers the satisfaction to be had from doing the job and doing it well. For the first time in a long while, she's actually enjoying herself.

Keeping up with demand means they're soon in need of clean glasses. As she washes up a batch of tankards, she continues to observe this Frank. She notices how he gives Mrs Perkins the briefest of smiles as he hands over her change and how the woman's face reddens in response. Despite her advanced years, and the fact that her husband is only a few yards away, the old lady looks positively coquettish as she gives him her gap-toothed smile.

Frank comes over to take the glasses she's just dried. He doesn't say much, just something like 'Ta, Grace,' but then he goes and smiles down at her and, with that, his whole face takes on such a look that she has to avert her eyes back to the task in hand. Wouldn't you know it, now she can feel her own cheeks blushing; an awareness of him running through her body like it really, really oughtn't to.

Grace always considered herself to be a realist and it's not hard to size up the situation. The most sensible course of action now would be to thank this man for his hard work and then, once he's been paid his week's dues, get Dennis to inform him his services are no longer needed. In truth, they've always managed well enough between them with the help of young Jack on the busier nights. The boy's slower about his work than she'd like but he's willing enough. Frank Danby's certainly a better worker by far, he may even be good for trade, but without a doubt he's a luxury neither of them can afford.

Frank goes off to collect more empties and her attention is drawn towards a thin figure standing in the passageway to her right.

Arnold Kirby tips his hat at her. 'Evening, darlin',' he says in that smarmy voice of his – the one he puts on when trying to appear charming. 'I'm after a word with your Dennis – in the back, is he?'

The little weasel takes a drag on the cigarette pinched between his fingers, his pale eyes narrowing on her. Without waiting for an answer, he says, 'I see you're busy. I'll find the way meself. Just got a little spot of business to discuss with your hubby.'

He turns away with every intention of carrying on towards their private rooms.

She steps out to stop him with a hand to his arm. 'I'm afraid that won't be possible, Mr Kirby.' Keeping her voice as steady as she can, she adds, 'You see he's not in at the moment and I'm really not sure when he'll be back.'

The odious man looks down at her hand resting on his jacket sleeve and all the way up again until his eyes reach her face. 'In that case, perhaps you'll tell him I called.'

He takes another long drag on his cigarette before dropping it to the floor and grinding the butt beneath the sole of his polished brogues. 'Tell him I'll be round to see him again sometime soon. Maybe I'll have better luck with finding him in, the next time I visit.'

Kirby gives her a twitch of a smile then raises his hat. 'Be seein' you again soon, Mrs Stevenson. Goodnight to you.'

She watches him go, and makes damn sure the man has left the premises before she bolts the side door behind him.

'When you've got a moment, Mrs S...' Without even turning round, Grace recognises the raised voice of Mr Tomkinson the undertaker. 'I'll trouble you for a Double Diamond, if I may?'

'I'll be right there,' she tells him, taking a moment to collect herself.

She grabs the bottle of beer on her way through, snapping its cap off with one swift and satisfying movement. 'So, how are you tonight, Mr Tomkinson?' It's odd that she doesn't know or can't recall the man's first name.

'Oh, I'd say fair to middling, as they like to say up in the north.' He nods his head towards Frank. She guesses that it's not just because of his profession that the other men shy away from his company. Some of them complain there's the pong of death hanging about him and Grace has to admit that, on occasions, she's detected an unnatural chemical smell on the man.

While she's pouring the beer into the sleever glass the undertaker prefers, Thin Harry comes up for yet another refill. The two men greet each other with 'Evening.'

'Double Diamond is it?' Harry says, looking at the label on the bottle she's holding. 'What is it they reckon in that advertisement? *"A Double Diamond works wonders".*'

'And I'd wholeheartedly agree,' the undertaker says. 'I find it a very fine drink at the end of the working day. Most restorative.'

'Is that a fact?' Harry looks pointedly down at the crotch of the undertaker's trousers and smiles. 'So, you planning on raising a stiff tonight then?'

Frank leans over the bar. 'I'd ask you to be careful of your language in front of a lady, Harry.'

The culprit ducks his head, looking a tad shame-faced. 'Point taken. No offence intended, Grace.'

'And none taken, Harry,' she says with a broad smile. Grace is indignant – it's not like she needs defending from that sort of thing in her own pub. She's tempted to tell that barman she's heard far worse, though she thinks better of it and gets on with serving the next customer.

Coming up to last orders, the bitter starts to run out. Not enough dribbles to fill a glass. 'I'm really sorry.' She looks into the young fella's disappointed face. 'I can give you this drop for free, but that's it with the bitter for tonight, I'm afraid.'

Frank comes over. 'Has that barrel run out already? We really have been busy tonight.'

'Well it's too bad, they'll just have to drink somethin' else,' Grace says.

Frank looks at his watch. 'I'll nip down and swap the barrels over – if that's alright with you?'

'What and leave me on my own for last orders – I don't think so.' Although she can do it herself if pushed, changing a barrel is heavy work more suited to a man. It's a job Dennis usually takes a good twenty minutes over including a fair bit of moaning and groaning.

'Won't take me more than a few minutes, I'll have it back on well before the crush.' Frank looks down at her with an expression on his face she can't quite fathom. 'Trust me, Grace, I won't let you down.'

Before she can argue, he's heading for the cellar stairs.

'Young fella says the bitters gorn off, is that right?' Fat Harry's standing at the counter looking mournful. 'A rum do and no mistake on a Friday night.'

'I'm sorry about that. Frank's gone down to change the barrel if you can hang on for a bit.'

'Like I said, it's a rum do, darlin',' Harry's smile reveals his tobacco-stained teeth; 'because at such times only a rum will do. I'll have a large glass of Myer's, if you please.'

She smirks. 'So – shall I put some water in that for you, Harry?'

'Now then – don't you go taunting an old navy man with such a terrible thought, Grace Stevenson.'

It's not long before Frank reappears. He strides over to the pump and, after a few splutters, the new barrel begins to flow. He's about to pour off the first pint or two to check its clarity when she stays his hand. 'That's enough, Frank. I'm sure it'll do just fine as it is.' She meets his puzzled expression. Leaning in towards him she whispers: 'There's really no point in wasting any more of it – it's not like they're going to notice the difference at this time of the evening.'

Grace is about to step back when she feels his warm breath against her ear: 'Is that right? Well now, Mrs Stevenson, I see there's a whole hidden side to you I hadn't appreciated.'

She's taken aback, is about to reprimand him for his flaming cheek when his smile stops her dead. 'I could say exactly the same for you, Mr Danby,' she says, as she turns away.

CHAPTER SIX

Tonight, it's Grace who rings the small hand bell and calls out, 'Time, ladies and gentlemen, please!' Frank feels dispossessed, oddly resentful that the task has been taken from him.

He goes from group to group collecting up glasses and wishing everyone goodnight. 'That's it, folks. Have a safe journey home.' Like always, a handful of customers need a bit more persuading and he tries to chivvy them along with: 'Let's be having you, lads and lasses, I'm sure you've all got homes to go to.' He's careful to keep his voice affable – tanked up as they all are, it wouldn't take much to rile someone and at this late stage of an evening things can get out of hand in a flash.

A heavy arm is planted across his shoulders. 'So how are you, Frankie me old mate?' The cigarette dangling from the corner of Thin Harry's mouth has gone out. 'You know we'd all stay as quiet as little, tiny mice, wouldn't we lads, if you and the ever-lovely Mrs Stevenson wanted to lock us in for another half an hour or so. What's thirty minutes between pals?'

'I'm quite sure neither Dennis nor Grace would want to risk losing their licence, Harry.' Frank picks up the man's limb and gives him a friendly smile before he lets it drop away. 'And I know you wouldn't want them to endanger their livelihood over a few extra drinks none of you really needs. Am I right?'

Thin Harry nods and then shakes his head, casting his gaze

down at the floor like a beaten man. 'When I was younger, coppers round here were a decent lot, happy to turn a blind eye to a lock-in – 'specially of a Friday or Saturday night; some used to drop by themselves for a quick couple of pints at the end of their shift. We was all pals together in them days.'

His two mates are nodding in unison. 'You could say it was bit of a tradition in this part of London.'

'We haven't long fought a war that was supposed to be for freedom and what do we get for it?' Fat Harry stands with his legs apart, swaying like he might still be onboard ship in rough weather. 'Country's gettin' more like a bloody police state all the time.'

He hands Frank his empty glass and then, with as much solemnity as he can muster, puts on his cap and staggers off towards the door.

'Peace at last.' Frank pushes the heavy bolts across behind the last of them. 'That was a busy one and no mistake.' From where he's standing, her face is unreadable. He's been on tenterhooks all night wondering if he'll have a job come the morning – now for the reckoning.

But the woman remains mute, standing there biting at her top lip and not meeting his eye. 'Quite a homecoming for you,' he says. 'I bet you're all in and ready for bed.'

Grace raises her eyebrows though still giving nothing away. She looks past him to gaze into the mirror while she removes the grips from the front of her hair. Apparently satisfied with her appearance (and who wouldn't be?) she sighs and then wipes her hands on her apron more than can be necessary.

He can't stop watching her every movement as she unties it at the back, winding the two straps round and around the whole thing to make a small bundle, which she dumps on the shelf below the mirror.

At last she speaks: 'Certainly got a bit wild in here tonight.'

She goes over to the till and pulls out the loaded cash drawer. 'It'll be interesting to see how the takings are going. They ought to be up a fair bit with trade like this.'

Frank wonders if her tone is implying something more. She looks directly at him now and still there's no hint one way or another. 'You get on with the clearing up in here and I'll go and see where Dennis has got to with your wages.'

Without further ado, she walks off with the money and leaves him to it. It's clear as day that, despite their earlier cooperation, the two of them are no longer a team.

As he goes round collecting up the empties, he admits to himself the signs don't look good. Of late he's been able to send good money to Annie on a regular basis; if he loses this job, he'll let her down once again. Of course, he'd known all along it was more than likely Dennis would let him go when trade gets less busy come the autumn – in fact he'd planned to go back down to Kent for the hopping – but the neither of the Williams brothers will want him to show his face down there much before the beginning of September.

He's always loved the hop season down on Gorseleigh Farm but it has one obvious drawback – even for a poll-puller or a binman the pay's never been up to much. With regular money coming in, he'd thought he might be able to save up a decent amount between now and then. Hop work is always hard, that's for sure, but he's noticed just how much those East End kids enjoy running around in all that fresh air and freedom.

Of late, he's even been wondering if, once he's got together enough to pay for their fare down and a bit of extra bait, he'll write to Annie this year and suggest she and the lad might like to join him for a bit of a working holiday.

Frank's finished with the ashtrays and is wiping over the tables and yet there's no sign of Dennis or Grace.

Someone's left a cap on the shelf in the corner. He looks inside to find there's no clue to its owner. Frank puts it on his head – it's several sizes smaller than his own. The hat is yet another object to add to the collection of keys, lighters and umbrellas they hold behind the bar. Once or twice he's found a wallet and just the once a purse. He made sure to hand anything of that nature straight over to Dennis for safekeeping. It would be too easy to be tempted.

So, what is he going to do if he's dismissed tonight? He could look for work at the docks. At best it's backbreaking work and he might be hanging around for hours, days even, before he's given a shift.

Dennis finally appears as he's wiping over the counter one last time. 'Evening, Frank.' The publican's changed into his carpet slippers, shuffling along like a much older person. 'Grace tells me it was a busy one again this evening. Takings are on the up, that's for sure.'

Looking down into the man's florid face, Frank guesses Dennis Stevenson is probably no more than early forties. The landlord's hairline is retreating as fast as his waistline is expanding. By his manner and the deep lines etched into his forehead, he could pass for fifty. The age gap between husband and wife must be a good twenty years or so. Yes – the Stevensons are an unlikely match on every level.

Though he's dressed in shirtsleeves – and the temperature in the empty bar has dropped considerably – Dennis is sweating profusely, dabbing his face with his hanky like he was earlier. A charitable view would be that the man is coming down with something.

'By my reckoning,' he says, 'once you've finished up here tonight, you'll have worked sixty-eight and a quarter hours this week.' From his trouser pocket Dennis produces a brown envelope and holds it out. 'I think you'll find it's all there – though you're welcome to count it.'

'There'll be no need for that, Dennis; I trust you.' He can smell the whisky and cigarettes on the landlord's breath when he steps forward to take his wages. 'I'm quite sure it's correct down to the last penny – as always.'

Frank looks down at the envelope resting in his palm. His name is written on it in a neat, sloping hand that has to be Grace's. He weighs its contents. 'And what about this weekend – do you want me to work the usual hours?'

A moment passes while Dennis rubs away at his moustache. 'It's been decided we'll go on as we are for now, Frank. I can't say fairer than that, can I?'

The landlord gives him a wry smile as he pats him on the shoulder. 'You get off home now and mind you're back here in good time in the morning.'

He unhooks Frank's jacket and cap and passes them to him. 'After the run on things tonight, there'll be a fair amount of bottlin' up needed before we open.'

So – a reprieve of sorts; for the time being at least, he's still an employed man. How long it's likely to last will depend on a number of factors beyond his control.

'Thanks very much, Dennis.' He hooks his hat over his head. 'I'm much obliged to you.'

Frank knows he was dead lucky to secure this job in the first place; work all over the city seems to be in short supply right now and yet it rankles to be so beholden, always at the mercy of other people's inclinations.

'Night then,' he says, as the door is bolted to his back.

CHAPTER SEVEN

It's a long slog home on foot. The air's still warm and, despite the hour, there are plenty of people out and about; the headlights of the passing traffic spotlight each group in turn.

He stops at the corner where there's a closed-up chophouse. The alleyway behind the building is redolent with the smell of cooked meat. It's his habit to take this back route – a shortcut to his digs and the sleep he so badly needs. At least he'll have money for the meter when he gets in.

Away from the interference of the lights, he looks up at the array of stars peppering the sky above his head. The shallow arc of his torch beam picks out the narrowness of the way ahead. A family of rats – looks like a mother and her four young – are scampering along in the dry gulley running alongside the cobbled pathway.

From here the alley leads up a steeper incline. He's almost reached the top when the silence is broken by the sound of quick footsteps approaching.

He can just make out the silhouettes of two men; both are wearing broad-rimmed hats and, despite the temperature, long, dark overcoats. There's a marked difference in their height and build – a disparity that would be almost comical in other circumstances. The short one keeps spitting from the side of his mouth like he might be chewing tobacco.

Too late, Frank realises this detour was a very bad idea – that he's alone in a narrow alley with his whole week's money in his pocket. If these two were to start something, the odds would be against him.

He continues walking, aware that retreating might only entice trouble. Their torch beams flicker over him. 'Evenin',' the shorter one says before he spits again. They draw nearer and the bloke lifts his hat in an exaggerated gesture like you might greet a vicar.

Frank touches his cap's peak and mutters a greeting back. At the same time, he tightens his grip on his hefty torch.

With no further ado, they pass on by. Just as he's letting out a relieved sigh, their echoing footsteps stop. 'Here, don't I know you from somewhere?' one of them shouts, the tone anything but friendly. 'I never could forget a face.'

Frank considers his choices. He could keep on walking and pretend he hasn't heard the man's question; then again, if he does that, they'll be able to take him more easily from behind. Unfortunately, his only alternative is to turn and face whatever danger these two might pose.

As casually as he can, Frank swivels on his heels. Already, they've closed the gap and are standing just a yard or so in front of him – a fraction beyond arm's length.

The short man shines his torch up into Frank's eyes, temporarily blinding him. He puts his hand up for shade, angling his face away. The light lingers before it runs down the rest of him and back up to dazzle him again. 'Well if it isn't Frank Walton,' Shorty's cocksure voice declares. A streak of phlegm is aimed at Frank's shoes. 'What a turn up for the books – I haven't set eyes on you in a very long while; Thought you must have scarpered for good.'

'Sorry, pal, but you're mistaken,' Frank assures him, 'Whoever this Wilton fellow is, it's not me.'

Keeping his own torch beam low, he takes a half step towards the two men. 'Though I reckon it's an easy enough blunder to make in the dark; wouldn't you agree?' His heart racing, he transfers the heavy torch into his left hand. Though their features are half hidden by the shadow cast from their hats, he detects a slight movement of both men's heads that they've clocked what he's holding, how he's ready to confront them. Though he's outnumbered, he has the advantage of the higher ground.

'Well let's see now,' the taller one keeps his voice low, 'my young friend here was never very good at seeing things in bad light. Come to think of it, he's no better at seeing things in a good light – if you get my meaning?' A brief mirthless chortle. ''Praps things looks different from his level.'

'You taking the piss?' Another gob of spit hits the ground.

Lofty calms him with a raised hand. 'Look – it's late. This chap might bear a passing resemblance to this Wilton bloke you used to know.' He shrugs. 'What say we leave it at that, eh?'

'*Walton*, dammit – his name's Frank Walton like I–'

'We'll wish you goodnight, mate, whatever your ruddy name is.' Lofty grabs his companion's elbow and steers him on his way. 'Have a safe journey home now,' he calls over his shoulder.

Their footsteps continue down the alley. Frank hears a throaty voice mumble, 'For Christ's sake, Lenny, it's not like we've got time to waste on some pointless argy-bargy in an alley. Let it go, will ya?'

Frank turns to continue his walk. So, Lenny Murray is down from Manchester and seemingly operating in this part of town. In future, he'll know to avoid this particular route home.

Saturday 21st June

Frank's woken by heavy thumps on his bedroom door. 'I know you're in there, Danby, so you'd better open up.'

He rubs at his eyes.

'I'm not budging an inch – d'you hear me?' The person making all the noise sounds like a youngish chap. 'You're to open this flaming door right now. This minute or I'll –'

'Or you'll what?' Frank leaps out of his bed as the pounding starts to shake the dust from between the planks.

The thudding stops again. 'I want the back rent you owe my mum and I want – no, I bloody well demand you give it to me right this minute. *She* might be a soft touch, but you'll find *I'm* not.'

'Will you hold your horses for a bit, lad? Give a man a chance to get washed up and dressed, for pity's sake. I'll be more than happy to pay your ma what she's owed, *in full*, once I'm half decent.'

'Wot, an' let you sneak out of the house while my back's turned – I don't think so, mate. I wasn't born yesterday.' A short pause. '*If* you've got the rent money, you can pay me right now. And don't bother to dress first – I seen plenty of naked men during my National Service.'

Frank unlocks the door and flings it wide open. The boy immediately takes a step backwards, his pinched-in face not quite able to hide a flicker of timidity. By the look of him he's no more than twenty; still has a touch of acne he's trying to hide with a sparse, gingery beard. All that ruddy shouting was bravado.

'Boo!' When the boy jumps, Frank laughs in his face. 'I'm guessing you must be young Malcolm. Heard a lot about you. You've a proud ma in Mrs Harris an' no mistake. Stay right there. I'll fetch your ma's money – though I'd rather hand it to her in person.' When he touches his elbow, the lad withdraws as if stung. 'You can tell her from me there was no need for all this ruddy fuss – she must know by now I always pay my debts.'

Frank slams the door in the boy's face. The hammering continues while he's retrieving the cash from under the floorboard beneath his bed.

'I'll have you know I'm authorised to collect the tenants' rents on my mother's behalf,' the boy shouts through the door.

Frank pulls on his trousers. 'Then I'll need you to sign the rent book,' he says, opening up again. He counts the money out into the lad's unsteady hand. 'Hang on a sec.' He produces the book and a pen. Watching the boy sign, he's tempted to suggest he practice that signature so it's less easy to forge.

Slipping the money into his back pocket, Malcolm re-groups. 'Right, well I'm glad that's all settled then.' He retreats a few steps along the landing. 'We're not running a charity here; just you make sure you're on time with it from now on.'

'And a good morning to you too,' he shouts after the boy's back. Frank's bare feet are sticking to the oilcloth. Closing the door, he mutters, 'I'll remember this when the time comes.'

CHAPTER EIGHT

With it being a Saturday, her friend Dot won't be working. Grace could call round, maybe suggest a trip to the pictures later on – 'praps the new one at the Empire. No, she's determined to keep her promise; in her best summer dress, she sets out to visit to her Aunty Dora, though she'd much rather be doing just about anything else on such a fine day.

The tunnels in the Underground are airless and crowded and her packed carriage reeks of other people's bodies. With not a seat to be had, Grace is squashed against sweaty armpits at every turn. She fans her face with her best hat. Why on earth didn't she think to take the bus instead?

They're held up for ages at a signal, which means her journey to Mile End takes far longer than it should. And then, at the exit, she has to wait in a snaking queue for the ticket inspector.

Glad to be out in the open at last, she makes her way through crowded pavements towards the Roman Road. She passes the sorry site of the derelict bathhouse, its once grand façade boarded up and left to become a home for weeds and moss. Nothing much has altered. The bombsite – or bombies as all the kids used to call them – are engulfed in a sea of purple buddleias that are just coming into flower. These and the endless swathes of pink-spiked rosebay make for quite a cheery sight.

This being Saturday, the street market is in full swing. She stops to watch a pack of over-excited children dancing about to the tinny band music that's coming from a wind-up gramophone. Walking on, the jolliness of the tune fades and is finally drowned out when a screaming baby is wheeled past.

The younger women have shed their working clothes and are dressed in summer skirts and blouses. The more solid older ladies – some still in wraparound aprons – are sticking to their cardigans or even coats; their hair covered by headscarves. Cyclists weave in and out, ringing their bells to little effect. A knot of little girls are skipping inside a long, turning rope. Grace can still recite the nonsense rhyme they're chanting. At the height of the arc, she's almost tempted to jump in.

A couple of grimy sweeps walk past and then wolf whistle at her back. Stallholders and spivs call out to attract her attention; following this up with their *'ello, darlin'* or *'Two for five bob, I can't say fairer'*. Other men seem to be mooching around in doorways, smoking and looking on in an aimless sort of way.

Grace jumps over the chalked squares of an abandoned hopscotch game, trying not to step on any of the lines. A row of hand-in-hand kids chant *The big ship sales through the Alley Alley O* as they bend to "thread the needle" beneath the stretched-out arm of the tallest boy.

She crosses over to take a side street that's milling with shabbily dressed women and swarms of little children. It's hard to dodge around all the parked-up prams. At the phone box she turns left, taking care to avoid a heap of dog mess.

This alleyway finally leads her into a small courtyard. Every building is festooned with lines of drying washing, some of it little better than rags. The smell of sewage and cooked cabbage hangs in the air. Her gaze travels up the soot-blackened bricks to the small window of the flat where her aunt and uncle have spent all their married life. She's forgotten what a slog it is up to their flat. More drying clothes adorn each stairway like bunting.

It's almost a year since her last visit but Dora's greeting is as low key as usual. 'Come on in then,' she says, her tone more resignation than enthusiasm. The spreading grey in her hair makes her look much older. Not only that – close up, her whole face seems to have shrivelled in on itself. Over her baggy clothing she's wearing the same old wraparound apron that's been washed so many times you have to stare hard to pick out any of its original paisley pattern. Grace feels overdressed.

Nothing much has changed inside the flat; a stale, damp smell still hangs about the place. What else was she expecting?

Dora looks her up and down with a critical eye. 'New dress then, is it?'

Taking off her hat, Grace bridles at the implications. 'I should be so lucky, Aunty. No, I've had this one for ages – not often it's warm enough to wear it though.'

She smoothes down the back of her skirt before sitting down in the one chair that's not reserved. Brown stains are encroaching onto the wallpaper everywhere she looks. Though she'd never thought her aunty was much of a patriot, some-one's stuck a large, yellowing picture of the late King above the fireplace. Below that, there's a smaller one of his black-veiled mother, widow and daughters. Clearly, these must have been cut from some newspaper report of the King's funeral back in February. Below these, a sprig of dried heather sticking out of a vase completes the makeshift shrine.

Through the wall she can hear the couple next door having a blazing row. The woman scarcely stops to draw breath. Although a baby begins to scream for attention, the two of them keep at it hammer and tongs. Then finally it all goes suspiciously quiet.

The mantlepiece clock chimes the half hour. As if waiting for his cue, her Uncle Bill comes in, crowding the small room by planting himself in the middle of it.

He nods in her direction. 'Grace,' but doesn't spare a smile to go with it. Despite the heat, a shiver runs through her.

His pink flesh is bulging out of the stained vest he's wearing so that it's hard to look at him and not think of a pig. Almost midday and the man's not even bothered to put on a shirt.

'How's your mother?' Dora asks. She interrupts her attempt at an answer to ask if she'd like a cup of tea. 'There's just about enough for a pot between us, but mind – we've not a grain of sugar to go in it.'

'Water will do me fine on a day like this, thanks all the same.'

Bill scratches at his sparse hair. 'I'm sick to death of this ruddy heat; there's hardly a bit of air to be had, even with both the windows open. Be glad of a storm to break it up.'

The conversation continues in the same fashion. Grace knows she should feel some gratitude for the way they took her in when her mum went off with Gerry Blake, but being back in this place is beginning to give her the screaming habdabs. It's as much as she can do to stay for further half hour. How could she ever have contemplated returning to this sort of life?

'I'd best be off now,' she tells them, looking down at her watch. 'Dennis will be wanting his dinner. Then there's the bottling up.'

Neither of them seems disappointed when she leaves.

Grace lets herself in the side door to the pub. Peering through as she passes, she can see the bar's busy again. Frank seems to be in there by himself. Despite his solemn promise, her husband is nowhere to be seen.

There's no sign of him in the kitchen either. The room smells of frying and there's a pan soaking in the sink along with a plate and cup. The greasy scum on the water turns her stomach. She throws her keys on the table and calls out his name as she climbs the stairs to their bedroom.

At least he's made the bed for a change. She crosses the room to open the sticking window on what's left of the day.

The curtains hardly stir. She takes off her hat. With the weather like it is, she really ought to make a start on the pile of dirty washing that's built up in her absence.

Instead she retreats downstairs and switches on the wireless for a bit of cheer.

Bloody cricket again. After she's turned it off, she sits there drumming her fingers on the tabletop. Her rumbling belly is telling her it's time she had something to eat but right now she's no real appetite for food.

It's not long before she's pacing the floor – not easy in such a small space. Why on earth had she come back here in the first place? What was the point if things are only going to carry on exactly the way they were before?

She goes through to the bar. The place is thinning out as the punters remember they've got families and homes to go to. Frank is busy pulling a pint and barely glances up when she walks in. 'Morning; sorry, *afternoon*, Grace.' He straightens up. 'Another fine one today, though I've not seen a lot of it so far.'

She's in no mood to be cheered up. 'I see he's gone and left you to it, then.'

Not meeting her eye, he hands the beer over to an eager hand. 'Dennis was helping me earlier on – said he was just popping out for a bit. You've not long missed him.'

'Popping out for a *bet*, more like.' The words run out of her mouth before she can stop them.

'That'll be one and a penny,' Frank tells a young man who looks to her like he might be underage. She'll be having a word about that later.

Once he's deposited the coins in the till, Frank gives her his full attention. 'Reckon he'll be back before long. Probably just nipped out to buy a paper or something?' The barman's wide smile shows up that near perfect set of teeth.

They both know he's covering for the boss. Looking uncomfortable now, Frank begins to rub away at a scar running just below his hairline. From the way it's faded it must be from an old accident – funny how she hadn't noticed that before. And there's something else, something that's quite different about him this morning. She can't quite put a finger on it.

Wilf sets his empty glass on the counter. 'I'll just have another half in there before I get off home.' This is an old trick – most barmen put too much in a pint pot when they're aiming for a half. To distract Frank, the old man adds: 'Me missus'll give me earache if me dinner's gone cold again.'

Grace has to admit Frank's guessed the level just about right, though Wilf still lifts the glass to take the measure of it. The old man looks from her to Frank and decides not to quibble. He raises his glass. 'Here's to my wife's husband.'

After a few sips he puts down his glass. 'So then, young Grace, how was Brighton?'

Grace keeps her sigh to herself. 'I was busy with my mum, most of the time.'

'Never ever been down there meself; I hear it's quite the place for a bit of sea bathing?'

'Yes, it is. As a matter of fact, I did take a dip once or twice last week. Although the beach down there is all pebbles so it's a bit hard on your bare feet gettin' in. And the water was freezing at first; took your breath away, it did. But once you're in, you soon get used to it.'

She looks up to find Frank's listening. 'There really is nothing better on a hot day than to just be floatin' on your back in the sea, starin' up into the sky. It feels so grand to be weightless. You know, like you could let yourself drift far away from everything and everyone.'

'Mmm.' Wilf shakes his head. 'I heard – mind you this was during the war –there was some poor fella who fell asleep on a train heading down south, missed his bloomin' stop and woke up at the end of the line in Brighton station. Course he wasn't a resident, so he had no right to be down there on the coast – not back then. Poor bugger got arrested before he had chance to catch a train back home.'

Frank starts mopping up some spillage with a beer towel. To no one in particular, he says: 'I've often thought I'd love to have a good cool down in that lake in the park.'

'Well you wouldn't catch me in no slimy lake,' Fat Harry plonks his empty glass down on the counter. 'Beats me why any bugger would choose to go swimmin' just for the pleasure of it. Did I ever tell you about the time we were on convoy duty and –'

'Another pint is it, Harry?' Frank's interruption puts paid to that particular saunter down memory lane. He aims a conspiratorial wink at Grace.

Despite her best intentions, she's amused. Watching this barman as he works, she can't help but notice the way he fits that shirt, filling it out in all the right places.

The penny drops – it's the beard, that's what it is; he's gone and shaved it all off. It's so obvious; she can even see how much paler the skin around his jawline is against the rest of his tanned face. Makes him seem younger. He's looking straight at her now, his eyes dancing with such a liveliness. There's even a dimple in the middle of his chin you couldn't have seen before. He puts her in mind of Kirk Douglas, though he looks more like Alan Ladd. She has to fight an impulse to reach out and trace a path around that little indentation with her finger. Yes, Frank Danby certainly is a handsome man.

'Are you two goin' to just stand there gawping at each other all ruddy day?' thin Harry's reedy voice demands.

'Just you watch your manners, Harry Bishop.' Grace can feel herself reddening. 'One of us will be with you soon enough.'

'Mmmm; well, when you've a mind to turn your attention to your paying customers again, I'd like a pint of mild, if you please, *Mrs* Stevenson.' His gaze goes from her to Frank and then back again. 'This sort of weather can bring out a raging thirst in the best of us.' Seeming to look right through her, he adds: 'Ent that right, Dennis, me old mate?'

Grace is taken aback to find her husband standing right

behind her. He must have come in through the side door; how long he's been standing there she's no idea.

Dennis drapes his arm around her shoulder and gives her a proprietorial squeeze. 'There's really no need for you to help out in here, love; especially dressed like that. The two of us can manage just fine between us; can't we, Frank?'

She's surprised by the animation in his voice. He's pressing the top of her arm now, his grip awkward and insistent. 'You deserve a few hours away from this place.'

His eyes look a bit wild and she wonders if he's been drinking, though, for once, she can't smell it on his breath. He lets go of her to rummage in his wallet before pressing a couple of pound notes into her hand. 'You could go an' get your hair done. Or go an' do a bit of shopping with Dot – whatever takes your fancy, my darlin'.'

He steps back. 'Go on, gal – off you go. Enjoy yourself.' And now his hand is right in the small of her back almost pushing her out of the way.

CHAPTER NINE

Frank tries to get on with his work, with what he's being paid to do here, for Christ's sake. He lifts up the hatch and goes off to collect the empties, glad to have a bit of space around him. There's no denying that seeing Dennis with his arm around Grace was a surprise – a shock even; yet he'd known exactly who she was almost from the moment he'd laid eyes on the girl.

Another feeling takes over the pit of his stomach – disgust. Is it that, or is it closer to a sense of outrage that such a young and beautiful woman could have settled for the likes of Dennis Stevenson?

Just before her husband's sudden arrival, Frank had held Grace's gaze for that one moment and what he saw in her eyes had stirred something in him. It wasn't only physical arousal – although he has to admit that was part of it – it was a lot more besides.

Once both hands are full of glasses, Frank heads back towards the counter determined to put aside any such thoughts. What's more, he should remember that none of the rest of it is his concern. Whatever it is that's going on between the two of them or what Dennis might be getting up to – it's their affair. This is a just temporary job and, if he's lucky, it might tide him over until he can escape The Smoke in September.

He only needs to stick it out for another five or six weeks and then he'll be gone.

Wilf surrenders his empty glass with a loud burp, doesn't bother to cover his mouth. 'That's me done – or done for.' The old man chuckles and pats him on the back before he turns to his friends. 'Be seeing you both. Come on then, Harry me ol' mate, you'd best get off an' all or you'll find yourself in hot water with the old trouble and strife.'

Frank nods a farewell to both men and watches them stagger together out of the door. He carries on washing up, wiping each glass with unnecessary vigour. Once he's back down there in the Kent countryside, everything will have altered again and he'll be able to see things here for what they truly are – none of his ruddy business.

He moves on to the ashtrays – dumping each mound of butts in the bin until it's pretty much full. You'd have thought, after all this time, he'd have learnt not to give in to distractions however attractive they might be.

'There's no need for you to stay right till closin' up today.' Dennis's eyes dart towards the door and back. 'Once you've finished washing that little lot and done round the tables a bit, you can get off home. I'll see to the bottles. And don't worry – it'll all be shipshape and ready for you when you get back this evening.'

'Oh right; well if you're sure.' What else can he say? The clock above the fireplace tells him that's likely to amount to a good half hour off this morning's money.

'Tell you what – you hold the fort for a minute while I just nip to the lavvy,' Dennis says. 'Be back in a tick.'

Frank calls last orders, though, in truth, the place is almost empty anyway. By the time the landlord's returned, he's finished most of the clearing up.

'You can leave everythin' to me now, Frank. Away you go.' The man even flaps his hands at him like you might shoo away a dog or a wasp. 'I've got to hang around here for a bit anyway – I'm expectin' my accountant to call round.'

Frank grabs his jacket. Stuffing his cap into a pocket, he takes his leave. Outside in the street, an unspoiled afternoon greets him. Not ten yards away from the pub, he passes a man coming the other way dressed in a dark suit and tie and carrying a silver-topped cane. The man's face is half hidden beneath the brim of his trilby.

Curiosity makes Frank glance back to watch this chap look carefully right and then left before he enters the side door of the Eight Bells. He'd be the first to admit he's no expert on that class of person, but this fellow seems a most unlikely accountant. Strange too that he would be conducting business with a client on a Saturday afternoon.

Once Frank's clear of the main road and all its noise and fumes, he finds himself heading towards the park. He's still had no chance to buy any swimming trunks but he's a mind to at least dip his feet in the water. The lake in the park is silted up around the edges, even so there's bound to be a place to dangle his feet in.

On the other hand, with this bit of extra time on his hands, he could take himself off to Tower beach. Why not? He's never been there but, judging by the photos he's seen in the newspaper, they've laid a proper sandy beach over the foreshore running south of the Tower of London. Shouldn't take him more than a quarter of an hour to get there on foot if he goes via Jamaica Road.

It's an extraordinary sight – if you could ignore the mass of crane jibs and the famous bridge itself, you might think you were on a regular beach. Right now, it's low tide and every yard of sand is teeming with near-naked kids. They're rushing around in every direction carrying toy boats or slopping buckets of water back to fill the moats they've dug around miniature castles. Many of them are paddling and splashing in the shallows, churning up mud that clouds the water till it looks like tea. The river itself smells of rotting weed, and worse.

Despite all the screaming and calling, their mums and dads are sitting back in deckchairs, many with their eyes firmly shut. Some of the men are shirtless though most remain fully dressed except for their bare feet. The women are in their summer frocks and skirts. A line of young girls walks past him looking self-conscious in their swimwear; holding onto each other's hands as they finally take to the water and shriek at its iciness. Everywhere he looks, newly exposed, pale skin is on its way to turning red and sore.

With no other choice, Frank finds a small space in the thick of it and sits down. He takes off his shirt and folds it with some care before laying it to one side. He rolls up his jacket to a make a headrest of sorts before he lies back to enjoy the sun's warmth on his chest. Despite the endless racket going on around him, it's not long before he falls asleep.

Frank becomes conscious of something dripping onto his leg, then a shadow blocks out the light. 'D'you mind if we sit here?' a woman's voice asks. When he opens his eyes, he sees two women about his age along with four soaking wet children of varying ages.

Both women have dark, curly hair and pleasantly regular features. They're equally slim and well turned out – one of them in a floral dress, the other in a pink one with a black band around her narrow waist. Their similarity suggests they might be sisters. Both women are wearing wedding rings.

'Go ahead,' he tells them, his dried-out throat making his voice sound like a stranger's.

Two of their boys are quarrelling over a plastic cowboy. The woman in the flowery dress spreads out a striped towel. The other one kneels down before opening a large basket from which she produces a pile of tin plates and mugs. She pops the lid off a biscuit tin and takes out a parcel of sandwiches. Once unwrapped, Frank can see these have a brown filling that looks and smells like Bovril, or possibly Marmite.

The children's sand-covered hands are upon them before she can distribute the plates. At least they're quieter now their mouths are filled.

Frank sits upright. Looking at the space these people are occupying, it's clear they'd have had enough room for this picnic without the need to wake him up.

'It's a grand day,' the woman in the pink dress says. She pours orange pop into each of the mugs. Frank's not sure who she's addressing. 'Not a cloud to be seen.' She looks up to the sky to illustrate the truth of it. 'The kids all love it down here, don't they, Winnie?'

'They'd be down here all day every day, if they could,' Winnie passes the pack of sandwiches back to her. 'Mind you, Sal, who can blame 'em; it's so nice to get a bit of fresh air for a change.'

Sal takes another bite and chews it for a moment before she says, 'We haven't seen you here before.' She's directing her words and what's left of her sandwich in Frank's direction.

'No, you won't have done.' He clears his throat. 'I've not been down here till today. Truth is, I didn't realise it would be quite this crowded.'

'Where are my manners – would you like a sandwich, mister, um –?' Winnie thrusts the biscuit tin under his nose and, like he's a ruddy dog, the smell of fresh bread makes him salivate.

'Frank,' he says, 'and I'm just fine, thank you.' He pats his empty stomach. 'As a matter of fact, I've not long eaten.'

'Well, if you're sure. Sal's made too many again. They're so nice and fresh it would be a shame to waste any.'

He notices her wristwatch. 'Have you got the time?' he asks her before regretting his choice of that well-worn phrase with all its implications. 'It's just I've forgotten my watch and I've been asleep, so I've lost track a bit.'

The women notice his embarrassment. Not quite hiding a smirk, Winnie glances at her watch. 'It's just coming up to four.'

The freckled little boy sitting next to her holds out his mug. 'You look hot, mister – d'you want a sip of my pop?'

Frank shakes his head. 'No – but thanks all the same, lad.' He feels a rising panic that he's getting himself embroiled with these people.

'I'd best be going.' He stands up, slips on his shoes and tucks his socks in his jacket pocket.

'Hope to see you again, Frank,' Winnie shouts after him.

He makes sure he's well clear of them before he slows down. There's no point in going back to the pub just yet – in fact there's still time for a bit of a paddle.

He rolls up his trousers until they're above his knees intending to wade out past the children into the less crowded part of the river. It's too awkward carrying his clothes in one hand so he takes the risk of leaving them tucked up behind one of the wooden groynes along with his shoes.

The water is shockingly cold and murky, but it cools him down. Under his feet the sticky riverbed oozes between his toes. He can't decide if the sensation is pleasurable or not.

Just as he's about to turn back, he hears someone cry out for help. He's not sure if it's a joke until he hears it again. 'Help me somebody!' A young boy who looks about ten is doing the shouting. 'My brother's gone under and he can't swim.' The lad's face is running with snot and tears as he frantically scans the surface of the water over and over.

With no other adults in the vicinity, Frank half wades, half swims, over to the boy and grabs his shaking arm. 'Where? Where was he when he went under?'

'Just there.' The boy points to a spot about ten yards away where the current is stronger. Frank takes a breath and dives under the surface. The water's too thick with sand and mud to see much. He thinks he can make out a darker ridge along the bottom where the river deepens.

He's forced to come back up for air; takes a deep breath and dives back down into the foul water. Just as the air in his lungs is giving out, he spots something lighter lying on the riverbed. It takes on the shape of a child's foot.

With no time to re-surface, he dives down and grabs at it. Working blind, he feels along the skinny leg to the rest of the boy's body and scoops him up.

Frank kicks for the surface and holds the child's head high above the water.

Treading water, he shakes the boy. 'We need a doctor,' Frank bellows. 'Somebody get him a doctor.'

He reaches the shallower water. The little lad's mouth and nose appear to be clear of mud at least. On the riverbank the shocked crowd part as he wades to the shore with the lad in his arms and, almost as if he were a fish, lands his limp body onto the sand.

A dark-haired woman rushes up and takes charge. 'I'm a nurse,' she announces. 'Quiet now everyone, please.' She puts her ear to the boy's nose and then checks his chest. 'He's not breathing. Help me turn him over.'

Together she and Frank roll the boy over onto his side. Using the fingers of both hands, she pushes the boys jaw forward until it's jutting out. Just as Frank is despairing, the lad throws up a quantity of pungent water. A second later he brings up some more.

'Quiet again,' she demands. 'You check his breathing while I hold his jaw.' Frank bends his ear to the boy's nose and mouth. He's sure he can hear a faint sound. There it goes again. He turns his head until he can see along his little chest and it rises just a fraction and then falls again. 'Yes, yes he's breathing.'

The crowd cheers as the boy's distraught brother is thrust

forward to witness the miracle. Through his tears he stammers: 'Our mum's goin' to wallop me good an' proper when she finds out about this.'

'An ambulance is on its way,' someone shouts out from the back.

A sturdy woman standing over them turns to the crowd, hands on her hips. 'Where was that bloody boatman – that's what I want to know. He's supposed to keep an eye on all these kiddies. This wouldn't have happened if he'd been doin' his job proper.'

There's a general chorus of 'that's rights' and lots of nodding.

The boy's face has turned more of a normal colour at last. While the nurse takes over, Frank flops back onto the sand. A wave of nausea overcomes him and he throws up some of the foul water he must have swallowed. Exhausted and sobbing, he shuts his eyes.

A rough hand shakes him. 'Now then, there's no need for all that blubbing –the boy's okay and you're a bloody hero.' The speaker is a fat man with a bristling moustache. 'That young nurse is an' all. If it hadn't have been for the two of you, the poor little blighter would have died.'

Frank comes to his senses, gets to his feet, though he's a little unsteady with it all. 'I've got to get back to work,' he tells the circle of spectators.

The fat man seems to have appointed himself as their spokesperson. 'What, half dressed like you are and soaking wet – do me a ruddy favour. You can't turn up for work looking like Robinson bloody Crusoe; you're gonna need a bath, sunshine, and some dry clothes. An' what about your ruddy shoes?'

A woman pipes up: 'Here, this man should have 'is picture in the Evening News – he ought to get a medal or something.'

Frank notices Winnie and Sal amongst the crowd at the far end. The bell that's been ringing in the background gets louder and then abruptly stops. A minute later two men carrying a stretcher come running along the beach. Spreading their arms out wide, a couple of bobbies aided by the fat man force everyone to step well back. 'Come on, folks – let the professionals do their job.'

Their patient blinks and then opens his eyes. A collective sigh issues from the crowd as they lean forward to witness the boy's first reaction. 'Flamin' hell,' he says.

Amongst the general laughter, Frank slips out through a gap between the spectators. Aside from his wet and muddy trousers, his underpants cling to his body as he walks. He hurries as best he can along the beach looking for the groyne with the two black stripes near the bottom – the place where he'd stowed the rest of his clothes.

Once he's located his clothing, with everyone still caught up in the drama at the far end, it's easy enough to dress without attracting attention. He pulls on his shirt despite all the sand stuck to his back. Getting his socks over the muck and sand still clinging to his feet is more of a struggle. For good measure he puts on his jacket.

A few yards away, someone has left a light grey fedora on the seat of an empty deckchair. He rolls up his cap and stuffs it inside his pocket. Looking around he can see there's no one close by. He walks past the deckchair and, as casually as he can, picks up the abandoned hat.

It's a near perfect fit. Before leaving the beach, Frank adjusts the brim with care, pulling it down so that it might shade his eyes from any passersby.

CHAPTER TEN

When Grace gets back from her shopping trip, she hears the cricket commentary droning from the wireless upstairs. Dennis's hat is hanging up in the passageway. Upstairs she finds her husband slumped back in his armchair with his mouth half open, the smell of whisky on him. It's comical how, with each whistling exhale, the hairs of his moustache lift just a fraction. He used not to snore like this.

For want of something else to do, she goes back down to the kitchen to make a cup of tea. Looking through yesterday's Evening News she finds nothing of interest. In this heat it's hard to concentrate on anything for long. She flicks through the pages of the Picturegoer but finds she's already read most of the articles.

In the quiet that follows the kettle's whistle, she hears noises coming from the bar. It seems a tad early for Frank to be back. Perhaps he's trying to impress her with his punctuality. Or maybe someone's broken in. Should she go and wake Dennis, just in case?

Instead, Grace decides to investigate herself. She slips off her shoes before easing open the door to the passageway. Maybe she should be taking this more seriously – what if she's about to disturb a burglar in the act of stealing their stock? Turning the corner, she bumps straight into Frank.

Both of them take a step back. 'I'm really sorry – didn't mean to scare you like that,' he says.

'I was surprised, that's all.' There's the oddest smell about him; it's not pleasant, that's for sure.

Grace retreats a couple more steps to stare down at the man's soaked through trousers. There's even a strand of what looks like pondweed dangling from one of his pockets. She can't contain herself and bursts out laughing at the sorry state of the man. 'Well now, if it isn't Old Father Thames himself.'

She straightens her face with some difficulty. 'I see you've bin wetting your whistle this afternoon.'

'You'll forgive me if I don't find it a laughing matter.'

'You know, Frank, dressed like that, the world could be your oyster.'

'I'm glad to be the cause of so much amusement to you, Mrs Stevenson.'

'Come on now, joking apart, how on earth have you got yourself in such a sorry state?'

He looks down at his trousers. 'I was down at the lake – you know, the one in the park. Thought I'd cool off by dangling me feet in the water. As I went to get up again, I slipped on the wet concrete round the edge and fell in.'

'So I see.' She holds her nose. 'Well, in all honesty, you smell worse than three-day-old fish.'

'I would have gone home to change first but there wasn't enough time.' He holds his hands up. 'Sorry.'

'You'll stink the whole bloomin' pub out if you stay like that. There's nothin' for it – you need to have a bath before you're fit to serve anyone.'

When he looks reluctant, she waves him along the passage-way. 'Come on – you can use ours. It's just out the back here.' She ushers him on through the kitchen into the bathroom beyond. It's so strange to see the barman standing there in their private space, to have him so close to her dressing gown hanging off the back of the door, the row of nylons spaced out along the towel rail.

'Soap's there on the side.' Rather than fetch a clean one from upstairs, she hands him the small towel they keep by the basin. 'You can use this to dry yourself. The Burco's not been on so it'll have to be a cold one, I'm afraid. Still, you did say you wanted to cool off.'

He finally appears to see the funny side of the situation and gives her a wry smile. Her eyes dart to his trousers, how they're clinging to the shape of him. 'Those will need a good soaking too before they can go out on the line. At least they'll dry soon enough in this heat. Fortunately for you, Frank Danby, my Dennis has some old ones you can borrow in the meantime.'

'This is really good of you, Grace.' He's already unbuckling his belt when she closes the door.

The mantle clock shows it's just gone twenty past – only ten minutes until they need to open. Up in their sitting room, her husband's still sound asleep and missing the commentary of Middlesex in action. There's no point in waking him, she already knows his castoff clothes are in the bottom drawer of the wardrobe.

She rifles through what's there. Dennis can't get into any of it these days, but he insists on keeping everything for some mythical time in the future when he plans to lose the weight. Frank's the taller man so any of these trousers are likely to come up a bit short on him.

Back downstairs she knocks at the bathroom door. 'Are you decent?'

There's a splashing of water from inside. 'I am now.'

'These should do the job. I brought you a clean shirt as well. You'll have to manage without underpants.' She opens the door just a fraction, not looking at anything below ceiling level as she offers the clothing in her extended hand.

'Thanks a million for this,' he says, taking the bundle. 'You've really saved my bacon.'

Her resolve weakens for a moment and she glances down. The towel around Frank's waist is covering the essentials but little else besides and what a body the man has on him! She's aware of the colour that's already sprung to her cheeks. 'I'd better go and open up,' she tells him.

Grace unbolts each of the three outside doors in turn and the city-warmed air pours in. For once there's not a soul waiting outside. She opens a couple of windows and props each door wide to create a bit of a through draft hoping there's one to be had.

Her mind's eye keeps going back to the sight of Frank standing there in just that towel and looking every inch the man she'd imagined he might be.

To clear these thoughts, she sets her mind to checking the bars, making sure all the ashtrays are in place and the clean bar towels are spread along the countertops ready for what's likely to be a busy night ahead.

A couple of spirit bottles in the saloon bar have run dry and need changing. Grace takes down the empties and fixes the optics into the neck of each one in turn before hanging them back up. It's odd that the labels on both bottles – a Bell's and a Gordon's – seem to be a bit skewwhiff.

The inner door creaks and she wonders if Dennis has finally woken up. She knows he'll want an explanation as to why their barman is sporting his old castoffs.

Frank is standing there in the room behind her wearing her husband's clothing in a way *he* never did. He smells and looks a great deal fresher than when he'd walked in a half hour ago. 'So – how do I look then?' he asks, turning around so she gets the full picture.

'A lot better than you did, that's for sure.' As she expected, those trousers are too short on him. She can see he's had to pull them in with his belt at the waist. The shirt's much too tight across his chest and one or two of the buttons have already popped open. Perhaps it's her familiarity with a garment she's washed so many times that makes her reach to button them up for him.

At least that had been her intention. She hadn't planned for her fingers to go stealing through that opening to explore the contours of his chest. Nor had she intended to press herself up against him, her free hand stretching up to encircle his neck and pull his lips down towards her open mouth.

When Frank grabs her wrist the shock of it jars her back to her senses. 'Don't,' he says. 'We mustn't.'

Overcome by a sensation that's close to, but not quite, shame, she withdraws her hand from his shirt.

What on earth had she been thinking to behave in such a reckless way? How could she have contemplated kissing another man – a man she scarcely knows – and right here in the middle of the saloon bar with the door propped half open so anyone could walk in?

They still could for that matter – her hips remain pressed against his and, regardless of his words, she can feel the extent of his physical arousal through the thin materials separating them.

In truth, doesn't she still want to take the risk of it, allow the possibility of this one act that would blow apart everything in her life so that it could never be the same again?

Frank bends to her ear: 'At least not in here, Grace.' His lips stray into her hair, stirring desire to an urgency that shocks her. 'Not like this.' He drops her wrist and turns away.

'Is anybody serving in here?' a man's voice calls out from the public bar.

Could they have been seen in the mirror? 'Be with you in just a sec,' Frank shouts sounding far cooler than he ought to.

Unable to master her own feelings, Grace strides out, doesn't stop until she's walked right through the building and can lock the door of the bathroom behind her.

With trembling hands, she opens the window and gazes out to where Frank's hung his rinsed-out clothes on their washing line. He must have swilled them out in the bathwater but really, they need a good scrubbing with some Oxydol.

She stoops to pick up the damp towel from where he's draped it over the side of the bath and buries her face in it – in the faint smell of him that still clings there.

Sitting down on the sharp edge of the bath, she tries to think through what's just happened; the enormity of the risk she'd taken in a moment of madness. Is she even glad Frank had stopped things before they could go any further?

When she finally glances down to the drained bathtub, she sees a quantity of yellow sand lying along the bottom. Strange. She's familiar with the boating lake in the park; she'd walked past it many times while they were in the process of repairing some of the wartime damage. It seems unlikely, improbable even, that all this sand could have come from an artificial lake.

If she had to put odds on it, she'd say Frank had lied to her about what happened to him. Where could he have gone off to in the short time they were closed? Had he been on a building site somewhere? Why didn't he tell her the truth?

Grace turns on the cold tap, taking care to swill every last grain of telltale sand down the plughole.

One thing's for certain – she can't stay in here all evening. She turns to the mirror, adjusts her hair until it looks under control. Her compact is on the shelf below and so she dabs her cheeks with powder. A little lipstick and you'd think there was nothing amiss.

Now she'd better go and wake Dennis, and explain why Frank is wearing his old clothes before he walks into the bar and sees for himself.

'Not like this,' Frank had said; she's sure those were his exact words.

And now, God help her, she's imagining the two of them in a bedroom that isn't hers or his. This one is big and sump- tuously decorated. The bed has real silk sheets. There's a tray with a cooling bottle and glasses full of half-drunk champagne filling her with Dutch courage. She's slipping off the straps of her petticoat, first one and then the other, while Frank watches her every move.

Is he standing in the shadows next to her? No, better than that he's already naked, lying back in that wide bed with those smooth-as-anything sheets draped across the lower half of his body.

Through the ceiling Grace hears an orchestra strike up on the wireless followed by the sound of someone walking about. She'd better go up and explain to Dennis what's happened; the last thing she wants is to arouse his suspicions.

CHAPTER ELEVEN

He chews at the inside of his cheek, doesn't stop until he can taste the blood in his mouth.

'Pint of mild, if you please, Frank.'

It had been a shock when he felt Grace's cool hand exploring his chest. Tempted as he was – and what man wouldn't be by such a beautiful woman – it had taken him every ounce of self-control to stop things going any further.

'I said, I'll have the usual please; if you don't mind, Frankie.'

'Sorry, Charlie – I was miles away. A pint, is it?' He should have shown more restraint, told her it was never going to happen; that he isn't the kind of man who fools around with another man's wife.

Charlie Metcalfe peers at him over his specs. 'You seem a mite preoccupied this evening, son.' The old man always smells of the Brilliantine he uses to slick back his iron-grey hair, and is never seen without a tie. 'Got yourself a new shirt too, I see.' He takes a sip of beer. 'A tad tight across the chest – if you don't mind me saying. If you were a woman, they'd describe an outfit like that as *leaving little to the imagination.*' Charlie chuckles to himself. 'I dare say old Ma Perkins' eyes will be out on stilts if she comes in 'ere tonight.'

More chuckling brings on a coughing spasm. Once he can catch his breath, the old man clamps his unlit pipe between his teeth and goes over to join the cribbage players in the far corner.

A quarter-to-seven on a Saturday night and there's still no more than a dozen customers in the place. The cribbage players are concentrating on their game, supping very little between them.

The same can't be said for the two college types who are having a stab at playing darts, their arrows flying in every direction but the board. If they're still at it when it gets busier, he'll have to have a word or someone might get hurt.

Frank polishes up a few glasses that are looking a bit cloudy. Is he imagining it now or had someone at the beach been brandishing a camera? He keeps trying to picture the scene again but it all happened so fast that he can't be certain what he saw and what he didn't.

'A couple more glasses of your finest ale, please barman.' One of the dart players – the lanky, fair-haired one – is standing right in front of him, though he hadn't seen the chap approach. The bitter's running a little frothy tonight; Frank's careful to tilt the glass a fraction more than usual as he draws it.

'My friend and I feel certain that a touch more alcohol will help to steady our aims.'

'That's an interesting theory, which has one benefit at least,' Frank sets his full glass down on the towel mat in front of him, 'it certainly can't make it any worse.'

Laughing, the lad takes a sip from his bitter and then flexes his arm. 'You know, I do believe I can feel the old brachialis loosening up already.' Once he's counted out a dozen or more coins into the damp patch on the counter, he picks up his friend's glass. 'Now, my dear chap, watch and prepare to be amazed.'

Frank is prising the last coin from the counter when a kerfuffle breaks out at the end of the room. 'That bloody dart just missed me hand by a gnat's whisker.' Bert Matthews is demonstrating the distance with two nearly closed fingers. 'Playing reckless like that, you'll take someone's eye out next.' Egged on by his fellow card players, he's refusing to hand the offending dart back. Chairs are scraped as half a dozen elderly men get to their feet, fists tightening in defense of their territory.

'Calm down, everyone.' Frank strolls into the midst of it with his hands raised. 'Come on, settle down now, gents.' He turns to the two youngsters. 'With respect, lads, I think we may have established darts may not be your game – your forte.' He waves down their protests. 'Whereas quoits – now that's a game that requires superior skill. You need a good eye and subtle judgment to master it.' He offers them a set of rubber rings. 'Maybe you'd like to try your hand?'

'A sound suggestion, old chap.' Swaying a little, the lanky one snatches up the quoits. 'You can all witness me thrashing my good friend here.'

'As if we didn't have better things to do,' Bert mutters.

Finding themselves equally poor at quoits, the two students eventually sup up. 'Au revoir, good sirs,' the lanky one says, almost overbalancing as he gives a low bow. 'Á bientôt.'

'Off you go – toot sweet.' Bert watches them saunter out. They steady themselves on the doorframe as they go. 'Let's hope that's the last we see of them ruddy dingbats,' he says.

'Evening, Frank; I've come to give you a hand.' Dennis is carrying a plate with two hefty sandwiches on it. 'My wife's been telling me about your little incident.' A smirk is playing on his lips.

'Yes, Mrs Stevenson was very kind – very helpful. I hope you don't mind me borrowing your clothes like this.'

The landlord looks him up and down. 'Not the best of fits, I'll grant you, but at least you're halfway to being decent.'

'My stuff ought to be dry before too long.'

'There's no need to fret about that.' The landlord grips his arm. 'Whole thing's given Grace a good laugh this afternoon, that's for sure. Brought a bit of colour to her cheeks for a change.'

He releases Frank's upper arm. 'Oh, and these are for you.' He hands him the food. 'Grace reckoned you must have missed your tea and you'll be no good to us half starved. Only dripping, though, I'm sure they'll be tasty enough.'

'That's very decent of you, Dennis – of you both that is. As it happens, I haven't eaten since breakfast.'

'Then I'd say you need to look after yourself a bit better, young man.' Dennis pats him on the back. 'Mind, don't you go eating these in front of the customers or they'll all be demanding food. Best you take them out the back now before we get really busy. Off you go.'

A smarmy looking chap in the saloon bar is waving a pound note to get attention. Dennis makes a beeline for him. 'Good evenin' to you, Cyril; Johnny; Arnold. I heard you wanted a word. But first off – what's your poison tonight, gents?'

Frank wolfs down his supper surrounded by crates. Mixed in with the dripping there's a fair bit of lamb. Was this down to Grace's kindness or her husband's? Though he's enjoying his meal, the afternoon's events play on his mind. Despite the way the wet material dragged at his limbs, he'd set a brisk pace once he'd left the beach; keeping away from the main road by weaving in and out of various side streets. He's fairly certain the few people he passed had been too caught up in their own business to notice him.

Dennis is still chatting to the men in the saloon when he slips back in behind the bar. Straight away, Frank has to deal with a disgruntled and demanding queue in the public bar.

The last person in line is Charlie Metcalfe. 'I reckon that ruddy lot over there are cheating.' The old man jerks his thumb towards the cribbage players in the corner. 'Another half in there, if you'd be so kind. I must say it's a poor job when a man can't trust his own friends.'

He carries on squinting at Frank through his glasses. 'Remind me again – were you in the army durin' the war?'

'Me? No, I did my bit in the Home Guard; I couldn't leave the family farm.'

'But you have now?'

'When my old man died, we lost the tenancy.'

'Unlucky that,' Charlie says. He moves aside to prop up the bar at the end.

Though he carries on serving, Frank's aware of being under his scrutiny.

Bert comes up for another half. 'Will you look at old eagle-eyes over there.' He nods in Charlie's direction and receives a scowl for his trouble. 'Never known such a sore loser. The man can't shut his flamin' gob for more than two bloody seconds at a time. Keeps bendin' our ears about how he used to be a Clerk of Works before he retired. Must be why he can't stop pokin' his ruddy nose in where it's not wanted. Sulkin' now. Look at him.' He glares at Charlie again: 'The rest of us are bloody delighted to be shot of the old fool.' He heads back to his game.

Things settle down for a bit and Frank takes a breather. During the hiatus, Charlie beckons him over. 'A word in your shell-like, son.' The old man looks around to check no one's eavesdropping. 'I can't help but notice how well in you are with our friend Dennis over there.' Before he can say anything, the man raises his hand. 'Now hear me out. Thing is, I just thought I ought to warn you to be careful.' He taps his nose with a tobacco-stained finger. 'Things may not be all they seem in that direction; if you get my drift?'

Frank frowns. 'I can't say that I'm following you, Charlie. Dennis has always been straightforward enough with me. Though he can be a bit forgetful, he always pays me what I'm owed in the end. I'd call him a fair and reasonable man.'

Charlie's eyes dart across to check Dennis is still caught up in conversation in the saloon. 'I'm just saying that a fine-looking young man like yourself would do well to watch his back.' The old man's voice is now so quiet Frank's forced to lean in close. 'Before he married, rumour had it, Dennis Stevenson was a little *light on his feet*, if you get my meaning? There was even talk he'd been caught red-handed – in the act, as it were. And you know what the law has to say about that.' Frank feels the man's breath on his neck. 'In the end nothing came of it. Everyone round here reckoned he'd somehow gone and bought his way out of trouble.'

Fighting to suppress another cough, Charlie says, 'Not long after that he went and married young Grace, his barmaid. Even that didn't entirely put paid to all the talk.' He shrugs. 'None of my business either way – live and let live's my motto. Just thought you ought to be appraised of the lie of the land.' Nodding over towards Dennis, he says, 'I'm afraid that man's card has been well and truly marked.'

Frank's taken aback, not sure whether to believe what the old man is driving at. With his attention now secured, Charlie takes out his pipe and begins to light it. 'Course, like I said, I couldn't vouch for the veracity of these stories.' He prods Frank's sleeve with the wet end of his pipe. 'It may only amount to a lot of tittle-tattle.'

After a bit more sucking, his tobacco crackles into life. He draws hard on his pipe and with a knowing wink blows a stream of smoke through the side of his mouth. 'In my experience there's no smoke without there's a blaze going on somewhere close by.'

People are coming in thick and fast and Frank's too busy to stand chatting. Dennis hasn't moved from the saloon bar counter and is getting stuck into the whisky with those three men, topping them all up from one of the bottles he keeps under the counter in there. He doesn't appear to be taking money for any of it. From the distinctive shape of the bottle, Frank can see it's one of the malts.

It's gone nine before Dennis finally comes over to give him a hand. A half hour later, he's back at the saloon counter with his pals and starting on yet another bottle. By ten o'clock, the man's too pie-eyed to be of any use. It's a bloody relief when he staggers off to his bed.

On his walk home, Frank thinks back over his conversation with Charlie Metcalfe. He's reminded of an evening back in the spring of '41. With passes until 22:00 hours, they'd ended up going to a sad excuse for a dance at the local village hall. Under the resentful scrutiny of a handful of village men, a couple of the lads went off to chat up the local girls with varying degrees of success.

Frank got stuck into the cider with the others. Only thruppence a pint, it was a greenish gold with a sourness that caught in your throat and had them literally holding their noses as they gulped it down.

That stuff was way stronger than expected. On the way back to the base, they all tried to sober up a bit. The night was as black as ink. With only one blackout torch between them, they kept blundering into the hedges and startling the cows grazing on the other side. Poor old Ferguson threw up most of the way back. Turned out the lucky bugger missed his uniform each time.

Frank ended up walking arm over arm with The Doc – not that he'd have called any officer by his nickname – not to his face. They were a similar age and build but from very different backgrounds.

After one particular stumble, he felt the pilot's wet lips on the side of his face but assumed it was an accident. There couldn't have been anything accidental when a few yards on Doc's free hand rubbed at Frank's thigh and then his crotch. Not wanting to confront him, Frank pretended to stagger and shook himself clear of the pilot's grasp.

Afterwards, he tried to put it down to the drink. He'd been shocked, for sure, but no harm had been done. Frank didn't say anything to anyone about it, least of all to the man himself. You heard plenty of talk about how such and such was thought to be a queer or a Nancy-boy, but, to his relief, he heard nothing but admiration for Flying Officer Julian Scott-Foster.

With them all being so close together physically, after that, Frank began to notice things about the pilot he missed before – an almost indefinable something in the way he held himself and the manner of the gestures he made. None of it much out of the ordinary, and yet so obvious now he knew the man's secret.

Had he noticed anything about Dennis that might lead him to the same conclusion? In all honesty, he can't say he has. That didn't make it untrue.

It's late and he wishes he hadn't been reminded of The Doc. Unconcerned by his personal inclinations, he'd continued to admire the man. The pilot had been renowned for his good humour and meticulous preparation. Of course, none of that attention to detail could have prevented what was to come – the string of events that would end with the poor bloke burning to death just a week after they'd all celebrated his twenty-third birthday.

CHAPTER TWELVE

Sunday 22nd June

At precisely seven o'clock Frank opens up and a dozen or so regulars troop inside. He's found that Sunday evenings are generally a lot quieter – if the punters aren't already spent out, they're mindful of the need to be up early the next morning.

When the conversation in the bar stops abruptly, he looks up to see the two youngest Dawson brothers have strolled in off the street. Looking pleased by the general reaction, they tip their hats as they make their way up to the counter.

The ugly one they call Dicer takes off his hat – a fancy homburg – and places it on the counter. A section of his otherwise greased-back hair is sticking up at the back, putting Frank in mind of a displaying bird. 'Give us two double whiskies,' he demands.

'Would that be Bell's? Teacher's? Haig?'

His younger brother, Rinty, leans across the counter, eyes narrowing. 'What, that bloody hooch of Dennis's – you've got to be kidding, mate.' His high laugh is anything but funny. 'We'll have the proper stuff – the sort our Dennis keeps for his *special customers*.'

'Then I assume it's the malt you're after. Just give me a minute, gents.'

Frank's relieved to find most of a bottle under the counter in the saloon bar.

Like they're in a ruddy western, both men knock their drinks back as soon as he's poured them. 'Not bad at all,' Dicer licks his lips. 'Think we'll have the same again, mate.'

Glasses refilled, the brothers slap their money on the counter and then retreat to the back of the room. They keep looking at the door, as if they're expecting company. Frank hopes it's not the other three brothers.

A few minutes later, a smartly dressed young chap comes up to be served. Frank can smell his aftershave from a yard away. 'Pint of bitter and half a shandy for the young lady.' The lad nods towards a pretty young woman standing just inside the door. Even from this distance Frank can see the poor girl's looking self-conscious. Something that's not helped by all the male attention she's getting.

'We're off to the pictures shortly.' The lad gives him a crisp ten-bob note. 'Just thought a drink might take the edge off things a bit – if you know what I mean?'

Just as Frank is handing him his change, someone at the back of the room starts to sing. *Hey, hey there darling, hey now sweet miss.'*

Another voice pitches in with: '*Would you like to dance with me? How about a quick kiss?'*

Squinting through the smoke, Frank can see it's the Dawson brothers serenading her. He nods the lad's attention towards the back. 'I think you'd best go and rescue that girl of yours before she bolts.'

Beer slopping everywhere, the young man pushes his way to the back of the room. Frank hesitates before opening the hatch and grabbing the neck of the whisky bottle. He's careful to seem casual as he makes his way over to position himself between the Dawson boys and the young couple.

Facing the brothers, he joins in with the next part of the chorus. Frank shows them the bottle. 'Thought you gents might be in need of a top up. On the house, this time.'

Once the brothers are holding out their glasses, he turns to the couple as casually as he can. 'Shouldn't you two get going? I'm sure you don't want to miss the main feature.'

The lad has the sense to put down the drinks he's holding. 'You're right.' 'Fraid there's no time to sup up, Joanie – we need to go, or we'll be late.' Grabbing her hand, he leads her out through the door.

'Are you goin' to start pourin' that or what?' Dicer asks.

Rinty scowls at him. 'I don't think I caught your name the last time we was in here. Remind me again.'

'It's Frank,' he tells them, pouring just less than a double measure into each of their glasses.

'Down the hatch.' Dicer knocks back the malt and then smacks his lips. He looks down at his watch and nudges his brother's attention to it.

Rinty swallows his drink in one gulp. This time, Frank detects a slight watering in his eyes. He covers it by smacking his lips exactly as his brother had and wiping his mouth with the back of his hand. 'When you see Dennis, be sure to tell him the Dawsons say ta for *his* generous hospitality.'

'Right.' Dicer slams his empty glass down on the table. 'Let's fuck off outta here.' He picks up his hat, takes a moment to adjust the crown before putting it on.

Both brothers stroll towards the open door. Pausing at the threshold, Dicer tips his hat. 'Be seeing you again, *Frankie.*'

Once the Dawsons have left, the atmosphere lightens although Frank can sense a lingering unease about the place.

It's a much shorter shift – they close an hour earlier on Sunday evenings. Even so, the time seems to drag on. He's kept busy serving a steady stream of customers in the public, though few are feeling flushed enough to buy a round. The saloon bar is pretty much deserted all evening and there's only the occasional rap on the hatch of the jug and bottle from men wanting packs of fags or baccy or an empty bottle filled up.

During last orders, the few remaining customers come up

for their final halves or bottles to take home. The place has already emptied out by the time he locks up.

Frank's managed the whole shift easy enough by himself. He bolts the last of the outside doors. All things considered, he wonders if it might be for the best this way. As long as they get young Jack in for the busiest hours on a Friday or Saturday, he'd have no objection if both of the Stevensons want to leave him to his own devices in future.

"Spect it was a lot quieter tonight.' Grace is standing in the shadows of the saloon bar. He didn't see her walk through.

'You're right – the usual Sunday evening – always the day after the night before. Lots of people regretting things they might have done in haste when they think back on it, I shouldn't wonder.' He gives her a long look.

Grace steps forward into the light with her arms full. 'Here, these are yours.' She hands him back his clothes, folded and ironed and smelling a good deal fresher than for some time.

He's touched by the effort she's made. It's a long while since anyone's laundered his clothes for him. 'There was no need for you to go to such trouble.'

'It was no bother.' Her skirt is swaying with her hips in that way she has. 'Besides, we couldn't have had our barman standin' there lookin' half drowned in front of the customers now, could we?'

He notices her use of "we" – the solidarity it suggests between the two of them – man and wife, after all.

'Well, it's very kind of you; very much appreciated,' he says. Whatever their domestic arrangements, he has no business even thinking of coming between them. 'I'll give Dennis back his clothes once I've had time to wash them.'

Grace seems amused by this. 'There's no rush – he can't get into 'em no more so I'm sure he won't be fussed either way. He barely made it into his bed tonight. I've left him dead to the world up there.'

She puts down the bundle of clothes before advancing a step towards him. 'The amount he's drunk this evening, a bomb could drop in the next street and it wouldn't rouse him.'

Noticing his changed expression, she says: 'Don't look so concerned, there really is nothin' that's goin' to disturb us tonight.'

She leans in closer and he inhales her perfume; notices how the light is falling to one side of her face, leaving the softest of shadows beneath her lips. There's no denying the woman's beauty. The vivid red of her lips seems to make her mouth float away from her face.

'I like you better without the beard,' she says, her words sounding a false note, like she's playing a part. Now her fingers are straying across his face, tracing a line down his cheek and then slowly and with increased pressure along his chin. 'Mmmm, so smooth.'

Despite himself, he becomes aroused when her finger continues its way along his lips. There's an increase in pressure as she dips the tip inside his mouth like she wants him to suck at it. 'So now we're alone, Frank Danby, aren't you going to kiss me?'

Frank's resolve is quick to crumble. He reaches out to stroke her hair and, seeing the movement, she closes her eyes and tilts her face up towards his just like before.

Dammit, he can't stop now. With a force he hadn't intended, he kisses her. His tongue begins to explore her mouth. She tastes sweet and minty. His hand soon strays down to the softness of her breast though it's difficult to feel much through the thick material of brassiere.

But then, for some reason he can't fathom, she begins to pull away. 'Stop! Frank – stop! Please.'

'What's the matter?' He pulls her close again, kissing the side of her face; his nose nuzzling against her ear, his hand running down to explore the silkiness of her stockinged thigh.

She pushes on his chest with some force. 'No, Frank – not

so fast. You need to slow down. I'm not ready to – well, you know.'

He doesn't know; can't fathom out what the hell it is she wants if it's not this. Recovering, he steps back to look at her. He sees how her lipstick has spread so that her mouth had lost it hard edges. There's an expression in her eyes he hadn't expected – like she's wary of him. He's reminded of the way that young girl looked when the Dawson's were advancing towards her.

'I'm sorry,' he tells her. 'I don't know what it is you want from me.'

'No,' she says, her voice cracking, 'I don't expect you do.' She turns away but not before he sees a tear slide down her cheek.

Frank's dumfounded. Neither of them speaks. Her distress moves him more than he can say. His jacket is hanging nearby. He delves in a pocket and hands her his handkerchief. 'It's a clean one, I promise.'

He waits until she's dabbed at her eyes before he rubs her shoulders. When she doesn't resist his touch, he pulls her into his chest. 'I'm sorry if it's me that's upset you, Grace,' he says kissing the top of her head.

CHAPTER THIRTEEN

Frank's quite the gentleman again; shaking his hanky out like a white flag before he hands it over to her. She dabs under her eyes, hoping her mascara's not in streaks down her face. It's too dark to see if she's left black marks on his hanky. Her nose is running with tears, so she wipes it, decides not to actually blow or she'll sound a comical note. In the state she's in, she couldn't bear it if he was to laugh at her.

He hugs her to his chest and it's like a wall pressed against the side of her face, so utterly different from the soft fat on every part of Dennis. Despite serving in the pub all night, there's none of that fags-and-whisky stench about him. She breathes in his smell – that faint tang of fresh sweat.

His arms encircle her. He kisses the top of her hair and she relaxes into him. Her head seems to fit right into the hollow below his chin. Close up, she can see the contours of those muscles running under the sleeve of his shirt.

'Do you ever wish, sometimes, that you could go back to when you were young and start all over again?'

She feels him nod several times. 'All the bloody time.'

Grace takes a deep breath then decides to say it anyway. 'I once saw this film at the pictures; I must have bin about seventeen at the time. It started with this woman shootin' her husband dead on New Year's Eve. You don't really know why.

Anyway, when the clock strikes midnight, she really wishes she hadn't gone an' done it, and so she gets her wish granted; finds herself right back at the start of that year when he's still alive.'

It takes her a moment to continue. 'But you know, even though she keeps trying to stop it from happenin' again, things just keep repeatin' themselves whatever she does. She's trapped.'

He squeezes her arm ever so gently. 'It doesn't sound like there's a happier ending second time around.'

'No, there isn't. It ends up that this man – who's her friend and the only one who believes her about what's happened – *he* goes and shoots the husband this time but with *her* gun.'

She can't speak for a bit, has to take a long steadying breath. 'So you see, she couldn't escape her fate no matter what she did or how hard she tried to.'

'You know, Grace I don't hold with all that nonsense about fate. There is *always* a way out, even from the worst of traps.'

'Do you honestly believe that – because I don't?'

'I do. You just have to be brave enough to take it.' He strokes her hair while she sobs into his chest.

They stay like that for a long time, neither of them speaking and it feels so nice to be hugged standing there in the quiet of the half-darkness. Finally, Frank looks down at her face and she lifts her head up so he can kiss her again. This time his lips feel different – gentler and less urgent. Their kiss goes on for so long she has to remember to breathe through her nose.

His mouth breaks away but only to kiss down her neck. When he starts on her ear, she gets that feeling again – like her insides are about to melt away. Inch by inch he kisses along her collarbone.

Grace feels reckless, yearns to let go and allow his hands to touch her bare skin. Her own fingers fumble to undo the buttons down the front of her dress one at a time until it's wide open all the way to the waist.

He takes a step back, looks at her like he's checking she really did mean to do this. *She* feels wide open now; meeting his gaze to answer the question in his eyes without saying a word.

His hands are on her shoulders and then he's pushing the material right down, baring her upper arms. He reaches around to undo her bra; has it unhooked in a trice – like it's something he's done many times before. Should she be worried about that?

Next minute all she can think about is the pathway his kisses are taking over her naked breasts. She groans aloud with the pleasure of it. Pressed up against the wall, she's overtaken by desire, shocked and yet thrilled to think that this is a man she barely knows. His wet mouth moves across her skin and it feels so good she moans even louder.

Frank's hand comes up over her mouth to stifle her cries. She opens her eyes and comes to her senses, aware of the sound of voices just outside the door. Some people have stopped out there and now they're laughing and singing. She can see the shape of them through the ornate glass.

There's a moment of peace and then the racket starts up again. This time it sounds like they could be jeering. The lights behind the bar are still on – can they see right into the room? One or two of them seem to be bending forward, foreheads touching the windowpane. Can they see her, see exactly what the landlord's wife is getting up to with the new barman? Her face grows hot with the shame of it.

'Hold still, lass,' Frank whispers in her ear, like she might be a horse about to bolt. 'They'll move off in a bit.' She does what he says; has very little choice in the matter. His touch continues to excite her even when someone tries the door handle and she watches it spin round and then back again.

A deep voice says something that causes the others to laugh. She catches his next words: 'Yeah, well I thought I could hear people in there, but you can see for yourself, the place is empty.'

Another man says something but all she can pick out is the word *shame*. She hears the sound of running water and realises that someone is actually piddling against the wall like a ruddy dog.

Gradually, their voices recede and she can breathe again.

'That was a close one,' Frank says. 'Now then, where were we …'

'No don't. This is far too risky,' she tells him. 'I don't know what I was thinkin'. They might have woken Dennis up with all the noise they were makin'. He could be on his way down here right now.'

'You told me the man's well out of it for the night.' His hands have stopped caressing her. 'Would you rather I just sling my hook? I'll go right this minute, if that's what you really want.'

Though his face is in shadow, she can see from his cocksure expression that he's confident she'll say no. 'It's your decision, Grace,' he says. 'You're the boss here; if you ask me to go now, I will.'

'Well, as your boss, I'd say that would be the most sensible thing you could do.'

'The most sensible thing – you're right. I can't argue with that. But is it what you want?'

'Yes; yes it is,' she says.

Grace steps away from his grasp and pulls up the top of her dress, fastening each button with care. Still adjusting her clothing, she walks through the hatch towards the side door. She unhooks Frank's jacket and then stops to pick up the grey fedora hanging next to it, which can only be his. 'This is new, isn't it? Very nice – can I see it on you?'

He doesn't meet her eye as he shrugs on his jacket and plonks the hat on his head. His expression is sullen when she hands him his bundle of clean clothes.

'Not like that,' she tells him stepping back into the saloon bar to view him. 'The angle's wrong. Here, let me.' She reaches up only to adjust the fedora. 'There, that's better.' Grace takes a step back with her hands on her hips as she appraises him. He looks every inch like a film star – a real leading man. 'I'd say that's pretty much perfect.'

'Right, well then, I'd best be off.'

She grabs the sleeve of his jacket. 'Wait a sec, there's something else you need to take with you.'

'And what would that be?'

In his ear she says, 'I'll come home with you tonight, if you'd like me to.'

Smiling now, he tries to slide his free hand onto her bottom. She steps well back from his reach. 'No, Frank, not here, I couldn't bear it.'

'It's quite a walk to my digs and, I have to warn you, it's not exactly the Ritz.'

'But you do have a bed?'

He nods. 'Only a single.'

'Well then, we'll just have to squeeze up, won't we? At least we'll be well away from this place.'

He gives her a crocked smile. 'You'll have to sneak in dead quiet like, so we don't wake up my landlady or her hawk-eyed son. And I suppose you'll have to slip out early an' all.'

'Well now, I'm game for it, if you are.' Despite the bravado of her words, she thinks about how they'll have to pass by the houses of people who know her. To be on the safe side, Frank ought to walk a few yards behind. 'Maybe I should disguise myself – hang on a minute.'

Grace goes out the back to find a headscarf. Choosing one she's seldom worn she wraps it around her hair and ties it in a knot at the front like some of the factory girls do. In the mirror she could almost be anyone.

'So, what do you reckon?' she asks, turning this way and that in front of him. 'With any luck they'll think I'm some floosy you've picked up for the night.' Saying such a thing excites her.

Frank's all smiles now. She grabs a small bottle of Martell and slips it into his pocket. 'Thought we might share a nightcap,' she says – a line from her favourite film. Though it's hardly champagne, it'll do.

CHAPTER FOURTEEN

Monday 23rd June

So hot, her flesh is running with sweat. Frank's naked body is pressed against hers. Outside the birds are already singing. When Grace moves away an inch or two, he nudges up and his heavy arm comes to rest on her shoulder. She can hear someone through in the next room snoring away.

In trying to disentangle herself, she practically falls out of the narrow bed. God, what madness had possessed her last night? Her wristwatch tells her it's ten to five. She guesses it'll be a good forty-minute walk back to the Eight Bells. She can't go home like this, not with the smell of sex all over her the way it must surely be. Looking around she spots a small Belfast sink in the corner; if she can find a flannel, she can at least clean herself up a bit.

Light is stealing into the room and she's appalled by the state of her surroundings; the brown and peeling walls and that threadbare oilcloth on the floor. Last night she'd draped her headscarf over the standard lamp, hadn't stopped to notice the drabness of his bedsit. Now her eyes range over the ill-fitting curtains he'd yanked across the window; not a single mat to put your feet on and nowhere else to sit but the bed. It's clear Frank does his best with what he's got, keeps it tidy in

101

here, like an ex-military man might, but everything's so utterly depressing whichever direction she looks in. The whole place makes her shudder.

She daren't run the hot water – those Baby Burcos make a lot of noise. It'll have to be the cold tap then. At least there's some Palmolive balanced on the edge of the sink to take the smell of him away.

The mismatched cups they'd drunk their brandy from are still there on the small table. 'Cheers,' they'd said as they'd clinked them together – laughed too much over nothing. Frank seemed as nervous as she was until the alcohol warmed her stomach and blunted her conscience. She can see now he'd hardly touched his. The bottle is still there – more than half full.

Her mouth is parched and there's a growing ache behind her eyes. Last night she'd used the lavvy on the half-landing but she can't use it again until she's fully dressed.

She hears the bedsprings go. Next thing, he's standing behind her pressing himself into her bare flesh. 'I must say, Grace, that were quite a night,' he whispers into her ear. His hands come round to cup her breasts like he has every right to keep touching them. 'How're you feeling?'

'It's hard to say,' she tells him, keeping her own voice low. Recalling their lovemaking, she's almost tempted to respond. 'I need to get goin',' she says stepping well away, busying herself with filling the washing up bowl with water. 'Do you have a flannel I can use?'

He finds one in a drawer along with a small, raggedy looking towel. 'Don't worry, they're clean enough,' he tells her.

Grace would like some privacy to wash but she knows that would be impossible and a bit ridiculous given all the things they did together last night. It's a shock to feel the cold flannel on her skin. She puts more soap on before she runs it over her face then her neck and shoulders, swilling it in the bowl and rubbing more soap on it before she does her underarms. With care, she washes between her legs, the tenderness she finds there shocks her with the memory of what they'd got up to.

'Here, let me help,' Frank says, taking the cloth away from her before she can protest. He swills it in the water and then runs it over her shoulders and on down her back and it feels so good. After he's rinsed it again, he runs it across her backside in a circular movement. When the wet cloth delves in between her arse cheeks she finds herself becoming aroused all over again.

'That's enough now,' she tells him. 'I need to get dressed; get out of here before it's too late.'

Her clothes are scattered around the room and they both set about retrieving them. 'I'll come with you part of the way,' he says, handing over her brassier. He delves under the bed. 'I suppose you'll be needing these again, Mrs Stevenson.' Her knickers are right there in the palm of his hand.

As she dresses, Frank begins to wash himself. He shows no self-consciousness even when he's rinsing around his private parts. Here and there on his torso she can see paler lines that look like the threads of old scars. Now she can see him more clearly, she notices how his chest is peppered with a variety of marks. Aside from these imperfections, she has to admit, his body is a thing of beauty – if you can say that about a man. With not a spare ounce of fat on him; he's like one of those statues her and Dot used to giggle over. In Frank's case, you'd have to find a good-sized fig leaf to cover him at the front.

Despite the risk, now she's half decent, she relieves herself in the lavatory on the landing; it's not like she could have held it in all the way back.

Frank's standing guard when she emerges. 'The coast's clear,' he tells her, leading the way. 'Go carefully down the last few steps, they creak like anything. I reckon the old dear must have loosened them on purpose.' This time she ties her headscarf tight at the neck in the regular way.

Once they're clear of his boarding house, she begins to

relax a bit. A milkie gives them a knowing grin and tips his cap with a 'morning' as they walk by. Just gone five o'clock and the streets are coming to life all over again. A large group of men dressed like stevedores walk on past them without a second look.

Though the sun's still low in the sky, the air's already warm; looks like it's going to be another hot one. They must be near to the river; she can smell the rotting debris left high and dry by the outgoing tide. Frank tries to hold her hand, but she won't let him.

The docks up ahead are a hive of activity. Everywhere men are shouting instructions or warnings as they load or unload cargo of all sorts of shapes and sizes. Their route takes them into a narrow alleyway. Once they're inside its high walls, Frank grabs her shoulders and pulls her to him. 'Give us a kiss, Grace,' he says.

'Not likely.' She pushes him away. 'Someone might see us.'

'Right.' He peers down at her. 'I see.' After that he walks some way ahead, hardly looking back over his shoulder. The streets are becoming more familiar; she knows where she is now. 'I can manage on my own from here,' she tells him. 'Thanks for seeing me this far.'

He pulls her into the locked and barred entrance to a tannery, 'I can only speak for meself, but I just want to tell you something.' He clears his throat. 'I can't think how to put it exactly without it sounding crude.'

She can't help but smile. 'Then I'll try not to be too shocked.'

'For me, last night weren't just about the sex – though I'm not saying there were owt wrong with that – far from it, I mean...'

'You certainly know how to sweet talk a girl, Mr Danby.'

'Just hear me out, will ya?' He looks into her eyes. 'It meant something to me. And I think, though I can't be certain, that it meant something special to you an' all.' He looks down at his hands. 'Any road, I thought that you might think I was just taking advantage of you when you were vulnerable but the truth is you made me feel – you *make* me feel – like I haven't felt in a long while.'

'I see,' she says.

'I've been thinking about that film you told me about – how the woman kept trying to get things right the second time around. It seems to me, if there's owt to be learnt from the past, it's that you should tell people how you feel about 'em while you have the chance. So, I thought, if I didn't say anything to you this morning, I might come to regret it later.'

She looks into the depths of his morning-blue eyes. 'I think you'd better kiss me goodbye,' she says.

CHAPTER FIFTEEN

The Eight Bells is in sight. Alone now, Grace takes a deep breath and steadies herself as she approaches her home. She passes only a handful of people and no one she especially recognises. Nevertheless, as she knows well enough, when you're the landlady of a busy pub, lots of people know who you are even if you don't know them.

Her wristwatch tells her it's just gone a quarter to six. Of course she's aware of how suspicious it must look her coming home at this hour; but then again, she could have woken up early and gone for a bit of a stroll around in the cool of the morning. People sometimes do such things.

Trying to look for all the world like she hasn't got a thing to hide, Grace lets herself in through the side door. It's such a relief when she shuts it behind her. So far, so good.

In the narrow passageway, she turns on the lights, takes her headscarf off and then adjusts her hair in the mirror. Checking her reflection, she can see nothing about her face that's especially different from any other day – that's if she doesn't look herself in the eyes.

Thankfully, there's no sign of Dennis downstairs. As she puts on the kettle, she rehearses her story again. She'll keep it simple – slept badly due to the heat, went outside for a stroll round. Now she's stretched her legs, she feels better for it. If he should come down the stairs right this minute, she'll say exactly that, and then mention that she's planning to take a bath before trying to catch up on a few more hours' sleep.

To her relief, all is quiet up there. She makes Dennis a cup of tea – strong the way he likes it – and takes it upstairs.

He's still lying there in the dark snoring away. When she puts the cup down on the bedside table, it feels like she's establishing an alibi. Dennis turns over in the bed, like he senses her presence. She holds her breath and waits.

After a bit of snuffling, he settles down, breathing with his mouth open in the same untroubled rhythm as before. With as little noise as possible, she pulls out a drawer to get out some clean undies and stockings. Her skirt and blouse are still on the back of the chair.

Downstairs in the kitchen, she sips at her tea while the bath water's running. The warmth of the cup seems to steady her nerves.

She locks the bathroom door before undressing. The water feels so good on her skin. Soaping herself all over, she's relieved to be cleaner on the outside at least. She shuts her eyes and tries to pretend she's floating on her back in a sun-warmed sea.

Once she's dressed again, Grace rinses her smalls twice over in the basin. Her hands are wrinkled from the water and she stares at them. One day her skin will no longer be smooth and what will she have to show for all the years in between?

Her old wraparound apron is hanging on the back of the door. She puts it on over her clothes like she's a regular housewife. Sackcloth and ashes comes to mind. If anyone is looking out of a window, they'll only see her taking a bit of washing out to the line in the yard.

So what? You wouldn't think twice about something like that.

They always send the sheets and towels out to the laundry, but the rest of the dirty washing has piled up in her absence. She really should make a start on it; it is Monday morning after all and a fine day at that.

The stairs creak and groan and she turns to face Dennis. 'You're up bright an' early this mornin'.' His face is still puffy, his hair all over the place. 'Ta very much for the tea; it was a bit tepid by the time I woke up, but I drank it all the same.' Nothing about him suggests he's suspicious.

'Couldn't sleep – it was so close,' she says. 'I even went for a bit of a stroll around outside to see if that would help.'

'And did it?' He rakes his hand through his hair missing the worst of it at the back.

'A bit.'

He seems distracted by something, hardly listening as she prattles on about her disturbed night.

'You look all-in, darlin',' he says. 'Why don't you go on back up to bed; see if you can catch a couple more hours' kip?' Dennis takes various keys from the hooks in the passageway and puts them on the table. 'We've got that delivery coming shortly. I can handle it. And I can manage to get my own breakfast.'

'Well – if you're sure.' She feigns a yawn, which turns into a real one. It's odd but she's almost disappointed to have got away with such an act of betrayal so easily.

Grace pulls the bedroom curtains though they're too thin to block out all the glare of the sun. She takes off her top clothes and gets into bed still wearing her petticoat and underwear. It's so nice to stretch out in comfort. She's dog-tired. Even with everything in such a quandary, it's not long before she's drifting into sleep.

Grace is woken by noises from outside. Well used to Alfie the drayman calling, she knows his booming voice and the familiar sound of barrels rolling along the cobbles. This is something different. She can hear a petrol engine idling for a moment before it cuts out. Dennis is talking to someone down in the side alley, but she can't hear what they're saying.

Her curiosity roused, Grace goes out onto the landing and peers through the bottom of the net curtain. From here she has a good view of the tops of their heads though the other man is wearing a cap. The two of them are standing beside a lorry. Along the side of it she reads: *C. Lloy.* Then: *Son.* Then: *al Builders.*

Grace knows who Cyril Lloyd is – he comes into the saloon bar sometimes; likes to doff his trilby at her in a smarmy way and call her Mrs S. She assumes the man must be doing well for himself – he's always smartly dressed; wears that thick gold ring on his little finger. The only thing she has against him is he seems to be thick as thieves with that little snake Arnold Kirby.

So, if that's his lorry – which it obviously is – what are those two up to down there?

The man in the cap pulls back the tarpaulin covering the back of the lorry. With Dennis's help, he unloads half a dozen cardboard boxes. He puts the first two onto a sack truck, which he wheels in the direction of their bottle store. Dennis trots along behind him.

Once all six boxes have been unloaded, she expects the man to drive away but instead he waits there by his lorry. Dennis hasn't yet emerged. The man lights up a fag and then looks up at the building as he smokes it. She has to duck down behind the sill.

When she steals a look again, Dennis has come back out and they're standing around chatting and smoking together. Then the man in the cap abruptly grinds his dog end under his boot and climbs up into the cab. Before he shuts the door, Dennis takes something out of his pocket and hands it up to him. At first, she can't see what it is and then the sun glints off a set of keys.

Grace gets dressed, intending to go down and ask Dennis

exactly what he's up to giving the pub keys out to other people.

She can smell burnt toast before she even opens the kitchen door. His plate is still on the table with the cut off crusts and two empty eggshells.

Dennis must be out in the bar. The passageway is too dark, so she turns on the light to check along the row of hooks where they keep the sets of keys. Grace is pleased to see the main ones for the pub are all there safely. It's only that small bunch at the end that's missing. They're the ones for that old lockup of his under the railway arches.

Grace knows exactly where the lockup is, though she's never once set foot inside it. Dennis has always dismissed any interest she's shown, telling her it's full of nothing worth keeping, just all sorts of bits and pieces that used to belong to his parents – things that, now they'd passed on, he doesn't have the heart to throw away.

She opens the door and hears her husband whistling in the bar. At least the man sounds happy for a change. It would be easy enough to go in and demand he tells her exactly what's in those cardboard boxes – though she's already got an idea what the answer to that question would be.

If Dennis doesn't know she's caught on, it might be easier to check what the ruddy man's up to and, especially, why he would give the keys to that lockup of his to one of Cyril Lloyd's men. What exactly have those two gone and cooked up together?

She goes through into the public bar where Bessie is mopping the floor in her usual less-than-enthusiastic manner. Dennis is through in the saloon leaning against the counter reading something. Straight away, Grace can see it's The Sporting Life. 'You're up then,' he says, folding the newspaper to hide the page he'd been studying.

'Yes. I feel much better now I've had a rest.'

She's quick to change the subject. 'I saw you out the window talking to one of Cyril's chaps.'

From the corner of her eye, she sees Bessie straightening up, a hand in the small of her back while she stops to listen. Nothing much gets past that one.

Grace can see her husband's discomfort, that way he has of eyeing up the ceiling just before he conjures up a whole host of half-truths and lies to cover his tracks.

'That was just Bernie,' he begins. 'He was delivering something down the road so I waved him down. I asked him to ask Cyril if one of his roofers could take a look at the gents' roof sometime. It's not so obvious in this dry spell, but there's damp getting in down the far corner.' He looks more directly at her now; his colour is up, that's for sure. 'Bernie thought it was probably somethin' blockin' the gutter or maybe a few slipped tiles. As a matter of fact, he was very helpful.'

Granted, the man can certainly think on his feet when he needs to. In truth, hasn't she always allowed him a few secrets?

'I could see as much,' she says. 'You two looked as thick as thieves out there.'

Grace stares directly at Bessie now. The old woman dunks her mop and then twists it round and round hoping to hear more before she reluctantly starts on the floor again.

'You need to be careful.' She's looking him straight in the eyes and for once he can't hide the alarm in his face. 'He's a sly one that Cyril Lloyd. Just you make sure he doesn't take advantage.'

With that she walks away; leaves him to it. Who is she, after all, to insist on the truth and nothing but the truth between them when she's ready to spin a pack of lies herself?

Maybe this time, it might be as well if she knows next to nothing about what Dennis Stevenson has gone and got himself mixed up in.

CHAPTER SIXTEEN

The sun is higher now, already skipping along the edge of the rooftops. Heading in no particular direction, Frank walks and walks; the cobbles around the dockyards unyielding beneath the worn soles of his shoes.

The usual arrangement is that he goes in to work a bit later on a Monday morning. 'There's no point you gettin' here any sooner,' Dennis had reminded him more than once. 'Bessie won't want you under her feet while she's doin' the floors. Eleven is plenty early enough.'

People crowd the pavements or speed past him on push-bikes – off somewhere in a hurry at the start of the working week. Turning the corner, a great ship looms above the warehouses and wharfs like a cathedral dwarfing all before it. Through the gaps between buildings, he glimpses all manner of ships and boats crisscrossing the river. Light patterns the surface of the water and bounces off soot-blackened walls. For a long moment he stares at those restless shapes forever forming and then dissolving again.

'Kiss me goodbye,' she'd said and he'd done just that; but it wasn't the long lingering kiss he'd hoped for. She'd broken away from him too soon, turned her back and not looked round once as she hurried away. Now he thinks about it, Grace's final words could have meant something entirely different.

Frank gets to the pub just before opening time. For a change the place smells of furniture polish and disinfectant. Grace is nowhere to be seen but Dennis is already in the bar messing about with the sign on one of the pumps.

'Mornin', Frank,' he says, hardly looking up. 'I trust you enjoyed a few extra hours in bed this mornin'?'

The question catches him unaware. Something about the man's tone doesn't sound right. 'Ah – yes, I did, ta,' he tells him, wondering if Dennis might have his suspicions. 'I've brought back your clothes. Bit hard to wash them in my digs or I would have. Thanks again for helping me out.'

The landlord barely looks at the small pile. 'My wife's idea entirely,' he says. 'That woman can never say no when somebody needs help; always did have a soft spot for someone in trouble. A soft touch, some people might say. Course there's always some who'll take advantage of a person's gentle nature.'

This almost sounds like a thinly veiled accusation but, then again, he could be imagining it. Frank can't think how he should respond, so he says nothing. It's all he can do to look the other man in the eyes. Dennis appears to be his usual self only a bit redder in the face. Large beads of sweat are forming on his forehead and running down the side of his nose. He can smell the Brylcreem that's keeping the man's hair under control. That moustache on his upper lip once again puts Frank in mind of a Fox Moth caterpillar.

In the silence that follows, he finds himself blathering. 'Another fine day out there. Quite a dry spell we're having.' When Dennis fails to respond, 'Is there owt I can help with before we open up?'

The landlord turns his attention back to the pump label. (The man always insists on them lining up exactly.) 'I think you'll find it's all in hand. As you can see, I've done all the bottlin' up, an' the optics are fine.'

Dennis's eyes dart up to the clock on the wall. 'Two minutes past, you can open up, though I doubt you'll be trampled in the rush.'

When not a soul walks through the door, the landlord smiles at him in an I-told-you-so manner. 'Well, I'll leave you to it,' he says. 'Grace's got her head down. Catchin' up after a disturbed night.' He rubs his hands together. 'I'm off out for a bit. Just got a spot of business to see to.'

The morning drags on. Frank keeps hoping Grace will come through and talk to him but she doesn't. Around half past one, he catches sight of her leaving through the side door. The woman doesn't even glance in his direction.

After that he can't help himself, he keeps checking the door hoping to get a glimpse of her returning. If only he could talk to her, find out how she's really feeling.

In his afternoon break he dawdles in the street outside hoping to bump into her as she returns home. He passes a crowded café and then turns back. This is the most likely route she'll take; if he sits near the window, he might catch a glimpse of her. He's got enough change in his pocket for a cup of tea.

A skinny redhead looks up from behind the counter. 'Afternoon, love,' she says. 'Just you, is it?' She nods him towards a vacant table near the back.

'Mind if I sit here by the window instead?'

'Take your pick, darlin' – it's a free country.'

Frank decides not to argue with that statement. The girl's quick to bring him his tea. There's even a biscuit in the saucer – a Marie. 'Don't worry, I won't charge you extra.'

He's obliged to thank her. 'Anything else I can tempt you with?' This time she adds a flirtatious smile. Her freckled cheeks redden as she waits for his answer.

'Not right now,' he tells her. 'This will do me fine, thanks.'

Stirring his tea, he begins to contemplate his immediate future. After what happened last night, everything is up in the air again and there's no knowing where things will land.

The entrance bell rings out and an old chap in shirtsleeves

and green braces comes in. Without asking, he sits down at the table opposite him. Frank continues to check the street while in his side vision he sees the man take his specs from his pocket and clean the lenses with his hanky.

A gaggle of laughing women pass the window, dressed up to the nines and in a hurry to get somewhere. None of them looks remotely like her.

Once he's ordered a tea and a crumpet, the old man extracts a rolled-up newspaper from his other pocket and fans himself with it. 'Goin' to be another scorcher.'

When Frank remains mute, the old chap adjusts his specs, flattens out the paper and turns his full attention to the inside pages.

The man's tea arrives first. He carries on reading, holding his newspaper – The Evening News – inches away from Frank's face.

The headline on the front page reads: GUILTY SPY TO GO FREE. His curiosity aroused, Frank looks away from the window to scan the article. Seems a Russian spy was caught red-handed in a London park with top-secret stuff on him.

He has to lean forward to read the smaller print about how this man had been sentenced to five years on Thursday, only to be released at the weekend because of his "diplomatic immunity".

The old chap looks up and catches Frank's eye before checking to see what he's been reading. 'Terrible, ent it? They catch the ruddy fella at it; he gets banged up like he should be and then the bugger gets let off scot-free. Would you ruddy Adam and Eve it? If you're a bloody foreigner, you can get away with murder. Diplomatic immunity – wouldn't we all like a bit of that? Makes a bloody mockery of the laws the rest of us have to follow.'

'You're not wrong about that,' Frank says, more to shut him up than anything. The street is empty save for a couple of chaps on pushbikes.

The old man holds his gaze. 'Here now, take a look at this.' He folds the newspaper over to reveal one of the inside pages. OUR SEARCH FOR A HERO the headline reads. 'See there; the fella in this photo – the one they're lookin' for – he looks a bit like you, mate.'

Frank stares at a blurred snap of the crowd on Tower Beach. They've drawn a thick black circle around his head. 'I suppose there is a passing resemblance,' he admits. 'Though you could say the same about half the men in London.'

'I 'spose your hair's a bit lighter than his is,' the old man concedes. 'Says here this chap saved a kiddie from certain drowning.'

'Afraid I can't even swim.' Frank shrugs, the lie coming easy. 'I've always had a terrible fear of water.'

The old man finishes his drink then puts down the newspaper to take out his tobacco tin. 'Paper's offerin' the lucky bugger fifty guineas if he comes forward. That's more than half my pension for the year.' When he laughs his front teeth fall down from his gum. 'Eh – if *he* don't come forward you could always dye yer hair and go an' claim it.'

He takes his time rolling a cigarette and then runs his tongue along the flimsy paper to seal it. 'Ah, it's a funny old world,' he says, inserting the roll up into the corner of his mouth. 'Comes to somethin' when a villain can get away with his crime and a genuine hero don't seem to want his just reward.'

Frank spots a girl with the same shade of hair as Grace disappearing around the corner. His first instinct is to run. As he gets up to leave, the old man mumbles: 'A man could do a lot with fifty guineas.'

CHAPTER SEVENTEEN

Tuesday 24th June

Dot comes to the door with a towel draped over her head and a row of skinny curlers poking out of the front. Thinking of sardines, Grace stifles a giggle.

'Don't you start,' her friend says. 'I'm just tryin' out this new perm. Pin up, it's called. Cost me a guinea with the rollers as well so it better look good. Mind you, they do promise you your money back if it doesn't work wonders.'

'I need to talk to you,' Grace tells her once they're safely inside.

'Why – what's happened now?'

'Are your mum and dad in?' That chemical smell is already making her eyes smart in the confined space of the hall.

'D'you think I'd be doin' this if they were? I'd never hear the end of it if our dad saw me lookin' like this. Don't you go tellin' 'em how much it cost, neither.' They move through into the small kitchen and its cloying heat. 'I've got to wash this off in ten minutes,' Dot tells her. 'Don't let me forget, will ya?'

She finds her cigarettes and lights one – knows better than to offer one to Grace. Her face looks different with her hair away from it – her dark eyes much more prominent than usual. 'So, what did you want to tell me then? Have you had another bust up with Dennis?'

'No, not that.' Grace wonders if this is such a good idea after all. Maybe she'd be better off keeping it to herself. No – it's no good, she just *has* to tell someone about what's happened, or she'll burst.

'I don't suppose you've seen our new barman,' she begins.

Dot turns her head to blow smoke off to one side. 'As a matter of fact, I spoke to him when I called round last week to ask Dennis if you were back from your ma's. To tell you the truth, it was a bit embarrassin'; I could barely take me ruddy eyes off the man.' After another drag on her cigarette she asks, 'Is he married?'

'No. At least, I don't think so.'

Dot pulls a face. 'Then there has to be a reason why a man of his age, who looks like that, is still a bachelor.'

'Maybe he just hasn't found the right girl yet?'

'Or maybe he's one of them?'

Grace frowns. 'One of what?'

'One of them – you know; men who don't like women much; least not in that way. Them who would rather be with other men, if you get my drift.' Though there's no one else around, she lowers her voice. 'Our Reg reckons he knew lots of queers in the army and they're usually the best lookin' ones.'

'You shouldn't go calling them queer. I mean –' Grace stops herself. 'Besides, what about Clark Gable? Or Alan Ladd? Tony flamin' Curtis even. They're all really handsome so, by your reckonin' all of 'em must be –'

'Nancy-boys?'

'Oh, for Pete's sake, Dot – the word is homosexual.'

'There's no need to get your hair off; I was only suggestin' your barman might not be a ladies' man.'

'Well I can tell you he is. Alright?'

'Oh, I see.' The smoke from Dot's fag is rising into her face. 'Got proof of it, then, have ya?'

'No.' Grace can feel herself blushing. 'Of course I bloody well haven't – not in the way you're suggestin'. I can just tell he likes women, that's all I'm sayin'.'

'Well then – that's good. Maybe I'll call round an' have a drink with you in the saloon bar one night this week an' hope he takes it from there. That's if you've no objection, like?'

'Why on earth would I mind one way or the other?' Grace does her best to look unconcerned.

Dot looks up at the clock. 'So, what was it you wanted to tell me about your oh-so-handsome barman then?'

'Only that we're not sure whether to keep him on or not. Now I'm back, me an' Dennis can probably manage by ourselves without him.'

Dot stubs out her cigarette. 'Be a cryin' shame to get rid of a bloke like that unless you really have to.' She pokes at a curler. 'He's done nothin' wrong, has he? Not been fiddlin' the till or summat like that?'

'No – the man seems honest enough.'

'Well then, if you want my opinion on the matter, you'll hang onto him for as long as you can.' She lifts the towel from her head. 'Besides, it'll give me a chance to turn his head with this new hairdo of mine.' She dips her head down so Grace can get a better view. 'Look, I've put this row of medium sized ones along the top bit so it should stick up a bit like Piper Laurie's does.'

Grace looks up at the clock. 'That ten minutes is nearly up. I'd better leave you to it.'

Dot looks crestfallen. 'But don't you want to stay an' see what this turns out like? Witness the brand new me?'

'Oh, all right then.' She can never stay cross with her for long. Dot's been a good friend to her. In fact, since she married Dennis, the girl's been the only friend that's stuck by her.

Her husband's hat and jacket aren't on the hook. Grace checks the row of keys and the set for the lockup is still missing. The smell of fish and chips lingers in the kitchen; a few burnt chips still nestle in some crumpled and oily newspaper. A couple of teacups lie on their side in the bowl. He hasn't put the milk away and a quick sniff tells her it's already on the turn.

Propped against the bread bin, a scribbled note reads: *Gone to see our Stanley. Will probably be back late. No need to wait up.*

It's possible he really has gone to see his brother in Bromley this time, but she doubts it. She runs the kitchen tap until the water's cooler and then gulps down a full glass. Feeling better, she makes herself a fish paste sandwich, which she takes upstairs to the living room.

Straight away she can see their things have been disturbed; someone's rifled through all the papers on the top of the bureau and a couple of its drawers are sticking out. The stuff they keep on the mantelpiece is all topsy-turvy. When she checks the drawers and cupboards in the bedroom, it's clear the whole lot's been pulled about.

There's no sign of a break in, though the window in the living room is wide open. It would be easy enough for someone to stand on one of the bins and shin up the drainpipe.

It's not like they keep any valuables up here, not since Dennis disturbed a burglar a couple of years back. After that, they've been meticulous about locking up and storing any overnight cash in the safe. Any pub's a target for thieves; they even discussed putting bars on the upstairs windows. Grace had vetoed that idea – if there was a fire, they'd have no means of escape.

She runs downstairs to check the small safe hidden behind a picture on the kitchen wall. Thank the Lord it's still firmly shut. She dials the combination, is relieved to see the black cash tin is in there. There's no money inside, but why would there be? Dennis always puts the day's float in the till just before opening time. He ought to have paid the weekend takings into the bank on his way to the station.

Behind the empty cash box, there's a stack of papers – insurance stuff, their various certificates, both passports and, on top of the lot, their ration books. Everything's where it should be in a neat pile.

The most sensible explanation for the disorder upstairs is that Dennis himself had been frantic to find something – might have been a betting slip he'd lost.

Midway through the afternoon and the stale heat of the day is closing in on Grace. She's not used to sitting idle in the middle of the day; it makes her feel like a ruddy prisoner in her own home. Somewhere outside a group of kids are laughing and squealing in their backyard. A pigeon lands on the windowsill not a yard away from where she's sitting and begins a rhythmic cooing. Its curious eyes stare at her while its restless feet shuffle this way and that along the sill like an act in the music hall. Grace shoos the bird away and closes the window in case it has ideas about hopping inside once her back is turned. She drums her fingers on the tabletop. It's no good – Frank or no Frank, she has to go in there.

The afternoon shift is ending and there's barely a handful of customers left in the public. The saloon bar appears to be empty.

Frank looks up from washing glasses and smiles at her. Despite her best intentions, the sight of him moves her. His pleasure at seeing her is written all over his face like an open letter anyone might read if they had a mind to.

Grace is careful to keep the gap between them to a respectable distance. She nods to Fat Harry and Wilf, puts some cheer in her voice as she says, 'Good afternoon, gents.'

'There's nothin' *good* about it,' Harry tells her. 'The missus 'as got me decoratin' our kitchen – in this flamin' weather! Paper's dryin' out before I can hardly get it on the bloody wall.'

'Oh, stop all your moanin, will ya?' Wilf nudges his drinking arm on purpose. 'She's hardly held yer nose to the grindstone, 'as she? You've been in here a good hour or more.'

'You don't know the half of it, mate. I've only been let out on strict instructions I'm to have no more than a pint in case I fall off the flamin' stepladder.'

''Spect it'll all be worth it for the end result,' Grace suggests.

'Will it buggery – 'scuse my French, sweetheart – lime green and blue little squiggles everywhere you look.' He finishes his pint and slams it down on the counter. 'Hurts yer eyes, it does. Fashionable, she calls it. All them years at sea I was never sick, but I reckon that wallpaper's gonna do it for me.'

Wilf looks at his watch. 'Come on, Harry – sup up, mate. I dare say these two young people are keen to lock up.'

'No need to rush your drinks,' Grace tells them though she can see there's only a couple of minutes to go. She flips the hatch over and goes to collect the handful of empty glasses dotted around the place.

With the counter safely between them, she addresses Frank. 'I just wondered if Dennis had left you the usual float this mornin'?'

His eyebrows come together. 'Aye: five quid in change – same as always for a Tuesday morning.' His gaze sharpens. 'Is there a problem?'

'No, no, it's fine.' She tries to strike a casual note. 'I was just wondering if he happened to mention he was goin' to the bank?'

Her eyes are drawn to Frank's hands as he works the cloth round the glass, those long, elegant fingers that you wouldn't expect on a man of his size. The next second she's reminded of how those same hands caressed every inch of her naked body.

A wave of lust runs through her and straight away there's a new dampness between her legs like she's no more than an animal on heat, for goodness' sake.

'No – Dennis said nowt to me about what he was up to or where he might be going.'

'And he seemed quite normal to you, did he?'

He's frowning now. 'Far as I could tell, aye.'

On his way to the door, Wilf turns: 'Be seein' you both.'

Does she imagine that hint of suspicion in the look he gives her?

Once the last bolt is across, Frank turns to her. 'Grace, I need to talk to you.'

'What about?'

'Surely you can guess?'

'Am I supposed to read your mind?' Grace retreats from the glare of the windows, the swirling patterns of sunlight are showing up every flaw in the room, every scrap of dirt. She walks off, heading towards the door to their private quarters.

There's a thread of anger in his voice as he strides after her. 'I shouldn't need to spell it out.'

She turns with her back against the passageway door. 'Go on then, I'm all ears, Mr Danby; what is it you want to say to me?'

'Not like this – not when you're playing games.' She can see he's proper angry now. He takes a step closer looking like he might be about to slap her. Is this another side to him – this angry man already making his demands?

He grabs the top of her arm, pulls her towards him until his face is a hair's breadth from hers. Her heart's hammering in her chest as she stares up at him.

Grace breaks first; her mouth devouring the taste of him; her hands grabbing those perfect arse cheeks of his until he's pressed so hard against her it hurts.

She comes up for air. 'Dennis won't be back till late tonight.' Taking hold of his hand, she pulls him along the shadowy passageway.

He stops, yanks her towards him again. The edge of the coat stand is pressing into her flesh and likely to leave a bruise. 'We mustn't.' She has to force the words out of her mouth. 'We shouldn't do it – least not in our bed.'

Frank's smile reveals those perfect teeth of his. In her ear, he whispers: 'Well then, why don't we start with the kitchen table?'

Grace stands alone by the cooker. It's after opening time and Frank's already gone through to the bars. When she looks at the out-of-its-place table, the wall by the door and then on through to the still-full bathtub – all of them seem invisibly tainted by the acts they've just committed. They may not have slept in Dennis's bed but that was a rather hollow gesture given there'd been no sleeping involved. If Dennis were a dog, he'd smell her out – sniff the two of them together on every surface.

What kind of woman must she be if she's feeling no shame? In fact, when she thinks over what they've just done, the things that linger are to do with how good it felt to let go like that, give in to the demands of the flesh like there was nothing wicked in it after all.

At first, they'd both been too full of need, but then, even with the water sloshing everywhere, it felt tender, natural; like she was caught up in a dance her body had been waiting all these years to perform.

No, this time she feels no guilt and little remorse – what they've done is not a betrayal but an act of faith in what nature intended between a man and a woman.

Though she's almost reluctant to dispose of the evidence of their lovemaking, her sensible self takes control of the situation. She finds herself humming something as she cleans and then laughs out loud when she realises it's that Hoagy Carmichael song, *My Resistance is Low*. Ha – non-existent, more like.

Unable to recall the words, she ends up simply humming the tune. She lets out the tepid bathwater and mops up all the puddles on the floor below. It's a reminder of the previous time Frank was in this bathtub and that mysterious layer of sand he left behind.

Maybe he's really a merman? The thought tickles her imagination. Yes, Frank Danby's not really human after all; he's a sea creature walking amongst them in disguise – only borrowing those legs of his while he's on dry land.

In the kitchen, she rights the heavy table, having to guess the exact spot it was in before. It seems stable enough, unscathed by the going-over it's just had. She's not sure she can say the same about herself.

There's not much to do at the sink, only a few crocks to wash up. She throws Dennis's chip paper into the bin and is about to close the lid when something on the newspaper catches her attention. She extracts it again.

CHAPTER EIGHTEEN

Tuesday nights are normally slow to start with and so far the place is still half empty. A short chap Frank's not seen before comes up for half a mild. The man's eyes seem to be darting in every direction.

Frank looks up when Grace strides through, is careful to say: 'Evening, Mrs Stevenson.' She just stands there with one hand planted on her hip. Her skirt is hiding whatever it is she's holding down by her side. Grace looks flustered but doesn't say a thing until he's taken the money and rung it into the till.

Walking towards the other bar, she trails the smell of fresh soap in her wake.

'There's something I need to show you, Frank.'

'Oh really.' He follows on her heels, unable to wipe the smile from his face. 'I can't imagine what else that might be, Mrs Stevenson.'

Once they're in the small recess where they serve saloon customers, she turns to face him. 'Have you seen this?' She slaps a piece of newspaper down on the counter.

Someone must have crumpled the paper before she smoothed it out. He can smell the vinegar coming off it. A grease patch covers part of the sky, but the rest of the photograph is clear enough. She jabs a finger at his likeness. Once again he sees the black circle drawn around his head like a noose. 'They're callin' you a bloody hero,' she says.

He glances away – checks there's no one in earshot then frowns, shakes his head with some vigour. 'What are you on about? That's not me, though I grant you he looks a bit like me.'

As close as the two of them are she must have spotted the involuntary muscle spasm in his cheek. He finds himself rubbing the scar on his forehead like he tends to when he's nervous. Involuntary they call it – those little jerking movements that can give you away.

Grace moves nearer to whisper: 'Don't you dare tell me such a barefaced lie, Frank Danby, and expect me to believe it. D'you hear me?'

Words form in his brain, but he can't seem to express them. Throwing caution aside, he plants his lips right in her hair and whispers: 'What can I say to you, Grace? As you can see, I'm a wanted man.'

'You lied to my face about how you got in such a state on Saturday,' she hisses. 'All that business about falling in the lake when it was really the river.' Her red fingernail jabs the paper again. 'I'm guessin' you won't be claiming this reward. Why would that be, exactly?'

'We'll talk about it later,' he says, his tone deadly serious now. Before she can protest, he walks away.

Grace doesn't hang around. He hears the rustle of her skirt as she pushes past him. She slams the door behind her.

He spends the rest of the evening wondering how he's going to explain himself. It's likely she'll sniff out any lie but, on the other hand, the less she knows about any of it, the better it'll be.

Around nine o'clock the public door opens and Jack Dawson walks in. An audible muttering goes round as the man saunters towards the bar. Everything about him reeks of wealth. He takes off his fancy fedora and leans both hands on the counter, his gold rings glinting like knuckledusters. The tattoo of a raven peeks out from one rolled-up shirtsleeve. He fixes Frank with his pale blue eyes. 'Pint of bitter, if you please, barman.'

As he's pulling the man's pint, Frank notices a sizeable number of drinkers have already left the premises. The rest are watching the man's every move.

Dawson sniffs at his drink before taking a sip and weighing up the taste like a connoisseur. He spits it back into the glass. 'Tastes like piss.' The light bounces off his slicked-back hair as he leans in. 'Good job I'm not here for the ruddy beer.' He slams down his glass spilling the contents along the counter. 'Dennis in the back, is he?'

'Mr Stevenson went out early this morning. I'm not sure we're expecting him back for a while – could even be a few days.'

'Is that so?' Dawson pulls at his chin like he might be stroking an invisible beard. 'You're Frank, aren't ya? Frank *Danby*. My brothers tell me you're in the habit of givin' out free whiskies. Now why would that be?'

Without waiting for an answer, he picks up his hat. 'For the beer,' he says, throwing a shilling down on the counter where it spins before it settles. 'I always settle my debts.'

At closing time Frank is relieved to lock the doors and start the clearing up. He takes his time about each task, knowing when he's finished he'll have to go through and talk to Grace. Should he warn her in some way?

Someone's pounding on the door of the public bar. Frank decides to ignore whoever it is. 'Open up, for Christ's sake!' He recognises Thin Harry's voice. 'I've got Dennis out here an' he's in a bad way.'

Frank flicks on the light and unlocks the door. As soon as he pulls back the last bolts the two men stumble inside.

Frank grabs hold Dennis before he falls. The metallic smell of blood hits his nostrils along with the whisky and cigars on the landlord's breath.

Between them they get Dennis onto a chair. Breathing hard, Harry says: 'I found him on the corner – he was sprawled out on the pavement outside the ironmongers.' The docker sits down to get his breath back.

Frank scrutinises the injured man. His right eye is almost swollen shut and his cheeks and the right side of his jaw are a mass of blood and bruising. To stop him sliding off the chair, Frank puts a hand to his chest and Dennis cries out in pain. 'Looks likely he's got a few cracked ribs,' he says, 'who knows what else besides.'

'Looks far worse in the light.' Harry stands up, starts pacing the floor. 'Reckon we need to get him to hospital.'

Dennis rouses himself, 'No bloody hospital.' He points a finger at both of them in turn. 'Don't want a fuss – you hear me?' He tries to shake his head then winces with the pain of it. 'Once I've had a bit of a lie down, I'll be right as rain.' He grabs at Frank's sleeve. 'No doctors – understand?' His good eye looks straight into Frank's before he lets go.

'Man's out of his wits – take no notice,' Harry mutters. 'You get him cleaned up a bit while I go an' phone for an ambulance.'

'No!' Frank pushes the docker's shoulder to sit him back down. 'The man knows what he's saying alright. He must have his reasons – we should go along with what he wants.'

'What's all this racket?' Grace demands from the doorway. Her hands fly to her mouth. 'Oh, my good Lord, whatever's happened?' She looks straight at Frank. 'You didn't –'

'Harry found him like this.'

'Came across him lying half in the road just round the corner,' Harry says. 'Bloody lucky some car didn't hit him.'

'Oh, Dennis, my love, will you look at the state of you.' Grace bends down to examine his injuries. 'What in God's name happened?' She gently squeezes her husband's shoulder. Turning to Harry she says, 'He might have bin run over?'

'Done over, more like,' Harry tells her. 'Look at his eye. You might check his pockets, see if he's bin robbed. There was no bugger around when I found him. I've no idea what sort of bastard would go an' do such a thing.'

Frank says nothing while Grace examines her husband's injuries. 'Who was it did this to you, darlin'?'

Dennis opens his one good eye. 'Too bloody dark.'

'We have to get him a doctor,' Grace tells them.

'No!' Dennis roars. 'I ent seein' no ruddy doctor – d'you hear me, woman?' He subsides from the effort. 'Wasn't no thief, that's for sure. It'd be more than my life's worth if the Old Bill started askin' questions.' He touches his wife's hand. 'Please, sweetheart, trust me, it's for the best.'

Frank and Harry wait for her response.

'Okay, we'll have it your way – for now, anyway.'

'Can you stand, are your legs alright?' Frank raises his voice to stop him drifting off.

The landlord's eyes remain glazed for a minute before he stirs himself. 'I think so.'

Between them, they manage to get him into the back kitchen. 'Hold up,' Harry says. 'Let me get me breath back.'

They lower Dennis into a softer chair. Grace finds a flannel to sponge the worst of the blood from his face. It's not much of an improvement. Harry squats down to the injured man's eye level. 'This may not be the right time to say it, but I'll say it anyway – you, Dennis Stevenson, are your own worst enemy. This here's bin a long time coming. Think of the bloody company you bin keepin', for Christ's sake.'

Dennis looks like he's drifted off. 'Why do I get the feelin' I'm talking to meself?' Shaking his head Harry straightens up. 'Not goin' to be easy but we better try an' get him up to his bed.'

'Wait.' Frank bends close to the landlord's wrecked face. 'Are you quite sure about this? We shouldn't be moving you around or owt before a doctor's had chance to check over them ribs of yours. I used to do a bit of boxin' – I know it can be serious if a broken rib punctures a lung or summat like that.'

The landlord opens his good eye. Looking at Grace he says, 'Don't you dare go callin' any doctors.' With an effort he swivels his head from Frank to Harry. 'Same goes for you two. We're all what you might call men of the world.' With an effort he taps his nose. 'You know what I'm saying without me havin' to spell it out.'

Grace tries to carry on sponging his face, but Dennis brushes her hand away. 'If you want to help me, sweetheart, you'll go an' get me a drop of whisky.' The landlord's attempt at a smile reveals several missing teeth. 'Need somethin' to deaden the pain before they start manhandling me up them stairs.'

Grace stands her ground. 'Looks to me like you've had more than enough booze. I'll fetch you some aspirin, if you like.'

'Right then, well, we'd better get on with it.' Thin Harry rubs his hands together. 'Don't know about you buggers but I've got an early start in the mornin'. We'd better be getting 'im up them apples.' He looks at his watch. 'My missus'll be thinkin' it's me that's had a ruddy accident. We don't want her ringin' the Old Bill.'

It's quite a struggle to get him up the narrow staircase and into the bedroom. One final heave has him on the bed.

'I'm all in.' Harry doubles over, breathing hard.

'I can't thank you enough for everythin' you've done.' Grace squeezes his arm. 'If you hadn't found him lying there, Lord only knows what would have happened. You get off home now Harry – Frank and I can manage the rest between us.'

'I'll lock up behind you,' Frank says, following the docker down the stairs.

Harry retrieves his cap from the floor then stands on the threshold fiddling with it. 'You don't need me to tell you –' He points his cap at Frank's chest, 'You need to watch your step here.' He puts his cap on his head. 'I'll say no more. Goodnight to you.'

Frank ponders the man's words as he climbs the stairs. He helps Grace undress her husband down to his underwear. Hardly in good shape at the best of times, there's vivid bruising along both his forearms where he must have tried to defend himself. When Grace lifts his vest, his torso is purple and black; his attacker must have carried on kicking the poor man when he was down. Frank turns away, shaking his head – hadn't he done much the same?

As he lies there in the bed he shares with her, Frank notices Dennis's pale and scrawny legs – how they contrast with the bulk of his body and how, now they've finally got him onto his back, the man begins to resemble a half-squashed toad. He tries to banish the thought. The landlord groans a couple more times before noisily falling asleep.

'Thanks for your help,' Grace says, pulling the covers up over her husband and then turning them down with care like a nurse might. 'I'll see to him now. If anyone asks, say you've heard Dennis is restin' up in bed after a fall. Don't make it sound too serious.'

Her fingers sweep over her husband's forehead brushing his thinning hair away from his eyes. Frank's shocked by the tenderness of the gesture. He watches her every movement as she leaves the bedside to go over to the window and draw the curtains.

'You should go,' she says, not once looking directly at him.

CHAPTER NINETEEN

Wednesday 25th June

He doubles back in order to approach the newsstand from a different direction. Keeping to an unhurried pace, Frank looks at this and that like he's simply a man out for a constitutional on a fine afternoon. Up ahead, the vendor is strolling back and forth chanting something that sounds like *'Idiot sees flyin' saucer.'* Getting closer he realises it's: *'Yankee pilot sees flyin' saucer; read all abowt it.'*

Frank adjusts the angle of his hat. 'Evening News,' he says, handing over the exact money to prevent any further conversation. Stuffing the paper under his arm, he strides on trying to look as nonchalant as possible.

He's spent the morning going over everything in his head. That fifty guineas would open up so many possibilities; the way things are, he's wondering if he shouldn't just claim it and disappear again. What's stopping him? With that money he could go down to the south coast for a bit; spend a bit of time enjoying himself before he looks for another job. He could try getting work at a funfair or something like that.

He enters the park through the gate by the lido. In front of him the grass is teeming with kids – they run across his path trailing their kites or speed past him on their bicycles or push scooters. He's heading in the direction of the empty bandstand and the quieter fringes of the park. Clouds block the sun for a moment – once again a few cumulus humilis that have bubbled up in the heat. Perhaps a change of weather might be on its way.

And then there's Grace. How could he have imagined for one second they might have a future together? It became crystal clear last night that the woman still has tender feelings for that useless husband of hers. What with the Dawson brothers and everything, he really ought to get out of London, and fast. But then how can he just up sticks and leave her so unprotected?

Two men get up from a bench at the far end near the road and walk away in opposite directions. Despite the humidity, they're both formally dressed like they could be a couple of ill-disguised spies. Frank entertains the thought as he walks through an avenue of gnarled old plane trees to claim the bench they've just vacated.

At last he can spread out the newspaper. Ignoring the enticements of the front page, he scans every inch of the inside section. At first, he can't find it, but then halfway down page six a headline catches his eye.

TOO MANY 'HEROES'

Sadly, this newspaper has been forced to suspend the reward money offered to the man who saved the young boy from drowning in the river at Thames Beach last Saturday after a great many 'gentlemen' stepped forward claiming to be the hero in our photograph. Fortunately, the Evening News has since uncovered more clues to real man's identity. If the genuine hero of

the day would care to get in touch at the address below, our lawyers will establish the truth of his claim. The Evening News remains eager to reward this man with those fifty guineas for his selfless and heroic deed.

Frank studies every word and the implications behind each. The most straightforward, less worrying explanation is that some reporter's talked to the two women he met on the beach. Maybe the sisters have offered to identify him in person. He was sloppy when he told them his first name but he's sure he told them nothing more than that.

Frank's hands are trembling as he folds the newspaper. All those imagined possibilities are dead in the water; there's no chance of any of that now. If he contacted these lawyers, they'll want cast iron proof of his identity before he can get within sniffing distance of the money. They'll eagerly plaster the story of who he was and how they found him all over their bloody rag. He'll stay at the Eight Bells for the moment but only as long as it takes for Dennis to get back on his feet.

As he leaves the park, Frank drops the newspaper into the nearest bin.

There's no letup in the pub. 'Here have you seen this picture of that bloke they're lookin' for?' Wilf produces the same damn photo and someone holds it up to Frank's face while they all look from him to it and back again.

'Apart from the hair, it could be him,' Bert decides.

Wilf draws on his pipe as he cogitates. 'No offence,' he says, releasing a stream of smoke into Frank's face, 'but that fella's a lot better lookin' than you.'

'They've already had loads of blokes tryin' to claim it.' Fat Harry burps into his pint. 'Frank here would have to join the queue.'

He's careful to carry on drying the glass in his hands. 'Aye, well anyroad, I can safely say it's not me.' It's a struggle to keep his smile looking natural. 'So you lot can all bugger off and stop taking the piss.'

'You could still have a go at it,' Bert suggests. 'Worth a shot. I would if it was me.'

Frank shakes his head. 'As you said, it's obvious it's not me, more's the pity – fifty guineas would come in dead handy.'

'If I had fifty guineas, I'd go up West.' Bert's eyes glaze over with nostalgia. 'For a start I'd have meself a slap-up meal in some fancy restaurant. Then I might go on to one of them clubs you hear about where there's a woman barin' her all on the stage an' the other girls hang off yer arm – all of 'em practically half naked.'

Wilf snorts the froth off his pint. 'If you was to find yerself surrounded by half naked women, Bert Matthews, your eyes'd be spinin' so much you'd have a ruddy heart attack.'

To Frank's relief this takes the conversation in an altogether different direction.

Frank's attention is drawn towards the saloon bar where Cyril Lloyd has his hand raised. 'Two double malts when you've got a minute,' he says, the light glinting off the heavy ring on his pinky finger. Leaning an elbow on the counter, he turns to say something to his companion. Frank recognises the other man – Johnny Davidson.

He goes over to serve them and is struck by the way their expensively tailored jackets are unable to disguise those protruding paunches. 'No, I insist, these are on me,' Davidson says brandishing a fiver.

Once Frank has counted out his change, he leans in. 'Could you tell our friend Dennis we'd like a quick word when he's got a minute?'

'I'm afraid I can't do that – Mr Stevenson's in bed recovering from a very nasty fall.'

Frank registers what seems like genuine surprise on both their faces. 'His injuries aren't too serious, I hope?' Lloyd looks anxious now. 'Any idea when he's likely to be back on his feet?'

'Hard to say at present.'

'Perhaps we could come through and have a quick word with him,' Davidson suggests.

"Fraid not, gents. Mrs Stevenson's left strict orders he's not to be disturbed – under any circumstances.'

Lloyd's eyes narrow on him. 'Your name's Frank, isn't it?'

'It is.'

'Well now, *Frank*, while it's only natural for a wife to feel protective towards her husband, I'm quite sure Dennis wouldn't object to a couple of old friends paying him a visit.'

Davidson adds, 'No need to disturb his beauty sleep for more than five minutes.'

Frank squares up to them. 'I'm afraid I really can't let you through, gents – poor bloke's in quite a state and needs to be left in peace right now.'

'Then perhaps we could have a word in *Mrs* Stevenson's shell-like.' Lloyd lowers his voice. 'It's a business matter of some urgency. I'm sure Grace will understand.'

'Sorry, gents. I'm happy to tell her you were asking after her husband, but I'll do nowt else.' Frank stares down one and then the other. 'I take my orders from the boss.'

'So we've been hearing,' Davidson mutters. 'I think you'd better watch your step, *Frank*. It seems to me you're getting somewhat above yourself.'

His friend pulls on his elbow. 'Let's not get too carried away, Johnny. I'm sure our barman here will inform the *lovely* Mrs Stevenson of our pressing desire to have a quiet word with her husband.'

Davidson finishes his drink and slams the glass down hard on the counter. 'Tell Grace we'll be round to see Dennis tomorrow afternoon.' He puts on his hat. 'You can assure her that, whatever the poor man's injuries, he'll want to hear what we have to say.'

It's nearing closing time when Frank's attention is drawn to a movement to his right. She's standing in the doorway, doesn't come any further than the threshold. 'I'd like a word once you've finished up.'

She looks down, fiddles with her wedding ring, turning it round and round with a nervousness he hasn't seen before. When she finally looks at him her eyes are red-rimmed and her face is drawn and anxious.

'How's Dennis?' he asks to her disappearing back.

She doesn't even turn to answer.

CHAPTER TWENTY

Grace paces the kitchen waiting for Frank, her mind reeling from lack of sleep and worry. When she'd last checked Dennis, he looked worse if anything; the bruises covering his skin make him look like he's been coloured by a child's purple and mauve paint set. That closed eye seems to bring a new focus to the open one, like he's seeing right the way through her.

She goes to check on him again. It's hard to recognise the man lying there. Even when asleep, he doesn't seem to be resting; his fists keep curling or his legs thrash around like he's running. Though the movement makes him wince, it doesn't stop. He keeps mumbling, too. Try as she might, she can't make out the words though he seems to be re-living an argument. Has he been lying about not seeing who attacked him? He's shouted out the odd word but so far, no name.

Over on her dressing table, there's a framed photograph of the two of them standing outside the church on their wedding day. Grace picks it up. There she is – a scrap of a girl so awkward in the posh new dress he'd insisted on buying. The man beside her is looking proud as punch all dolled up in his suit – a lot slimmer, that's for certain. You'd never call him handsome, but he has a nice, kind-looking face.

To help the swelling round his eye, she fetches a cold flannel. The shock of it wakes him up. Dennis knocks it to the floor as he attempts to sit up. 'I've got to go out,' he keeps saying. Doesn't say where or why. His attempts fail. If he weren't confined by pain, he'd be out of the bed before she could stop him. Since this afternoon, and against her better judgment, she's been adding whisky to his tea to keep him calm enough to rest.

Grace goes downstairs to make him another cuppa. She's startled by the knock on the door, though it's gentle enough. When she opens up, Frank's standing there like a regular visitor – like he isn't the same man who only yesterday had her every which way in this very room. 'How is he?'

'No worse,' she says, 'least, as far as I can tell. He's certainly not happy bein' in bed – ill as he is. I've had a job to keep him from trying to get up.'

'Happen that's a good sign.'

'Maybe it is, maybe it isn't.'

'Cyril Lloyd and that Davidson chap were asking after him earlier.'

'Were they now.' Her sigh is heartfelt. 'I'm at my wits' end, Frank.' She rotates the wedding band on her finger – it seems looser than ever. 'I don't know what to do or what to think anymore. How did everything get to be such a bloody awful mess?'

She notices how he hesitates before coming forward. 'There, there, lass,' he says, his northern accent really coming out like it does at times. When his arms enfold her, she takes in the smell of him and, losing any restraint, sobs into his chest.

'I've gone an' made you all wet,' she says, pulling away, stepping back so he's properly in focus.

'That's not the least effect you've had on me.' There's a look in those pale eyes she's not seen before.

'I expect you think all kinds of things about me,' she says, 'a married woman ready to drop her knickers at the drop of a hat.'

'It's true I do think all kinds of things about you, but not those sorts of things.'

'Why not?' She lowers her voice to a whisper. 'Why wouldn't any man think less of someone who behaves like I've done right under her husband's nose?'

'Is that what you want from me?' She's noticed before how quickly his fists remember to curl. 'Do you think I'm the type of man who would judge you like that?'

'Most men would, and I can't say I'd blame 'em if they did.'

He touches her hand, his voice softening as quick as it hardened. 'But I'm not most men, Grace.' His fingers run up and down the thin material of her sleeve.

She looks away from the tenderness in his expression. 'I think you need to understand.' Her eyes trace the convoluted pattern on the rug beneath their feet. 'I do love Dennis in my own way, and I know he loves me too. He can be a bloody fool at times, I grant you, but he's a good man underneath it. And I'll be forever be grateful that he took me in, offered me this home, when I hadn't really got one to speak of.'

'Then I think 'praps I'd best be getting out from under your feet, Mrs Stevenson.' Not meeting her eye, he turns towards the door.

'Wait,' she says. 'Please, Frank, there's more I need to say to you.' She can't see his face. He remains bolt upright, hands at his side, like a man about to take a dive from a high platform.

'Go on.'

'Just so you know, I'm not in the habit of goin' to bed with other men. But me and Dennis, we don't–' She can't think why she's shying away from the words, not in front of a man who's made her groan in ecstasy. 'We haven't done it. I mean it's bin a long time since we've bin properly man and wife – if you get my meaning.' Loyalty stops her elaborating on their disastrous and perfunctory fumblings; how, for them both, it had been a chore neither of them wished to endure again. 'He's not bin interested,' she says.

'I suppose that's where I come in.' There's more than an edge of bitterness to Frank's voice.

'Don't be like that. It's not as if I haven't had plenty of opportunities before. Up till now I've always resisted.'

He finally looks at her. 'So why me?'

'Because – oh, for goodness' sake, you'll just have to use your imagination, Frank Danby.'

'But I want you to tell me.'

'Tell you what? You want me to list all the things about you that made me desperate to feel you inside me almost as soon as I set eyes on you?'

He's smiling now – a big grin that starts with his mouth and spreads all over his face. 'You could start there,' he says.

His hands are on her cheeks, in her hair, and he's kissing her so hard it's hurting. Before she loses control, she pushes him away. 'We can't – not with Dennis lyin' up there right above our heads in the state he's in.'

She pulls her blouse back into shape. 'And besides, I really need to tell you somethin' else.'

Frank doesn't say a thing. He folds his arms across his chest, his face only half serious.

'I think, in fact I'm pretty certain, there's somethin' wrong with all the spirits we're sellin'.' She takes a steadying breath. 'I think it's hooch and Dennis has bin gettin' it from somewhere he shouldn't.'

Frank's eyebrows go up but at the same time he's nodding his head like none of it's a big shock to him after all. Seems like he's already worked it out for himself. She studies his face. 'Did you know about it?'

'No,' he raises both hands like he's surrendering to an enemy. 'I swear to you, he's said nowt to me about it.' He looks to be telling the truth.

'An' that's not all of it,' she says. 'I saw him with my own eyes give a bunch of keys to one of Cyril Lloyd's men. They were the keys for this storeroom he's got – well, it's more like a lockup – but a big one. You know them ones under the railway arches off Ragnall Street?'

Her fingers go back to her wedding ring; she can't seem to stop turning it round and round. 'He's had the place for years just for storin' a few bits of old family furniture an' that.' It helps to pace the floor. 'Now I think he's lettin' Cyril store things in there – things he wants hidden. Could be stuff off their sites – materials he's claiming to have used. There again – it could be somethin' else altogether.' She comes to a standstill in front of him. 'What d'you think I should do?'

'Seriously, Grace,' he grabs her shoulders, gives her a sort of shake: 'It'd be best – safer by far – if you try to forget whatever it is you've seen or you think you know. Look what's just happened to Dennis.'

She shrugs him off. 'You mean to say you think the two things are connected?'

'I'm not saying they are or they're not; what I *am* saying is, for your own safety, it's best you know nowt about any of it. In this sort of situation, ignorance may not be bliss but it's a darn sight better than knowing too much.'

CHAPTER TWENTY-ONE

Thursday 26th June

Frank keeps his head down – carries on with his work like there's nothing out of the ordinary going on. No one in the pub mentions Dennis's absence. The regulars are unlikely to be suspicious since Dennis is so often not around – his constant presence would be far more noteworthy. The subject hasn't even cropped up; it seems unlikely Harry will have said anything to anyone.

His morning shift over, Frank resists the urge to go through and speak to Grace. He locks up as usual before heading east towards Ragnall Street, whistling as he goes, his jacket slung over one shoulder. It's an easy, ten-minute stroll. Frank stands at the busy junction looking over at the row of arches under the bridge – all exactly as Grace had described.

He's surprised by a train as it comes rattling overhead. There's no knowing which of the lockups belongs to Dennis. Various doors are propped open and a fair number of people are going about their work. Some are sitting outside at work-benches; one man's stooped over a small lathe. From across the road he hears the whine of the machine, can already smell hot metal and grease. There's a squeal of brakes as another train passes; under his feet the ground vibrates.

A couple of units are closed up. A good many padlocked iron bars brace their stout wooden doors. He won't be able to see a thing through those painted over windows.

A middle-aged chap in overalls is working on an upturned motorbike next to the two locked units. The sun's rays are bouncing off the machine's silver paintwork. He's pretty sure she's a Triumph Tiger.

'Nice bike,' Frank says, kicking a stone as he wonders over.

The bloke looks up. Those grease stains on his face could be war paint. 'It would be if the silly bugger who owns it would learn not to take bends too ruddy fast. This time he's buggered up the front wheel and bent both front forks. I ask you. The bloody idiot always comes runnin' to me to fix things up again.'

'Do these really do a ton?'

The man takes a rag from his pocket and rubs away at the oil on his hands. 'So I'm told. Bloke I know reckons he got over a hundred an' five on one up the A1.'

Frank whistles though his teeth. 'I had a go on a Speed Twin just after the war. A beauty she was. Course, she didn't have these fancy telescopic front forks.'

After that he can barely shut the man up. It takes him a while to steer the conversation around. 'I do a bit of light welding for people from time to time. Was wondering if I could maybe rent one of these places meself.' The shine off the metal is making him squint. 'Those two over there looks pretty shut up – d'you know if anybody's using either of 'em?'

Straight off the man's demeanor changes. 'I wouldn't know one way or the other.'

'So you've not seen anybody coming and going from them lately or owt like that?'

'Like I said, mate, I wouldn't know.'

'Maybe I could, you know, ask somebody if they're vacant – that's if you wouldn't mind telling me who I should get in touch with.'

"Fraid I can't help ya there, mate. Chap comes round here

once a month an' I pay him in cash. That's it.' He picks up a large wrench. 'Everybody's happy and that's the way we'd like it to stay round here.'

He weighs the tool in his hand before he points the blunt end at Frank. 'I need to get this done by five, so if you wouldn't mind –' There's an unmistakable threat in his eyes as he flicks his balding head in the general direction of the road.

Frank takes the hint. 'Fair enough,' he says. 'No harm in askin', eh?'

The man continues to watch him until he's out of sight. What next? He dawdles along heading in no particular direction. Perching on a low wall, he stares down at the cracks in the pavement. The unrelenting sun beats down on his head making it hard for him to think straight.

On his way back to the Eight Bells, he calls in to Eddie's though he's not sure he's in the mood for the man's perpetual cheerfulness. Forty yards away and he can already smell frying fish. A small queue has built up as they wait for the next batch to be ready. Joining the line, his stomach rumbles its impatience.

'Afternoon, Frank.' Eddie looks like he's melting in the heat. 'What can I do you for today?'

'Just some chips.' Frank's thoughts go back to Grace and how, with all her worrying, she's unlikely to be looking after herself. 'Hang on – you'd better make that a couple of portions.'

Eddie's scoop is poised in the air. 'D'you want 'em all in together or wrapped separately?'

'Separate.'

The chippie puts a generous portion in the first bundle and, knowing Frank's tastes, dusts it with salt and a good dose of vinegar. 'And the other one?'

'What about it?'

'Is he, or I'm guessing it's a *she*,' he winks, 'partial to a bit of seasoning or happy to have it just as it comes – *unadulterated*, as you might say?'

Frank looks away from the man's knowing smirk. 'A smattering of both will do just fine, thanks.'

A fierce heat from the chips permeates the newspaper and several times Frank has to swap the bundle from one hand to the other to allow his fingers to cool down. He's just reaching the final corner when a fancy black car pulls up alongside him. A young chap he's never seen before rolls the window down like he's about to ask for directions. He glimpses two shadowy figures in the back seat.

Frank keeps walking.

'Mr Danby?' In the past, he wouldn't have broken his stride even if he'd heard his name called out by a stranger but, this time, he hesitates for a split second. Behind him, he hears car doors opening. With one hand still cradling the food, he's not ready when they come at him from behind.

He drops the chips to ram his fist into the driver's gut. Winded, the bastard lets go. Someone else grabs his arm and he turns to aim a knee into the man's groin. Doubling over, the bastard still doesn't give up his grip. Frank's almost worked his arm free when the other two come at him again.

Too many at once. His shoulders are pinned back so hard any further struggling risks dislocating them. He kicks out wildly as they drag him towards the car. The short one opens the back door and they push him inside.

With one sitting upfront and the other two lumps on either side of him, Frank knows it's pointless to struggle. The driver turns round. 'Really, Mr Danby, such a fuss was quite unnecessary.' His posh voice sounds genuine enough. 'A friend of ours merely wants to have a word with you in private.' Frank concentrates on memorising the man's face for another time. Mid-twenties; dark hair, long on the top and swept back. Green eyes. Long lashes a woman would be proud of. Skin's too smooth; he hardly has to shave at all.

'Shame about yer chips, mate.' The fat one to his left, is dead easy – forty-odd, big nose, gravel rash, tattoo poking out from his shirt sleeve of what looks like a fish or maybe a mermaid's tail.

As the car speeds away, Frank turns his attention to the other scumbag but a sack is thrust over his head.

The rough material is too thick to see anything but shadows. He can feel its loose fibres already tightening his throat. Frank coughs, tries not to breathe in too much, better to remember the sounds instead – anything that might give a clue to where they are.

Traffic must be heavier now. He hears various engines, bus brakes hissing, someone leaning on a horn. The clop clopping of a horse and someone shouting the same thing over and over. *'Rabone…Rabone.'* The trouble with rag and bone men is they move around the city.

Not long after that, the car veers sharply to the right and then he feels the shudder of cobbles underneath the wheels.

They've stopped. With the engine still running, they bundle him outside. Have him by the arms as they force him up four flights of stairs before he hears the groan of heavy hinges.

Quieter now – traffic noise muffled. They're inside and walking over uneven floorboards.

Someone spits. Without warning he's thrust forward and then released. He hears the door lock behind him.

At last he can pull the sack off his head. It's a flour bag with no tell-tale markings on it. The door's reinforced – too strong to kick in. He tries the handle but it won't open. Frank resists the urge to call out or bang on the door – to show any signs of weakness.

The room is cell-like – bare, save for a single wonky-looking chair. Daylight is coming in from a single barred window that's too high to reach. It looks out only onto more blackened brick. He can smell the damp in the walls. Could this be an old warehouse? The floor consists of wide dusty planks. When he walks around, he finds some of them have been softened by woodworm and are spongy underfoot.

A lone light bulb dangles from the ceiling. He notices it's swinging very slightly, its shadow creeping back and forth along the wall like a hangman's noose.

Someone's scratched FUCK YOU on one of the bricks in the far corner. 'Couldn't put it better,' he says out loud.

What if no one comes and they just leave him in here? His resolve weakens. A few more minutes then he's thumping the door with his fists.

CHAPTER TWENTY-TWO

Grace can hear lots of banging and thumping down there. What now? She goes to investigate and finds the pub is still locked up and there's no sign of Frank. 'Alright, hold yer ruddy horses.' She unlocks the door to a half dozen regulars in high dudgeon.

They spill into the public bar. 'It's almost six o'clock.' Wilf brandishes his pocket watch – holds it right in her face to prove his point. 'What in hell's name's goin' on?'

'I could say the same,' she tells him. 'Frank should have bin here well before half-five. Can't for the life of me think what could have happened to him.'

'Mmm, well, in my humble opinion, you can never fully trust a man who claims to be a conchie,' Fat Harry says, casting his eyes around in search of general agreement.

Peering over his glasses, Charlie wags a thin finger at him. 'You've gone and got the facts all round yer ruddy neck, as usual, Harry Jones. Frank told me himself he was in a reserved occupation during the war – workin' on his family's farm, as it happens.'

'An' how's that any flamin' different? Either way, it tells you the bloke's too fond of shirkin' his duty.'

'I'd call it vital work,' Charlie tells him. 'We all needed to eat – you more than most.'

Wilf prods at Charlie's arm with the damp end of his pipe. 'If you was to ask me, I reckon he didn't want to risk Jerry ruining those good looks of his.'

'Well now, aren't you all singing a different tune this evenin' with the man's back only turned for five minutes?' Grace knows she ought to contain herself but can't. 'It's bin all *Frank that* an' *Frankie mate* while you've watched him workin' like a demon in here every night.' She gives a hard stare to each of them in turn; every one of them looks away except Charlie. 'For all you know he could've had some kind of accident on his way here. How would you feel then, eh?' She plants her hands on her hips. 'Should be ruddy ashamed of yourselves runnin' the poor chap down like that when he's not here to defend himself.'

The men stay mute and, having made her point, she flounces off to turn the bar lights on and remove the towelling mats from where they've been draped over the beer pumps to dry. All the shelves are fully stocked so Frank must have seen to the bottling up before he left. Had he intended to be late back? If he had to go somewhere, surely he'd have warned her?

Something's amiss. Once she's pulled the first lot of pints, she'll check out the back, see if it's all looking okay.

Paying for his half of mild, Charlie takes hold of her hand and pats it like you might reassure some elderly relative. 'He'll be back with his tail between his legs before long.' Though he means well, the man's sympathy is worse than the others' scorn.

More early birds stroll in demanding cider and stout and who knows what else. Pouring the stout is a slow business. She glances up to the clock – coming up to half past and still no sign of Frank. When someone asks for a gin, she notices the label on this new bottle is a tad skewwhiff.

It's a good ten minutes before she gets the chance to check the stores and the side entrance. The door to the yard is still securely locked and the new combination padlock on the yard door is firmly shut with no sign it's been tampered with. She gives it a rattle and it holds well enough.

Graces hurries back to the bar and the impatience that's built up in her brief absence.

She's working at full whack when a commotion in the passageway draws her attention away. As bold as bloody brass, Johnny Davidson and Cyril Lloyd come strolling out of her kitchen. 'Bye, Dennis,' Cyril calls behind him. He raises his fancy hat to her. 'Evening, Grace.'

She rushes through to block their exit. 'Who the hell let you two in?'

'We could see you were rushed off your feet in there, couldn't we, Johnny? Didn't want to disturb you when we only needed to pop in and have a quick word with your hubby.' Lloyd's voice is all smarm. 'Glad to see your better half is on the mend after that nasty fall of his.'

Davidson slides past her. 'Didn't that good-looking barman of yours mention we were going to call round? He promised he would but I 'spect he forgot. Must have had other things on his mind.' She feels her colour rising. He doffs his hat, blatantly mocking her. 'I see you've got customers to serve; we really mustn't detain you any longer, Mrs Stevenson. Good evening to you.'

Both men have such an air of smugness about them; if she had a man's strength, she'd knock those stupid smirks right off their cocksure faces.

Around eight o'clock, Thin Harry comes in for his usual. Still in his working clothes, he stands there uncharacteristically quiet. 'I haven't had a chance to thank you for everything you did,' she tells him. 'We – Dennis and me that is – we really appreciate all your help.' Lowering her voice, she adds: 'I can't think what would have happened if you hadn't come along.'

He puts his hand up like a traffic policeman to stop her saying more. 'Anyone would have done the same.' Grace tells him his pint is on the house, but he insists on paying. After taking a long sip of bitter he says, 'No Frank tonight then?'

'No. I'm afraid he hasn't showed up for some reason.'

'*Right.*' Harry manages to give that single word any number of possible meanings.

She leans across the counter. 'Look, I really ought to go and check on Dennis; would you do me a favour Harry and hold the fort here – just for five minutes?'

Before he answers, he takes his time shaking out a Woodbine and lighting it. 'How d'you know I won't make off with all the takin's once yer back's turned?'

She pats the sleeve of his shirt. 'Because I trust you, Harry.'

He blows a plume of smoke down towards his boots. 'Well don't go trusting me too far.'

She finds Dennis fully dressed and sitting at the kitchen table. His face is all manner of lurid colours; the fiery ginger stubble doesn't help.

'You're up then.' She's pleased to see his bad eye has opened a fraction more than it had this morning.

'Ah well, I couldn't abide lyin' in that ruddy bed any longer. Had a bit of a struggle gettin' down the stairs but, as you see, I made it all right.' His attempt at a smile brings on a wince and a sharp intake of breath.

'What did Cyril and Johnny want that was so flamin' urgent it couldn't wait?'

He won't meet her eye. 'Just a spot of financial advice. As a matter of fact, it was very helpful; very good of them to go out of their way like they did.'

She plants herself in front of him. 'What sort of *financial advice?*'

Dennis looks away.

'Couldn't it have waited a couple of days?'

He continues to act like he hasn't heard. 'Come on,' she says. 'What was it then – a dead cert at Cheltenham?'

'Nothin' like that, woman.' To stand up he's forced to lean on the table. 'I'm goin' upstairs to watch the television. That alright with you, is it?'

When she tries to help him, he stays her hand. 'I can manage by meself.' He hesitates at the foot of the stairs. 'Oh, and by the way, Cheltenham's not on again till November.'

Back in the bar, she's still fuming; it's all she can do not to bite the customers' heads off, especially when they keep asking her where Frank's got to. 'How should I know?' she tells the lot of them. At least no one asks about Dennis.

The evening drags on, but she does her best to plaster on a smile and say a few words to each punter. She can't help but look over their heads because any second she's expecting Frank to come in through the door. And then there was that business of him hiding the fact that he'd gone and saved that little boy from drowning. Could he have scarpered for good?

Grace sighs as she slides the last bolt across. Where the hell can Frank have got to? With her emotions all over the place, it's hard to feel any satisfaction that she managed the whole shift by herself. Thursdays are always reasonably quiet but tomorrow night – Friday night – will be a different kettle of fish altogether. Though close to tears, she forces herself to consider the practicalities. If Frank's still AWOL by the end of the afternoon shift, she'll have to get someone else to help. Young Jack is only good for a bit of pot washing and such like. 'Praps her friend Dot might be persuaded to help out, just over the weekend. But surely it won't come to that.

When she's finished in the pub, she unties her pinny and goes through into their private quarters.

Grace is dismayed to see Dennis's hat and jacket are missing from the peg. She rushes to the street door hoping to catch sight of him, but she's left calling his name out in the dark and empty street.

CHAPTER TWENTY-THREE

The light slowly fades until the room is swallowed up by darkness. Determined not to sit on the chair, Frank has no other option but to lie down on the dusty, hard floor. There's no chance of him sleeping; to pass the time he looks up through the high window hoping to glimpse a few stars in the tiny section of night sky he's able to see.

At the sound of approaching footsteps, Frank scrabbles to his feet. He's blinded for a second when the overhead light is switched on from outside. He waits to hear the key turn in the lock, gets himself ready to rush at whoever is about to come in.

He runs headfirst straight into someone's flabby stomach but doesn't get more than a yard or more before others are tackling him. Between them, they drag him back into the room and pin him down in the chair.

The one he's winded takes his time straightening up and then comes towards him. He recognises him as the same fat git who'd wedged him into the back seat of the car. With his sleeves rolled up, the man's mermaid tattoo is fully exposed – too delicate a creature to decorate this lump of a man. The bastard takes his time as he checks that he's fully restrained before he plunges his fist straight into Frank's gut. The blow is well aimed – he can't draw breath, can't even double up pinned back like he is.

'Well now, what's goin' on in here, lads?' The voice belongs to Jack Dawson.

The man himself comes strolling in dressed in a jacket and tie like a toff about to go out on the town. A smile is tightening on the man's lips.

Frank forces air into his lungs as Dawson comes forward to stand directly in front of him; the man's crotch only inches from his face. He lifts up Frank's chin. 'No need for violence, I'm sure you'd agree, Mr Danby – that's what you're calling yourself these days, I believe.' Dawson steps back and nods to the two behind to release Frank. This outnumbered, there's no point in even thinking about fighting them. Glad to have his arms back, he rubs at each shoulder in turn and then rotates his neck.

'I think you've made a mistake,' he tells Dawson. He needs to be patient, bide his time until the odds are more in his favour. 'You've seen me yerself in the Eight Bells. I'm just an ordinary barman goin' about my business an' not interested in any bugger else's.' He looks the man in the eye. 'You're mistaken if you think I'm a threat to any of you lot.'

'Is that right?' A nod of his head is the signal to bring a second chair into the room; this one is more comfortable by far.

Dawson sits down on it, curls up his long legs and then starts swivelling the thing this way and that. He takes a while longer to adjust his cufflinks one at a time.

Finally, he speaks: 'Look at me.' He waits for Frank to oblige. 'That's better. Now then, tell me – do I seem to you like the sort of man who makes mistakes?'

The threat is clear enough. Frank shakes his head.

'Good. So now we understand each other a bit better. Don't you go pullin' on my chain, son, or you'll make me angry. You may be just a barman these days, as you put it, but I make it my business to find out about the people who move into my patch an' you, Frankie boy, are sellin' yourself short.'

The chair creaks as he leans back into the leather. 'For starters, I know you were goin' by the name of Walton back in forty-three – not long after you went AWOL, was it?'

He checks over his manicured fingernails one at a time. 'Got yourself a ten-bob boxin' license and even made a few quid at it. Despite you bein' a coward an' a ruddy deserter. Heard you was quite the hard man in the ring back then, though I can see you've gone a bit soft since.'

Behind Dawson, Fatty is grinning all over his face, enjoying the show. Out of shape like that, he has to be the weakest link, the one to go for when the chance comes.

'But then it all went horribly wrong, didn't it, Frankie boy? You got carried away one night – hit some poor bugger too hard.'

'It wasn't –'

Dawson springs from his chair, clamps Frank's chin in his hand and peers down at him eyeball to eyeball. 'Don't want to hear it, son – makes no flamin' odds to me whether it was a fair fight or not.

'However,' he releases his grip, 'you won't be surprised to learn, Frankie, that there's a few blokes up in White City who still bear a grudge to this day about what happened. Blokes who are dyin' – if you excuse my pun – to know the where-abouts of the man responsible for turnin' their little brother into a droolin' idiot.'

Regaining his composure, the man starts to pace back and forth in front of him. Frank looks beyond Dawson to where Fatty's standing with legs apart at roughly the midway point between him and the door. He can see a light shining down the stairwell. They're several stories up here – is it worth the risk of a beating if he makes a run for it and fails? It's unlikely the rest of the building will be empty; big place like this could be used for all manner of activities.

'No need for you to look so worried, sunshine – I had you brought here tonight just so we can have this friendly chat.'

Dawson sits back down. His laugh is far from genuine. 'I bin hearin' how you're quite the ladies' man.'

Leaning forward, he peers at Frank's face – those ice blue eyes inspect one side and then the other. 'I must say, I don't know how he's managed to keep his good looks. All that boxin' an' there's hardly a mark on him, is there, lads?'

The men say nothing. 'I'm sure our friend 'ere would prefer it stays that way. Well, you'll be pleased to know I'm not plannin' on roughin' you up no more, Frankie, not unless you was to disappoint me.'

He shakes his head. 'That bint of a landlady you've been knockin' off might not look at you twice at you if we was to rearrange those oh so handsome features of yours.' Dawson brushes at his trousers, picks off a piece of lint and drops it. 'Well now, Mr *Danby*, you and I will be doin' a bit of business together – somethin' that will be mutually beneficial to us both. I have a job that wants doin' and let's just say I'd rather it was done by someone not connected to me – if you follow my drift?'

'What sort of job?'

Dawson looks down at his gold watch. "Fraid I haven't got time to go into the details right now. Don't like to keep a lady waitin' for too long – never a good idea as I'm sure you'd agree. We'll just leave it at that for the time bein'.'

Leaning on the chair arms, he gets to his feet. 'Let's give you a few more hours to enjoy our hospitality – just to seal the deal, as it were.'

Halfway to the door he spins round, 'Don't forget my chair, lads, we don't want our new friend 'ere gettin' too comfortable, do we?' His eyes linger on Frank's face. 'We'll talk again later.'

The rest of them follow behind their master and the door is pulled to. Before Frank can react, he hears the lock turn and the next second the overhead light is switched off, leaving him in the dark.

CHAPTER TWENTY-FOUR

Friday 27th June

On the other side of the door, Grace can hear someone padding down the hallway. Heavy breathing and then the lock turning. Poking her head around the door, Dot's mum is still in her non-too-clean dressing gown; the back of her grey-brown hair sticking up in every direction. 'Hello, Grace,' she says. 'Not seen you in ages – how are you?'

'Fine ta. Really sorry to disturb you so early, Mrs Weston, I just wanted to catch your Dorothy before she goes off to work.'

The woman's interest is aroused, her brown eyes trained on Grace with undisguised curiosity. She opens the door wide. 'Dorothy!' she calls behind her. 'Get yourself on down here; Grace is at the door wanting to speak to ya.'

'Don't stand there on ceremony, come in.' Waddling on through, she asks, 'Cup a tea?'

Grace wishes she couldn't smell the woman's body odour. 'Just had a drink at home, ta all the same.'

'Come through to the kitchen, love. Mind, Ralf may not have his shirt on yet – though I dare say you've seen worse.'

The small room is in its usual state – stuff piled up on every surface and last night's tea things a tower climbing out of the sink. Smells like they had liver and onions. The curtains are still pulled tight giving everything such a peculiar red glow, as though they're all inside the belly of a giant beast.

At least Ralf is fully dressed and standing next to the table eating a piece of toast. 'Mornin', Gracie,' he says, his smile exposing those missing front teeth. 'They're sayin' on the wireless it's gonna be another scorcher.'

Mrs Weston aims another shout at the ceiling: 'Dorothy!' They busy themselves, trying to hide their curiosity as they wait for their daughter to appear.

'What the hell – you're up an' about early,' her friend says, buttoning up her blouse as she walks in. 'Nothin' bad's happened, 'as it?'

'Not really, at least I don't think so.' Grace moves a pile of clothes aside so she can sit down on a chair. The other three remain standing, each staring down at her.

'Dennis went out last night an' he hasn't come back; least not yet anyway.' She decides not to mention the beating he'd taken before that. 'He's done the same thing a couple of times in the past but not since I got back from Brighton. On top of that, Frank – our barman – has gone an' taken himself off somewhere without so much as a by your leave. I'll be on me own in the pub tonight. Being it's a Friday, I'll likely be rushed off me feet an' I've got no bugger to help me.'

She draws herself in, tries not to give in to the tears that are pricking the corners of her eyes. 'Anyway, I was wonderin' if you could give me a hand this evening, Dot? Otherwise I don't know what the hell I'm goin' to do.' It's a struggle to keeping her voice steady. 'I know you'll have bin to work an' you're bound to be tired an' all that. I can manage by meself till half six, or seven even, at a push. It would only be from then till eleven. I'd do all the clearing up meself.'

'My word, them men have left you in a pretty state, you poor love.' Dot's mum pours out a cup of tea and pushes it in front of Grace. 'Get that down ya, girl.'

'Tea's hardly gonna help,' Ralf says. 'Would you care for a drop of Pusser's rum in that?'

Moved by their kindness, Grace shakes her head. 'No ta – honestly I'm fine, just a bit worried about everything.'

Dot takes hold of her hand and sits down beside her. 'Of course you're not fine an' course I'll help you out. Anytime – you only had to ask.' Dot swings her arm, pulling hers with it like they used to when they were kids. 'Mind you, I'll be wantin' the goin' rate for the job.'

'Will you look at the ruddy time,' Mrs Weston shrieks. 'We'll all be late if we don't get a move on.' She starts to run a brush through her hair.

'Fancy the two of 'em just buggerin' off an' leavin' you to it.' Ralf shakes his head. 'You'd never Adam and Eve it.'

His wife is determined to yank that brush on through a tangled strand of hair. 'Bloody men, eh.'

'Don't you go tarring us all with the same brush, Lottie Weston.' Having finished his breakfast, Ralf starts to roll a cigarette, licking the edge of the paper and then pausing to pull a strand of stray tobacco from his tongue. 'Maybe the two of 'em have gone off somewhere together?' He twists the end. 'Have you thought of that?'

Grace catches the stern look his wife gives him. 'Don't go talkin' so soft, you old fool.' She waddles towards the stairs clearly intending to get dressed at last. 'I 'spect they'll both be back soon enough an' spinnin' all kinds of yarns to cover their misdeeds.'

It's as busy as it always is on a Friday night. Customers have spilled out into the street so there'll be empty glasses left on all the windowsills and probably a few broken ones on the pavement. Despite every door and window being open, the place has been like an oven all evening – so hot and smoky, Grace can barely draw breath.

Working alongside her, Dot's been doing a sterling job. With relief, Grace calls last orders; ringing the bell a half dozen times so it can be heard above the din.

There's a sudden commotion near the street door. Not a bloody fight, please Lord, not that of all things. The public's so packed out she can't see what's causing all the fuss. Finally, the crowd parts as he makes his way to the counter ahead of a gaggle of jeering regulars.

'Eh – see, what did I tell ya, Grace darlin'?' Charlie Metcalfe is beaming. 'The wanderer has returned.' He winks at Dot. 'Mind you, I have to say he's not nearly as good-lookin' as his replacement.'

'Frank.' Straight away she spots the fresh cut under his left eye. She lowers her voice unable to disguise her relief at seeing him. 'Where in hell have you bin all this time?'

Bert digs him in the ribs. 'Eh, you're in for it now, mate. If she's anythin' like my missus, she'll be gettin' the ruddy rollin' pin out later.'

Dot stops what she's doing to listen.

'Something came up,' Frank tells her. 'I'm really sorry but I had to deal wi' it. I'd no choice.' He looks over at Dot but says nothing as he flips the hatch up and steps behind the bar. 'I need to have a word wi' you in private, Grace.' His expression is deadly serious.

'It'll have to wait till we've finished serving,' she says. 'Why don't you go through to the back – I'll be through when I'm done here.'

He stays where he is. 'I'd rather have a quick word wi' you now, if you don't mind.'

Grace turns to meet her friend's curious gaze. 'Would you mind holdin' the fort on your own for two seconds?'

'Don't you go leaving me for any longer, will ya? I've got the hang of most of it but I'm much slower than you are.'

'I swear I'll just be two ticks.'

Once they're in the kitchen, Frank grabs her shoulders. She breathes in the familiar smell of his body. 'I wish I didn't have to say this to you, Grace, but I'm worried. There's things goin' on–' He bites his lip, then looks back towards the doorway as if he expects the Mongol hordes to come rushing in any minute.

She checks his eyes and then his breath to be certain he's not drunk. 'What sort of things?'

'I can't say owt – for your own good. You'll just have to trust me.'

'Trust you! You bugger off without a word of warnin'. Then Dennis ups an' vanishes into the night. Both of you leave me here to cope with all this whole pub on me own.'

She pulls away from him. 'An' now, out of the ruddy blue, you reappear and it's obvious you've bin in some kind of brawl, and after all that you still expect me to trust you about summat but you haven't said what, or put two words together that make any kind of sense.'

She makes to walk off, but he comes up behind her, spinning her round by her shoulders to face him. 'This is serious – I think you might be in danger.'

'Are you tryin' to scare me, Frank?' She shakes her arms free. 'For the life of me, I don't know what the hell you're goin' on about. I've got a pub to run an' the danger I'm facin' right now is stoppin' the buggers out there from riotin'. Dot can't manage by herself so I'm goin' back to help her. You can bugger off home or come an' give us a hand – the choice is yours, Frank.'

CHAPTER TWENTY-FIVE

Frank finds it difficult to concentrate on the clearing up with his mind still racing away in every direction. He can see that if he'd chosen to go home, the two women would have managed by themselves. The new girl – Dot – seems a nice enough lass and a hard grafter. Pretty girl, though her short, dark hair has been teased into a stiff style that doesn't suit her.

'I'm not sure I'll be needed again,' Dot says, 'not now she's got you back. Shame really, I could get to like it here.' The girl looks at him in a strange sort of way before going outside to collect more stray glasses.

Coming through with her hands full, she bumps up against him on her way to the sink then keeps peering at him through her eyelashes. The penny drops when she deliberately catches his eye while over-polishing one of the pump handles. Despite the present circumstances, he struggles to suppress a laugh, has to look away for fear of hurting her feelings.

'Can't thank you enough,' Grace says, giving her friend a hug. 'You really saved my bacon tonight, Dot, an' I won't forget it.'

Grace hands her some cash from the open till. 'It's bin a long day for you. I expect you're keen to get off home to your bed.'

'Not particularly. I mean I'd be happy –'

'No really, off you go now – we can manage the rest between us, can't we, Frank?'

There's some sort of kerfuffle going on in the street outside. 'Listen to that. You never know who's about these days, do ya?' Dot says. "Praps Frank might see me home safe – that's if you can spare him, Grace?'

'I'm sure he won't mind bein' a gentleman and escorting you.' A look he can't quite fathom runs between the women. 'Your place is only a couple of streets away, he'll be back in no time to help me finish up.'

It's good to be breathing the cooler night air. The streets around them are quiet for this time on a Friday, though Frank eyes up every passerby.

Their footsteps fall into an easy rhythm. 'Have you and Grace been friends for long?' he asks.

'Ever since we started school,' she says. 'The two of us used to sit next to each other at one of them double desks. D'you remember them?'

'Aye, I do.'

They walk on a few yards before Dot says, 'Back then, her name was Gretchen. Did she tell you that?'

'No.'

'You see, her dad was a German an' he called her after his own mum; daft idea, givin' her a name like that in the first place, if you ask me. Elsie – that's Grace's mum who lives down in Brighton – she must have gone along with it at the time, though she herself was a Cockney through an' through like the rest of us. Weird sort of name Gretchen – us kids had a job sayin' it, as you can imagine. She must have bin about seven, when we were all told to start calling her Grace instead.'

'I see – I didn't know that.' He stops walking, stands there under the streetlamp wondering what else he doesn't know about the woman he's obsessed with. Now there's a thing – how long has it been since he felt like this about anyone?

'Course, she had a tough time of it at school when the war

started.' Dot looks up at him. 'I felt so sorry for her, 'specially when they came an' took her dad away –

interned him over on the Isle of Man, so me mum said. Poor man died before the war ended. Caught pneumonia apparently. I remember that because it was a funny word I hadn't heard before. After he died, they moved away an' I didn't see Grace for a few years; not till she moved back again. When we left school, Grace started workin' in the biscuit factory like me. Course, that didn't suit her for long. Bit later on, she got a job as a barmaid in the Eight Bells instead and that's when she met Dennis.'

For a while they carry on walking in silence, their footsteps ringing loud in the empty streets.

'Well, this is it,' Dot says. There's only a step between her front door and the street. 'Thanks for seein' me home, Frank.' Though her face is in shadow, he can see from the way she's tilted her chin that she'd like him to kiss her.

When he doesn't make a move, she reaches into her pocket and produces her key. 'Maybe I'll see you again in the pub. That's if you plan on stickin' around.'

He knows she's expecting an answer one way or the other; that her friend will want to know the exact same thing as soon as he gets back.

'Goodnight then,' he says. 'Sleep tight.'

'I'm all in – anything else will have to wait till the mornin'.' Grace looks as weary as she sounds. 'I'll leave you to put the lights out.'

Frank follows her into the kitchen. When he goes to hold her in his arms, she doesn't resist. He buries his face in the smell of her, the way her head tucks into his chest as if that precise spot was made for her. He lifts her chin to kiss her and she responds at first but then pulls away. 'No, we mustn't.'

He opens his arms up. 'Grace, there's no one else here,' he

says. 'I can't stop thinking about you – the touch of you – everything about you.' Passion turns his voice hoarse. 'I missed you. I just want to fold you into my arms and –'

'It's all very well you sayin' you missed me when you buggered off who knows where without a word. I was half out of my mind frettin' over where you might have got to.'

How pale she is despite the heat, her forehead creased with worry. 'And then there's Dennis. Why on earth would someone beat him up like they did? I know he's a daft bugger in lots of ways but it's not like him to up and disappear like this.'

She moves around the room unable to settle into a task or a direction. 'I grant you he's stayed out all night in the past but he's usually back the next day.' She rubs her eyes. 'Something's not right, Frank – I just know it.'

'D'you want me to go out and look for him?'

'No.' She grabs his sleeve. 'You wouldn't know where to start. In any case, I don't want you dragged into the ruddy mess he's in. It's bin awful havin' to worry about the two of you at the same time.'

She sits down and eases off her shoes. Leaning on the table, she buries her head in her hands, a sea of brown hair. 'I wish I knew what to do. I've bin thinkin' 'praps I should go to the police an' report him missin' – though I know he'd go mad at the thought of me involvin' the Old Bill. Dennis reckons half of 'em are crooks and the other half sadists.'

Frank rubs his forehead, tracing the line of his scar over and over. 'Aye, I agree it's best not to say owt to the coppers.' He sits down on the opposite side of the table. 'They like to go poking around in things. From what you've told me, who knows what they're likely to turn up. You could be dumping the poor man in it good an' proper.'

Grace brings her head up. 'You're right.' She stands up, her chair scraping against the hard floor. 'I think you should get off home now – Dennis could walk through the door any minute an' find you still here.'

'I don't want to leave you alone. Like I said before, I've heard rumours – there's things going on and I'm worried. I don't mind kippin' on the sofa.'

'You can't do that – what would it look like if the neighbours noticed you were here all night as soon as Dennis's back is turned? There's enough talk already. I'm the one who has to live with all their stares and whispers.'

'This is serious, woman.' Without meaning to, he thumps the table and she jumps out of her skin. 'I'm sorry,' he says, 'but you have to understand you could be in danger. There are people out – I won't mention names – let's just say they're out to settle some debts with Dennis.'

'You're scaring me. Why the hell would they go after me? What is it you're not tellin' me?'

He grabs her arm. 'Please, Grace; idle talk can't hurt you nearly as much as they can.'

She looks down at how he's gripping her arm. 'Take your ruddy hands off me, Frank Danby.' She pries his fingers away and lets his hand drop. 'I don't need a man to look after me!'

'Under normal circumstances that might be true, but this is different. You saw how Dennis was beaten up. You're not safe here by yourself. I wouldn't say that if it wasn't true.'

She shuts her eyes, is taking a moment to think about it. He presses the advantage. 'You'll be much safer if I stay. I promise not to come creeping into your bed in the middle of the night.' He smiles across at her. 'Scout's honour an' all that.'

Finally, she grins back at him. 'I'd bet good money you were never a boy scout.'

In the end she takes him at his word. Finding the sofa too small for comfortable, he curls up on the rug with a cushion for his head – luxury compared to the previous night.

He's woken by the sound of floorboards creaking under someone's tread. 'Oww!' She stumbles over his foot. He grabs her by the waist before she can fall and feels something wet running down his arm. 'I only came down for some water,' she tells him. In the half-light he watches her put down her glass. 'All this heat – it's too much.'

'You must have had a yearning for something to cool you down,' he says, tightening his grip.

She drops to her knees, trails her fingernails across his chest. 'When a thirst comes over a person, it does make it hard to sleep.' She slides down beside him, her bare legs wrap around him. 'Just like drinking a cup of tea in summer – I find it's the things that make you hot that cool you down the most.'

Saturday 28th June

Someone's hammering on the street door. Frank reaches it first. 'Who is it?' he shouts, hoping on one leg as he pulls on his trousers. 'What's your business at this hour?'

'Southwark police; we need to speak to Mrs Stevenson.'

'What about?'

Grace comes up behind him tying the cord of her dressing gown. She squeezes his shoulder. 'It's alright, Frank – you can let them in.'

He unlocks the door and they both step back. A couple of bobbies are standing on the doorstep, the dawn chorus breaking around them. Both of them are holding their helmets in their hands and looking far from comfortable. 'Mrs Grace Stevenson?'

She nods. 'Something's happened, hasn't it? I just knew it. Don't just stand there – answer me.'

'If we could come in,' the fat one says, pushing his way on through. 'Maybe there's somewhere we can go and sit down?'

They all walk through into the kitchen. The big one says, 'I'm Sergeant Bradley and this is P C Hitchens.'

He turns to Frank. 'And you sir are…?'

Frank shrugs. 'I'm just the barman here. Friend of the family.' The copper looks from his naked torso all the way down at his bare feet but says nothing. 'And your name, sir?'

'Frank – Francis Danby.'

'What's happened? Just tell me,' Grace demands.

'Please sit yourself down, Mrs Stevenson.' The sergeant waits for her to comply. His podgy hands inch along the brim of his helmet, turning it slowly. 'I'm afraid we have some very sad news.' He takes a deep breath then lets it partway out before he adds: 'It concerns your husband, Mr Dennis Albert Stevenson. I'm sorry to have to tell you he was found dead earlier this morning.'

All colour drains from Grace's face. She tries to speak but her mouth's having trouble forming words. Frank goes to stand behind her chair though he daren't touch her. 'How?' At the second attempt she says, 'How did it happen?'

'It's a bit of a mystery at the moment. His body was found by a bargeman – floating in the river just past Rotherhithe.'

Grace turns on him. 'How can you be certain it's my Dennis?'

'He had his driving license on him. Luckily, it was sandwiched between all the other bits and pieces in his wallet and that kept it dry enough to read.'

'So he hadn't been robbed?' Frank asks.

The sergeant turns a curious eye on him. 'We didn't find any money on him – so it's possible he had been.'

Every inch of Grace is shaking now. 'Oh, my Lord, then he really has drowned?' Tears are wetting her cheeks. 'So, you're saying he fell into the water – the river?'

'He'd been in the water for some time,' the sergeant says. 'However, there are injuries on his body that remain *unexplained*.'

Frank's aware both coppers are now looking directly at him. He knows only too well they will have clocked the cut on his cheek.

'Oh, my poor Dennis.' Grace covers her head with her hands and starts to wail – a strange primeval sound. The younger copper goes over and hands her his hanky. After a while her cries subside into quiet sobbing.

Instead of comforting her, Frank clears his throat to ask, 'You think someone pushed him in?'

'Afraid we'll have to wait for the full medical report, sir.' The sergeant gets to his feet. 'Once we have that, Mrs Stevenson, we'll have a clearer idea of how your husband may have met such an untimely end.'

CHAPTER TWENTY-SIX

They bow their heads and stand there by the door to give her a few minutes to get dressed.

There's no time to wash. Upstairs she finds her clothes on the chair from yesterday. No – too colourful. She tries the wardrobe, finds a darker dress that'll be too hot in this weather. Dammit, she can't think straight, can't make zips and buttons do up with her hands so much out of control.

She has to grip the handrail on the stairs. All three men are standing around the table in the kitchen. A copper's helmet is sitting on the tabletop along with the morning post and a fresh bottle of milk no one's put away. Grace is tempted to do it herself, can't bear the thought of how it'll go sour in all this heat – Dennis can't abide it when it's turned like that.

She's pleased to see Frank's fully dressed now. The constable – the young thin one – has his notebook and pencil out. They must have been questioning Frank, but she can't think why. 'I'll go with her,' he says. 'She needs someone there.'

The sergeant is holding his hat under one arm like you might cradle a goose that's in danger of escaping. 'No need for you to fret, Mr Danby, a policewoman's on her way.'

The shaking starts up again forcing Grace to sit down. Above her, they keep on with their questions. 'Is there someone else we should inform? Are Dennis's parents still alive?

Someone you would like us to contact for you, Mrs Stevenson? A relative perhaps?'

Grace shakes her head. 'I don't know much about his family; he fell out with them years ago. They didn't approve – of his choices.' It takes her a moment to remember. 'He keeps in touch with his brother down Bromley way. Kenneth his name is, Kenneth Stevenson – but then it would be, wouldn't it?'

And now she can't see through the tears. She's still clutching that hanky as the copper's pockmarked nose swims into focus, mouth opening and shutting like a fish, saying something about an address. 'On the mantelpiece,' she says. 'Up there somewhere.'

'What is it we'll find on the mantelpiece, Grace?'

'They write to each other sometimes him and Kenneth. There's a couple of letters.'

A knock at the door and a youngish woman walks in. 'This is WPC Bartholomew.'

The woman pulls up a chair and sits beside her. 'You've had a nasty shock,' she says. 'Would you like a cup of tea?'

'My Dennis has just bin found in the bloody river an' you think a flamin' cup of tea's gonna help?' Grace sniggers. It starts small but then it grows in her throat until it takes over and all she can think of is how they're all standing there so stiff like they're in a pantomime or a musical with their silly hats and their daft uniforms.

And all so damn serious looking.

Nobody died, she wants to say – only they did, didn't they? And now there's nothing anybody can do to stop it happening or take things back or make him content to stay at home and not keep going out into the night like he does.

Frank's there. He drapes a blanket around her shoulders. She grasps his hand. 'Don't leave me,' she says.

She knows the chorus line will be singing about that.

CHAPTER TWENTY-SEVEN

Frank bangs his fist against the back of the door they've all just left by. A strange silence clings to the empty kitchen. He sinks against the wall without the first idea of what he should do next.

The most sensible thing would be to clear off right away while he's got the chance. Stashed under a floorboard in his room, there's a bit of cash for emergencies. If he's got any sense, he'll get going right this minute. With no identity cards these days, there's nothing to stop him calling himself any name he likes.

But then again, how will it look if the police decide Dennis was murdered and he's gone on the run? It won't take Sherlock Holmes to work out he's been having an affair with Dennis's wife – the poor man's widow. If he acts like he's guilty, won't they put two and two together and come after him?

And there's Grace to think of. She was in such a state as they bundled her into the back of that police car. With that scarf around her head, her face was hardly visible. She hadn't looked back at him once as they drove away.

On top of that, there's the ruddy pub to worry about. The morning shift's due to start in a couple of hours. Of course, it would be disrespectful, callous even, if he simply opened the doors and carried on trading like nothing had happened.

Rooting around in the table drawer he finds a pad and a fountain pen. He has to spit on the nib to get the ink flowing again. In large capitals he writes:

DUE TO THE SUDDEN DEATH OF

MR DENNIS STEVENSON

THE EIGHT BELLS WILL REMAIN CLOSED

UNTIL FURTHER NOTICE

With more than one entrance to cover, he copies the same thing out several more times. He can't any find sticking tape. After rooting around, he finds a roll of pink plaster and decides to use that instead. When he puts up the notices, the effect is unfortunate – each time he does it, the paper takes on the look of a bandage held in place over a wound.

It doesn't seem fitting for him to be hanging around in a house that's not his own and, in any case, he needs to go home and change his clothes. Did Grace even take a key with her?

Frank starts to walk away but then has second thoughts. Someone needs to stay in case Grace gets back while he's gone. In the end, he decides Dot would be the best person to ask.

It only takes a few minutes to walk the short distance. All the houses are identical and he can't for the life of him remember which one was hers.

Dot must have seen him through the window because she comes running out into the street shouting his name. It breaks his heart to see how happy she looks blinking up at him with the morning sun on her face.

A change enters her features as he starts talking and a few minutes later the poor girl is weeping so loudly the net curtains on her house begin to twitch. 'I'll have your guts for garters!' A stout woman rushes out at him with her fists raised. 'What the hell have you gone an' done to our Dorothy?'

The girl grabs her mother's arm. 'It's not him, Mum – it's what's happened.'

'What's that then?' she demands, looking from Dot to Frank and back again. 'Well?'

Frank repeats the same words, already sick to the stomach at having to be the messenger. 'They've taken Grace off to the police station so she can look at his clothes and that. I think they're hoping to get his brother to identify his body – so at least she'll be spared that.'

Between sobs and exclamations, the two women bombard him with questions. After a while they grow querulous, as if his lack of knowledge might be deliberate.

'I don't think they'll keep her there for long,' he tells them. 'Not given the state she was in. She'll need someone to sit with her when she gets back.' He holds out the side door key.

At last they make an effort and pull themselves together. Dot's mum takes a hanky from her apron pocket and blows her nose. 'We'll both go,' she says, almost snatching it out of his hand.

'I'll pop back in a couple of hours,' Frank tells them, 'I just want to make sure Grace is alright.' He sees a flash of suspicion enter their eyes.

Washed and changed at his digs, Frank feels more in control. He soaps his clothes in the small bowl and then runs down to the backyard to peg them out, relieved to find space on the washing line he has to share with the other tenants.

He returns to the pub but the kitchen's full of people, sitting around talking about Dennis like he's already sprouted wings and a halo.

Grace hardly registers his presence. She briefly lifts her

head to say, 'Are you still here, Frank?' When she looks at him, her blue eyes are clouded over like there's no life left in her. They keep adding brandy to her tea until her eyelids start looking heavy. Dot escorts her up the stairs for a nap. Halfway up, she turns to say, 'I think it's best if you to go on home now, Frank.'

Monday 30th June

Sitting on his bed the next morning, Frank is turning a half crown coin over and over. He looks at the profile of the King – George V1 – then flips it over to read the date: 1937. George was in his forties then – a man in his prime with a young family. The war was still two years away. He was a lad of eighteen at the time with all his life still in front of him.

That familiar feeling creeps over his scalp. When he holds his hands out in front of him, he can see they're trembling. He can't give in – can't let himself get into a state like he used to. For the first time in a long while he has no work to go to, nothing to keep him busy and his mind otherwise occupied. Being holed up in this drab, airless room is starting to get to him.

He hasn't been back to the pub since that brief conversation with Grace on Saturday. She'd thanked him for putting up the notices but hadn't said much else with all three of the Westons fussing around, trying to get her to eat or drink all manner of things to keep her strength up.

He'd heard them planning to have her stay over with them that night. 'Good idea,' he'd told them, though they'd looked at him as if to say *who the hell are you to be giving an opinion on the matter.*

Mr Weston – 'call me Ralf, for God's sake' – had been the one to offer to take any money to the bank's night safe.

'What about the pub?' Frank asked. 'If it's left empty

overnight people will soon get to know and, soon enough, someone's likely to have a go at breaking in.'

Ralf talked of getting a couple of sizable lads in to guard the place and seemed to know a few likely candidates. Before he left, Mrs Weston firmly told him, 'We can sort this out between us now.'

He puts the coin in his back pocket before shifting the bed to one side and lifting a section of the board hidden beneath it. That wad of notes is still there along with his ration book. On the cover he reads: Surname... *Danby*. Initials... *F*. Underneath the first one, there's another ration book – exactly the same only with the front cover blank. Such a simple document and so easy to forge: five quid or less in any city if you know where to look. In any event, these days he only needs to produce the thing if he wants to buy meat, eggs or cheese. He has no use for sugar.

There's a sharp rap on his bedroom door. 'Mr Danby?' A man's voice he doesn't recognise. Doesn't sound threatening but that's no guide.

'Hold up,' he shouts, 'I'll be with you in sec.' He puts the piece of board back in place and pulls the bedframe back, taking care not to make any noise.

Frank opens the door but keeps his left boot in place ready to close it in a hurry if he has to. The chap standing there is about forty, dark hair cut well, carefully trimmed moustache, no sign of a paunch. 'I'm Detective Inspector Collingwood; I believe you've already met Sergeant Bradley.'

The bloke walks straight in without an invitation. His sergeant's ample frame blocks the doorway. With no choice, Frank stands aside. Lurking in the corridor, Mrs Harris calls out: 'Is there a problem, officer?'

Collingwood spins on his heels, almost shoos her away with a wave of his trilby. 'None whatsoever, thank you.' He shuts the door firmly in her face.

Unable to offer them a seat except for the bed, Frank

decides to remain standing himself. 'I expect you're here about what happened to Dennis.'

'Quite so, Mr Danby; quite so,' the inspector says, in his irritating la-de-da voice.

'He were a good bloke; a fair one,' he tells them before they can ask his opinion. 'Drowning's a terrible way for any man to meet his end.'

'Well you see, that's the thing, Mr Danby – Frank, isn't it?' As if he didn't know already, the inspector waits for his answer.

'Yes, it is.'

'Well, Frank, as I believe you know, Mr Stevenson previously sustained a number of injuries on –' He takes out his notebook and flips through the pages until he finds the entry he's looking for. 'The night of Tuesday the twenty-fourth.' He looks up. 'Mrs Stevenson has told us you were by yourself clearing up in the public bar when he was brought home by a Mr Harold Bishop; by all appearances having sustained a fierce beating.'

'Aye, he were in a terrible state. We wanted to call the doctor out but Dennis wouldn't hear of it.'

'Did he mention to you anything about his assailant?'

'No – he said he hadn't seen owt. Said he had no idea who'd attacked him.'

'Well now, moving forward, Mr Stevenson – Dennis, if you prefer – left his home two nights later, on Thursday the twenty-sixth, sadly not to return. I'm sorry to say, we think he sustained further injuries before he fell, or was pushed, into the Thames. Although we're still awaiting the results of the postmortem that was carried out, we're currently treating his death as suspicious.'

'I see.'

The inspector walks over to the sink. From there, Frank sees his eyes range over the mismatched crocks on the draining board, across the stained wallpaper and back to the single wardrobe and the chest of drawers pushed up against it. Finally, his gaze comes to rest on the worn away oilcloth beneath his feet.

'I notice you've a slight Yorkshire accent, Frank. I happen to know that part of the country well. Beautiful scenery. Whereabouts do you hail from?'

'From York itself.' He clears his throat. 'Though I've not lived there for many years now.'

'When did you begin your employment at the Eight Bells?'

'Let me think now, it would have been around the middle of May. A Wednesday or Thursday I think.'

Collingwood writes this down in his notebook. 'So that's what – just over six weeks ago?'

'What of it?'

'And before that, where were you living?'

'I was moving around; doing a bit of farm work here and there.'

'Perhaps you wouldn't mind being more specific, Mr Danby?'

'Actually, I would mind.' Frank knows he should keep his anger under control, but it isn't easy. 'You said yourself, Inspector, Dennis Stevenson was still recovering from the beating he'd had only few days before. A severe beating. On top of that – and I've no wish to speak ill of the dead – the man was a heavy drinker. Ask anyone and they'll tell you he drank whisky like it was water. So, for all you or I know, being almost certainly drunk at the time, he could easily have tripped or slipped and fallen into the river.'

Collinwood holds his gaze for some time before he snaps his notebook shut. 'We'll call it a day, for the time being. Don't worry, we can see ourselves out.'

He takes a step towards the door and then turns. 'One last question, Mr Danby. I believe you failed to show up for the afternoon shift at the Eight Bells on Thursday the twenty-sixth and only reappeared the following evening – Friday the twenty-seventh. A period that seems to coincide with Dennis's disappearance.'

Frank knows what's coming, knows it would be like signing his own death warrant to mention Jack Dawson's name to a policeman. He's thought long and hard about what his answer should be.

'Would you mind telling us where you were all that time?'

'I was here in bed. I'd eaten something that didn't agree with me. I couldn't face work and I was far too rough to go round there and explain.'

'Can anyone here confirm your whereabouts at that time?'

'I'm not sure. I stayed in my room apart from when I had to use the lav. The people living here work all hours and so, as it happened, I didn't see a soul. It's just possible someone might have caught sight of me in the corridor but, being so under the weather at the time, I was in no state to notice.'

'Oh dear – that is unfortunate.' There's more than a note of sarcasm in his voice. Collingwood shrugs his shoulders, gives Frank another long look and then turns on his shiny heels. 'We'll leave you in peace for now, Mr Danby.'

Sergeant Bradley rakes his thinning hair back before he puts his helmet on. He nods towards Frank and walks out of the door ahead of the inspector.

Poised on the threshold, Collingwood turns round. 'One last thing, Mr Danby – please don't go leaving your lodgings here until we've concluded our investigation into this sad affair. Good day to you.'

Tuesday 1st July

For a long time after he wakes, Frank lies looking up at the spot on the ceiling where all the small cracks run together like a spider's web.

At this time in the morning, there's never much traffic noise to speak of and he can listen to the morning chorus. The old bombsites attract birds you wouldn't normally see in a city – the other day he even spotted a black redstart just down the street. With their second broods already hatched and no need to defend territories, the birds aren't singing like they were even a week back. Except for the sparrows that is – those little buggers never let up.

Putting aside all his other worries, the question of money can't be ignored for much longer. It's well over a week since Dennis paid him but then he's not done a full day's work since last Wednesday. Including that Thursday morning shift – before Dawson's men intervened – he's owed five and a half days' wages. Plus, there's the four days in hand Dennis made him work at the start. (A precaution, he'd called it, to make sure Frank didn't leave him in the lurch.)

Of course, he can't go and ask Grace for it; he'd never trouble her at such a time. Still, if he's to keep this room, in three days' time he'll have to pay Mrs Harris what he owes her. The last thing he's willing to do is break into that roll of notes under the bed. Troubling him the most is how he's to send money to Annie and the lad. Yet another promise he's about to break.

The shame of it gets him out of bed. With everything up in the air like it is, he needs to go and find some work and right now anything will do.

He's putting a shine on his shoes, when a rustling draws his attention over towards the door. Someone pushes an envelope underneath it. Though he's quick to unlock it, he's too late to catch whoever it was.

Frank picks it up and reads his full name across the front in what looks like a woman's hand. Perhaps Mrs Harris has finally lost patience with him. He tears into it, unfolds the pale blue notepaper inside to read,

I need to talk to you. Meet me at the bandstand in the park at 1pm. G

CHAPTER TWENTY-EIGHT

She'd written the note in haste and now Grace can't think what possessed her to choose this spot. Anyone standing up there on the raised platform can be seen from all over the park – that's the whole bloody point of a bandstand. Better then to sit on a bench not too far away and keep an eye out for him.

It's yet another sunny day and the parched grass is teeming with all manner of people. She's wearing her new sunglasses and a headscarf tied closely at the neck to hide most of her hair. She's not entirely sure why she's being so cautious – even sending that lad to Frank's with the note and sixpence for his trouble. Still, she's learning to trust her instincts – look how right she'd been about Dennis's disappearance.

In any case, with so many prying eyes about, she couldn't suggest they met at her place or anywhere near it.

A shiver runs through her every time she thinks of going back into that pub. The beer in the pumps will be souring already and there's all the rest of the stock to worry about. After what's happened, even the regulars must be thinking of taking their custom down to the Bridge or the King's Head. One thing's for certain, she can't keep the pub shut up like it is for much longer.

A nearby church clock is still striking the hour when she catches sight of him coming across the grass to her left. He's wearing the shirt she'd first seen him in – the one that brings out the colour of his eyes. The sun-bleached top of his hair is catching the sunlight. He's striding along, in his element out in the open; you only have to look at him to know he's not a city man and never will be.

She sets off in his direction, intercepts him with the slightest touch to his elbow. Noticing his confusion, she peers over the rim of her glasses. 'Yes, it's me. Who did you think it was accosting you?' And then, 'Let's go somewhere quieter.'

They turn off the main path into a shaded area where it's cooler.

'How are you?' His thigh keeps rubbing up against her and she wonders if she should break step with him.

'How do you think I am? The police think Dennis might have been murdered, for pity's sake.' A notice tells her that the path they're on is leading them towards the rose garden.

'I'm so sorry,' he says.

'Why? What have you done?'

They break apart to go through the narrow gate. The formality of the garden must make most people uncomfortable because, unlike the rest of the park, there's hardly anyone about. Halfway round, they sit down on a bench next to a white rosebush. Grace makes sure there's a respectable gap between them. She bends toward the nearest bush to take in the smell one of its blooms. The aroma reminds her faintly of Pond's cold cream.

'I've been going out of my mind with worry,' he tells her. It's true he looks anxious; nervous as a rabbit judging by the way he keeps pumping his left foot up and down.

'First things first,' she says. 'I found some cash Dennis had squirrelled away amongst his socks.' She holds out the envelope. 'It's the money you're owed plus the four days in hand from when you started,' she says. 'So, we're all square now.'

'It could have waited.' He frowns, is reluctant to take it. ''Praps you'd better hang onto it.'

Grace resorts to a lie. 'There's plenty more where that came from.'

'Well, if you're sure.' He seems relieved as he stuffs the envelope into his trouser pocket. 'Thanks very much – I won't pretend this isn't welcome.'

She looks away to focus instead on the man eating his sandwiches on the bench at the end. 'The police have bin asking me so many questions,' Grace says. 'Especially about you.'

'What sort of questions?'

'About everythin' really. That's not the half of it – they've bin nosing around, talkin' to all the regulars. I think they know we've –' She's uncertain whether the man with the sandwiches might be within earshot. 'I don't need to spell it out, not to you of all people.'

'Adultery isn't a crime,' he says. 'If it was, the jails in this city would be overflowing into the streets.'

She winces at his naming of what they – no, what *she's* done; a stark word for something so complicated. It takes a while for her to collect herself again. 'They wanted to know about money matters – whether Dennis had taken out a life insurance policy.'

Frank looks startled. 'And had he?'

'Yes – he fixed it up with Kenny Fletcher from the Pru not long after we got married. I remember him sayin' he'd got responsibilities to think of now.'

'Shit,' he says. 'They're trying to find a motive and financial gain is an easy one.'

When she takes out her hanky, Frank puts his arm around her shoulders. 'Don't,' she says. He doesn't say a word; just takes his arm away and stares down at the palms of his hands instead. She can see him studying those three lines that are meant to tell your fortune.

'I nearly refused to answer,' she tells him. 'They were so damn nosey, lookin' at everything. Then I thought I should show them I've nothing to hide. I handed over everythin' they asked for – all the paperwork from the safe, the whole lot.'

'The thing is,' abandoning caution, she leans into his ear, 'they showed me a piece of paper where it says in black and bloody white that I'm entitled to six grand in the event of his death.'

'You can't be serious?'

'I'm deadly series. Six ruddy grand.'

'Flaming hell's bells!' Frank cradles his head in his hands. 'That's a ruddy fortune.'

'I know – it's far too much. I remember tellin' him at the time it wasn't necessary, and that Kenny Fletcher was makin' a small fortune out of everyone round here. I suppose he must have bin thinkin', at the time, that we might start a family.' She stops short of describing how, even before the end of their first year together, Dennis never seemed to want her in that way again.

Frank stands up. 'Christ, this puts a totally different light on everything.' He starts walking in circles in front of the bench. It's making her feel dizzy. Finally, he stops and turns his face up to the heavens. 'You know the Old Bill – how their minds will be working. They've already paid me a visit. Now they'll think that I had a motive for wanting him dead and out of the way so I could get my greasy hands on your money.'

He pinches the bridge of his nose. 'This is all such a bloody mess.'

'Listen, Frank,' she says, 'there's no need to panic; it may not be that bad.'

Grace gets to her feet. 'I've already told them you knew absolutely nothing about the insurance money. How could you have done him in when those two bobbies saw with their own eyes you'd spent the night with me?'

She makes sure to stare him straight in the eyes as she spells it out. 'All you need to do if they ask, is tell them exactly where you were after half eleven on Thursday – when Dennis left home – and when you walked back into the pub on Saturday evening. Simple enough, Frank. I told them I'd just called last orders when you came in so it would have been just before eleven.'

He turns away. 'They've already asked me and I've already told them I was in my bed sick. That I must have eaten something bad. Trouble is, I haven't got an alibi.'

'So that's your story, is it?' She's so angry she can barely get the words out. 'If I can tell you're lying, they'll certainly be able to work it out.'

Grace puts out a hand to stop him following her. 'Don't,' she says louder than she'd intended. 'If you think for one minute the Old Bill are gonna swallow that load of shite you're a bigger bloody fool than I took you for, Frank Danby.'

Turning to leave, she almost trips over a chap kneeling to do up his shoelaces.

Frank gets in front of her, tries to block her path. 'Don't you dare touch me,' she tells him. 'I don't want you anywhere near me, d'you hear; not until you're ready to tell the truth – that's if you can still remember what that is.'

CHAPTER TWENTY-NINE

He leaves the rose garden just behind her, as she walks across the park at a brisk pace, not looking to her left or right and certainly not looking back at him as she heads through the outer gate and disappears out of sight.

Should he go after her? Frank's urge to unburden himself is almost – but not quite – overpowering. Instead, he strides off in the opposite direction – towards the north gate. People are everywhere and yet there it is again, a sixth sense that's telling him he's being watched. He can't shake off the idea that he's being followed. Whenever he looks back – like when you play grandmother's footsteps – everyone behind seems to be going about their own business and not looking his way for a second.

Once through the big gates, he turns left onto the main road. If he crosses over, he can take one of the smaller roads that leads down to the riverside. There's a pub he knows just at the end, right down by the water.

Lunchtime and he can see they're doing a roaring trade. His plan is to nip inside where he'll get a good view of the road he's just walked down to be certain one way or another.

Ten minutes go by and no one appears except for a woman in a bright headscarf pushing a pram.

Feeling calmer, he goes up to the counter. Though he's

pretty much lost his taste for beer these days, he orders a half pint and takes it outside.

Frank sits down on the low wall that bounds the riverbank. A sharp stench fills his nostrils as he looks across the expanse of shining water. Upriver, a big liner is closing on the bridge. The slaps of her wake reach the black groynes just in front of him and tilts the buoys marking the shallows. Down on the shoreline a group of gulls are squabbling over something that's washed up.

He wonders where all these ships and boats are heading. This city, like so many others, was built on this movement of goods and people; it waits here at the start or finish of all those individual journeys. The same giant ship now towering above all those cranes and masts will turn about before long. Once she's free of the river and then the estuary, she'll be dwarfed by the vastness of the open sea.

Since the end of the war, countless men and women have queued up to pay their ten quid and sailed off for a new life in Australia or New Zealand. *Ten-Pound Poms* they call them out there. He's read how you only had to be under 45 and healthy enough to be a good grafter. He's known a fair few who've taken up assisted passage and several times he's been tempted by their enthusiasm to make the break himself. Why not now? All that's needed is the right bits of paper – and Lord knows that's never difficult if you can find the cash. Who'd look twice at him boarding the ship along with all those other dreamers heading for a new life?

He takes a sip of his beer though the reek of the water seems to sour the taste. Observing the strength of the current, he pictures Dennis's body drifting on this same river at the whim of the tide. In the papers they talk about bodies being fished out weeks or even months after someone's disappeared, how they can even drift right out to sea on the tide. Might have been the case with Dennis if his corpse hadn't caught the eye of that passing bargeman.

A black-backed gull lands on the wall right beside him. It turns its head along with that sharp beak in his direction; the single yellow eye seems to be weighing him up.

It's time to make up his mind, do something before others decide his fate. First though, he needs to speak to Grace again. There's no shirking it – he has to tell her the truth. The truth eh? Well, he could start by admitting that he's hopelessly in love with her. He stares at the sunlight skipping along on the surface of the dirty water. Ten years of feeling nothing and now this. He shakes his head, smiles up at the sky and his own damned folly. What possible use can he be to Grace now? How can he protect her when he can't even protect himself? One thing's for certain – there's not the slightest chance of them finding happiness together if he stays here and waits for the law to catch up with him.

Wednesday 2nd July

'Who is it?'

'It's me, Frank. Can I come in?' It's a while before she unbolts the door. Without sunglasses shielding her eyes, he can see how red and swollen they are.

She leads the way into the Weston's back kitchen. 'Watch the floor – some of it's still wet.'

'I hoped you'd be alone,' he says.

'As it happens, I am.'

He's careful not to knock over the mop propped up in its bucket. Grace is wearing a wraparound apron that looks all wrong on her. The wireless is playing a lively big band tune he half-recognises. She turns it off. 'Dot and Lottie are at work down the biscuit factory,' she says, 'and Ralf's still out on his rounds.'

Grace folds her arms across her chest. 'I'd offer you a cup of tea but it's not my house.'

'Can I sit down, at least?'

She pulls out a chair for herself and nods him towards the one opposite. 'So, Frank, now you're sitting comfortably, I'm all ears. Are you planning to tell me the truth at last?'

He rubs at his forehead, his fingers chasing the shallow groove of the scar. 'It's hard to know where to start.'

'Is it, Frank?' She picks up the sock that's on the table and pulls out a darning needle with a grey thread still attached. 'You can start with where you went off to when you left the pub last Thursday afternoon.' She keeps turning the needle from end to the end.

'Okay, well, after I locked up, I went for a bit of a stroll round.'

She aims the sharp end of the needle at him. 'If you tell me you went off to paddle in that flamin' lake, so help me I'll clock you one.' He's pleased to see a bit of colour back in her cheeks.

'Will you hear me out at least?' He waits for her full attention. 'I popped into the chippy down the road. I'd just left wi' me chips still in me hands when this car stops and three blokes get out and set on me.'

'Swear to me you're not making this up?'

'I swear.'

She stares at him, her expression only half believing. 'Who were these blokes – did you recognise any of 'em?'

'I'd never seen any of 'em before. Needless to say, I didn't go without putting up a fight. Anyroad, they forced me into the back of their car and put a ruddy sack over my head so's I couldn't see where they were taking me.'

'Bloody hell, Frank.' She's frowning like she's far from convinced. 'Wait a minute, let me get this straight – you're saying these four blokes you'd never seen before kidnapped you from right outside the chippy in broad bloody daylight?'

'It was a bit further up the road, but yes, that's exactly what happened. They waited till there was no one around. I promise you, Grace, every word of this is true.'

'Okay, so supposing I believe you – what happened after that?'

'They drove me somewhere – before you ask, I don't know where. Then they marched me into this old building. Looked like an empty warehouse – something like that.'

'How could you tell? You just said you had a sack over your head, remember?' She looks pleased with herself for catching him out in cross-examination.

'Because they took the ruddy thing off when they pushed me into this room.' He stands up, affronted now. 'If you're not even willing to hear me out without doubting every word I say, I might as well bugger off right now.'

She tugs on his trouser leg. 'Sit down, Frank.' He's slow to oblige. 'Look, I'm sorry,' she says, 'it's just that, if you want to know the truth, it all sounds a bit far-fetched. Why would they do that?'

'They were acting on someone's orders – their boss. I'm not going to tell you his name because you'll have heard of him and it's better if you don't know who I'm talking about.'

She sighs. 'Right, so what happened when they got you into this room?'

'Their boss came in. He told me he knew all about Dennis's little capers with Cyril Lloyd and none of it was to his liking.'

'Why won't you tell me this bloke's name?'

'It's safer that way; trust me.' He starts to rub at his forehead again but she stays his hand. 'Anyroad, the bastard kept me there, locked me up overnight.' Unintentionally a note of self-pity creeps into his voice. 'Bastards gave me no food, not even a drink of ruddy water.'

She stands up; plants her hands on her hips. 'You're serious?'

'The next day the boss man came in with a mug of water and enjoyed watching how desperate I was for it.' The memory of it makes him angry all over again. 'Then he offered me what he called a *bonus* if I could get Dennis to sell him the pub. Said he'd been looking for a suitable free house and was prepared to pay a reasonable price *under the current circumstances.*'

Grace gets up and walks over to the window, that ruddy needle still poised between her thumb and finger like she's weighing his words. 'If this bloke was so desperate to get his hands on the pub, why would he go through you? Why not talk to Dennis directly?'

'That confused me at the time. I reckoned he probably knew Dennis was laid up in bed – in fact he was probably behind that beating he had. By kidnapping me and roughing me up, he thought I'd do a good job of convincing Dennis to take his offer.'

He can see she's pushing the tip of that needle into her thumb. He gets up to take it out of her hand and puts it back on the table.

'You just said that's what you thought *at the time*,' Grace says. 'So what do you think now?'

'I'm not sure.' His sigh is long and drawn out. ''Praps it might be best if neither of us speculates.'

'I want to know,' she says. Despite her red eyes and that awful apron, he's struck by how pretty she is.

'One thing's for certain – he knew about us.' He turns away. Should he say more? Was it right to worry her like this?

'Come on, Frank,' she says, 'spit it out, for pity's sake.'

'I reckon he was holding me there to make sure I had no alibi for Thursday night because being your lover makes me the perfect suspect.'

'You honestly believe that?'

'I've met his type before. They want to be king of the heap. Can't abide it if someone's setting up in competition. They don't get their own hands dirty – instead they use their henchmen to punish the offender as a lesson to anybody who might challenge them. You know yourself Dennis had been selling knocked off booze.'

Grace narrows her eyes on him. 'You're seriously telling me this bloke calculated that the police would put two an' two together an' make five and six? That he went an' kidnapped you so's he could set you up as Dennis's murderer?' She buries her face in her hands.

'That's about the long and short of it.'

'Oh, my good Lord.'

He touches her shoulders but she shrugs him off and instead starts pacing the room. 'And now with all that insurance money coming my way they might think I went an' put you up to it. Frank, you have no choice – *we* have no choice – you have to go to the Old Bill this minute and tell them who this bastard is and what he did to you.' She grabs hold of his arm. 'There's no other way out of this mess.'

'But I've already lied to them. Think about it for a second, Grace – if *you* didn't believe me just now, what ruddy hope is there that Collingwood will?'

He keeps on shaking his head over and over. 'Don't you see, I can't prove any of this? On top of that, believe me this bloke he's got people everywhere – he can get to anyone, anywhere. I've heard even a locked prison cell isn't safe.'

'So what the hell can we do?' Her hands are shaking.

He grabs her shoulders and this time she doesn't push him away. 'Listen, they would have arrested me by now if they had proof Dennis was murdered. That means we've got a bit of time.' He takes a deep breath, tries to sound more confident than he feels. 'I know where to go to get the right papers and passports – not just for me but for both of us. The two of us could be together. We could head off on the high seas and leave all this behind. There's nowt to stop us. In a few weeks we could be in Australia – or New Zealand even.'

She looks shell-shocked; her face unreadable.

'Think about it,' he says. 'You and me, we could start a whole new life together on the other side of the world. Places where there's always fresh air and sunshine, big countries full of opportunity, if you're not shy of hard work, big enough for

Frank Danby and Grace Stevenson to become Mr and Mrs anything you like.'

Frank pulls her towards him. 'Haven't you always wanted to start a new life?'

CHAPTER THIRTY

'Frank, this is madness.' The air's too close; it feels like he's squeezing all the breath out of her body. She pushes him away. 'I mean, is that your idea of a marriage proposal?'

'If you like. And why not, Grace? What's keeping either of us here?'

'We can't simply up and leave the country like outlaws on the run from the local sheriff. These days they can radio ships and send messages and photographs all over the world. They'd be sure to track us down.'

'Not if we're just Mr and Mrs Smith. Trust me – with the right papers in your pocket, it's easy to disappear.'

She winces at that one. Her head's beginning to spin like she's about to throw up. 'Here, sit down,' he says, guiding her back to her seat, as though that could make things any better. 'Can I get you a drink – water? A cup of tea?'

'Oh yes, because that's the answer in every bloody crisis – a brew up is bound to put things right.' She's so angry with him. Everything was bad before but now it's ten times worse. It's as well she's sitting down now because her legs have gone to jelly. Maybe it would have been better if he'd stuck to his other story.

She looks out of the window – at the cherry tree swaying in the breeze in the Westons' back garden. 'But what if Dennis just slipped and fell into the river – have you thought of that? We'd have left everything behind for no good reason.'

He keeps on shaking his head like she's the one talking nonsense. 'They beat Dennis up – almost left him for dead. Do you honestly think after everythin' I've told you, that his death could have been just an accident?'

'They still have to prove it.' She's the one shaking her head now. 'If we run, the coppers will assume we're both guilty. We'll be playin' right into their hands.'

'But they'll do that if we stay. I'll be put on trial and probably hanged for murder.' The look of desperation on his face frightens her; the old confident Frank has all but disappeared. 'Even if they don't prosecute you as an accomplice,' he says, 'you'll forever be seen as some sort of scarlet woman.'

Grace looks around the familiar, cluttered room. 'But what about Mum and me aunty; and then there's Dot and her mum and dad – the Westons have bin like a second family to me; I'd have bin lost without them these last few days. And what about the pub – Dennis and me worked bloody hard to keep that place goin' all these years.'

A bang at the door makes them both jump. From where she's sitting Grace can see the front door. Someone's just posted a newspaper through the letterbox and now it's lying on the mat.

Frank's slow to calm down – she notices the way his hands are shaking. Part of her is tempted by his offer of a new life, of a new identity she gets to choose for herself. Her head is buzzing. 'I need time to think,' she tells him. 'Look, you'd better go – Ralf will be back soon. It would be as well if he doesn't find you here.'

He kisses her wet eyelids before he leaves; promises everything's going to be okay again. In her heart she knows nothing will ever feel right again.

It's no good – she's finished all the chores and can't sit there twiddling her thumbs.

Grace grabs her handbag and sunglasses and steps out into a perfectly ordinary day. Out in the street, that sun beats down on her head like it's never going to rain again. A handful of little children are out there playing all the usual games, the littlest ones are wearing sunbonnets so, despite the shouting and arguing, they have the look of little angels.

There's no breeze and the houses at every turn are packed in too tight together. As she walks along the narrow pavement, she thinks she can spot a face behind every net curtain. When a black cat crosses her path, she watches it jump into a front garden and then starts to laugh so hard she has to lean against a brick wall to get herself under control again.

Without really thinking, she finds herself back in the street outside the Eight Bells. Now it's all shut up, the pub is a sorry sight. That chipped paint on the windows and sills looks worse than ever it did before. For the first time, she notices how a tiny tree has taken root in one corner of the front gutter. Those makeshift signs Frank put up in the windows have already begun to yellow in the sun.

She'd reminded Frank of all the hard work she and Dennis put into this place. How can she walk away from it now? What will happen to this pub once her back's turned? That villain – Frank's mystery man – is bound to snap it up; after everything that's happened, it'll go for a song and with her on the other side of the world powerless to stop it. He'll turn this place – *their* pub – into just another part of his crooked empire. Dennis would turn in his grave.

Behind her, someone clears his or her throat. She spins round to find it's only Charlie Metcalfe peering over his specs at her, cap in hand. 'I haven't had a chance to say it, but I'm very sorry about what's happened to your Dennis.'

'Thank you, Charlie.'

'He was a good man an' a decent landlord.' He fiddles with

his hat. 'I already miss the old bugger, if you 'scuse me French.'

Grace nods her appreciation, too moved to speak. Charlie looks as if he wants to say more but thinks better of it.

She finds the side door key in her bag and lets herself in. A pile of post is spread out over the floor. Some of it snags the door when she tries to close it until she yanks at a few of the letters.

Amongst them there's a large one with *Tomlinson's your friendly local undertakers* stamped across the front. Dennis would have roared at the cheek of it.

Mr Tomlinson begins by offering her his condolences. She reads on.

Your late husband was a fine fellow: a good friend to many and a good landlord to all. I've no doubt he will be sadly missed by everyone who knew him.

If I can be of service to you at this sad time, please get in touch.

Late husband eh. It seems to suit him well – late in life and now late in death. Poor Dennis. She's shocked at herself, at how she could have thought for one second about running away to a new life with Frank when her husband's not even been buried yet. Does he expect her to up leave before the funeral's even been arranged?

Grace takes the other letters into the kitchen and sifts through them one at a time. All the while, she tries to think about Dennis when he was still alive but it's not long before the other Dennis creeps back. His brother identified him but that hasn't stopped her picturing his cold body lying naked on a slab in the morgue.

To distract herself from such awful thoughts, Grace opens

the other letters. She's touched that most of the regulars have written and all of them saying such nice things. Each one adds a little something about how Dennis had made them laugh or helped them out or always had a kind word; and all of them say they'll miss him.

She goes through into the public bar and straight away she can picture him leaning on the counter with a glass of whisky alongside him, having a good old chinwag with somebody or other. The smell of stale beer and smoke is even stronger than usual.

Whatever the consequences, doesn't her Dennis deserve to have his death properly investigated? When all's said and done, he was her husband and, *if* he was murdered, the coppers ought to find out exactly who did it.

CHAPTER THIRTY-ONE

In truth, Frank doesn't know where to start. Since they scrapped identity cards, he hasn't had to worry about such things – not like he used to in the old days.

When he'd first come to London, some ten years ago, someone had tipped him off about a chap with a pitch in the market down in Bermondsey reputed to be able to supply you with any document you care to mention.

The recommended man turned out to be a thickset fellow with a bushy moustache going by the name of Robbie. He was understandably wary, wanted to know exactly who'd recommended his services before he decided to trust Frank. Robbie claimed to be the intermediary for his brother Gerald, and it was Gerald who could get you more or less any piece of paper you wanted for the right price. No one Frank knew had ever seen hide nor hair of this Gerald.

The street where they used to hold the market is empty. Could Wednesday be an off day? He pops into the newsagents right on the corner. Once he's paid for a Daily Mirror, he asks the balding chap in there about the street market.

'They packed it in a couple of years back,' he tells him. 'Not enough trade.'

'That's a real shame.' He doesn't need to act his

disappointment. 'Thing is, I was hoping to find my old pal Robbie. What with this and that, the two of us lost touch a few years back – you know how it is? He used to sell secondhand clothes and that sort of thing.'

'What, Robbie Harding?' The newsagent looks pleased as punch. 'You're in luck, mate; your pal's gone up in the world these days – got himself a fancy shop just off the square.'

The newsagent plants a hand on his shoulder and walks with him to the doorway. 'Turn left just over there, see. At the end of that street, turn left again an' you can't miss it.'

The sign over the double-fronted shop reads: *Harding's Fashion Wear*. Its proprietor comes towards Frank in a suit and tie, the collar digging into his broad neck. It's been ten years and Robbie's filled out in every direction; his moustache has been trimmed into submission and he's sporting a new hairstyle that's not dissimilar to Prince Phillip's.

'Can I be of assistance, sir?' He's even worked on his cockney accent.

'I don't suppose you remember me,' Frank says. 'Your brother Gerald helped me out a few years back.'

Robbie's face drops. He looks past Frank to the door. 'I'm sorry but my brother's no longer in that line of business.'

'That's a real pity. I always appreciated the quality of his work. I just thought he might be interested in doing a favour for a loyal customer.'

'Like I said, pal, my brother can't help you anymore.' Robbie stands there for a minute rubbing at his chin. 'However, I could give you the address of another chap in his line of work. This fella's just as fine a craftsman.' He scribbles the name *Arthur* on an old envelope – no last name – just an address. 'You should find him easy enough – his place is only a stone's throw from the tube station.'

He looks down at his fancy watch. 'He'll have knocked

off by now. Suggest you call round just after seven tomorrow morning if you want to catch him in. Be sure and tell him Robbie Harding sends his regards.'

'I hope Gerald's enjoying his retirement.' Frank holds out his hand. 'Thanks a lot, mate, I really appreciate your help.'

Instead of shaking his hand, Robbie nods his head. 'Now, if you'll excuse me, got some new stock to price up.'

Thursday 3rd July

It's drizzling when Frank leaves home – not the sort of rain you expect after such a prolonged dry spell. The way he's feeling, he'd prefer thunder and lightning to be crashing overhead; that would at least clear the air.

Despite the early hour, the city's already woken up. Crossing the road, he has to dodge between buses and cars and an endless stream of bicycles ringing out their warning bells.

He finds himself enjoying the exercise. It's refreshing to feel a fine spray on his face, though the rain's hardly enough to wet the pavements.

He's approaching the river; foghorns are booming out at regular intervals – they sound like the cries of prehistoric monsters hiding in the mist. Up ahead, Tower Bridge emerges out of the fog, both halves raised to allow the grey bulk of a cargo ship to pass underneath.

Fortunately, Frank's set aside plenty of time for his journey; time enough to admire the sheer scale and beauty of the bridge's vast metal structure. He wonders about the lives of the anonymous men who built her all those years ago.

Whitechapel isn't an area he knows especially well but he's confident he can locate the address without asking for directions. After a bit of toing and froing, he finds the sign he's been looking for on the wall of an alleyway.

There's no response when Frank knocks though he can see light shining through the thin gap between the two doors. A wireless or gramophone is playing band music. He cups his hands to the door and bellows: 'Hello, is anybody there?'

After a while longer, the right-hand door is wrenched open.

'What d'you want?' The bloke addressing him is tall and wiry. If he saw him in the street, he'd think he was a clerk with those tortoiseshell glasses and slicked back hair. He's young too – no more than twenty-five or so.

'Are you Arthur?'

The man scrutinises his face so closely he begins to feel uncomfortable. 'Who wants to know?'

'My name's Frank. Friend of mine by the name of Robbie Harding thought you might be able to help me.'

'Did he now?' The bloke remains where he is, blocking the view to the inside.

'Thing is, I'm looking to acquire a few bits of paper and Robbie told me how much he admired your work; said you were a real craftsman.'

His expression doesn't soften an inch as he peers at Frank's face and then his clothes. 'I don't work for nothin' – ain't running no charity here.'

'You've no worries on that score, mate – I've got the readies to pay for what I need; that's if the workmanship's up to scratch. It's got to pass muster.'

'I assure you it will.' Behind the lenses, Arthur's eyes are slits. 'Just so's we're clear – I'll need a substantial sum up front before I begin. A token of good faith, you might say.'

Frank weighs his options. 'Okay, mate, that's fair enough.'

Arthur opens the door wider – just enough to allow him to step inside the small workshop. Looking round, he can see it's quite a setup.

'Don't let the humbleness of my premises here fool ya,' Arthur says from behind him. 'I can assure you I'm pretty much the best in the business.'

CHAPTER THIRTY-TWO

Stepping inside the Eight Bells, Grace takes off her damp headscarf and shakes it. The sound of snoring greets her and she has quite a start. When it carries on, she follows the noise into the public bar.

Ralf had made all the arrangements – paid good money to this couple of so-called night watchmen. It's not like she hadn't made enough racket coming in, yet both men are sound asleep on their camp beds. Even at this distance the smell of their sweat is laced with their beery breath.

Empty glasses are lined up along the sticky counter. Had they invited their friends in or did they prefer to use a clean glass each and every time they helped themselves to another drink on the house?

She remembers their names – who could forget they're known as Fred and Ginger? It isn't hard to spot Ginger's head of fiery curls poking out of the sheet that's wrapped around his bulk.

She loudly clears her throat but neither one of them stirs. Resisting the urge to kick them awake, she picks up the hand bell they use for last orders and shakes it right next to their ears.

Wide-eyed with panic, the two men scrabble to their feet and stand there staring at her through bleary eyes. Grace wishes she had been spared the sight of their sagging bodies and far from clean underpants. 'You're being paid to keep an eye on this place and what happens?' She gives them no time to answer. 'Instead you betray Ralf's trust an' drink yourselves senseless at my expense.'

'Hang on a sec –' Ginger begins to protest.

'Don't you dare deny it. Any bugger could have strolled in here an' stolen half the stock, an' neither of you two sleepin' beauties would be any the wiser.' She's so angry she's tempted to clout them with the weighty bell she's still holding. 'You can clear off out of here right now.' It rings as she gestures towards the door.

'But Ralf said you –'

'I don't give a monkey's what Ralf did or didn't say. I'm the boss round here an' I'm tellin' you both to sling your ruddy hooks right this minute.' She puts the bell down before she gives in to temptation. 'And make sure you take all that rubbish of yours with you.'

Once she's heard their grumbling departure, Grace goes through into the public to clear up the mess they've left. She starts with the dirty glasses and continues to work out her feelings while scrubbing and polishing every sticky surface. After that, she fetches the bucket and some disinfectant and mops all the floors. Satisfied with the results, she tackles the glue from the sticking plaster that's still clinging to the inside of the windows. She has to use vinegar and old newspaper to remove every last bit.

It's less than a week since Dennis's death and there's plenty who might judge it too early to reopen the pub. Let them think what they like; she knows what he would have wanted and it's not that she should let all this go to rack and ruin.

Grace takes a final look to make sure all is shipshape before she puts on the lights. The big hand of the clock moves round to form a defiant V and she unbolts the doors as eleven chimes ring out.

No one is outside waiting. The drizzle that had started the day seems to have turned into a heavier downpour. With the drop in temperature, the air's a lot fresher. Across the street a handful of sparrows are splashing and squabbling in a pothole puddle.

Half an hour passes and still not a solitary customer comes in. With the beer on the pumps unlikely to keep much longer and the storeroom awash with those cases of spirits from who-knows-where, Grace is determined to keep the place open until closing time at two-thirty. Once word gets around, the regulars at least are bound to trickle back in dribs and drabs.

The clock chimes twice – the sound echoes in the deserted bar and Grace reluctantly accepts defeat. Not a single person has come in. Nobody's even ventured into the jug and bottle to buy baccy. She goes through to bolt the doors to the saloon bar.

Back in the public, she finds Wilf Barnet standing there by himself in the middle of the empty room. 'The missus told me she'd walked past an' seen your lights on,' he says.

'Pint of bitter, is it?'

The old man slowly shakes his head.

'Look, I know it might seem too soon,' she says, 'but Dennis would have wanted me to sell off the stock at the very least – get what I can for it. If I don't, it won't stay put for long.'

Wilf takes off his cap, holds it in front of him like a hearse might be passing. 'I dare say you might be right about that.' He goes to say something and then stops himself.

'I don't believe no one seems to want to drink in here any-more. Once they know the place is open again, they'll soon –'

'Don't.' He stops her with a raised hand. 'I'm afraid to say, you don't know the ruddy half of it, sweetheart.' That wry smile only makes his lined face look more serious.

She walks past him to secure the outside door. 'Then 'praps you'd care to tell me the half of it I don't know, Wilf.'

'I'll do that; only turn them ruddy lights off before they see the place lit up like a ruddy Christmas tree.'

Ever since she's known him, the old man has seemed so solid a figure; nothing appears to shake him. Now, for the first time, she detects fear in his voice.

Once Grace turns off the lights, they stand there facing each other in the gloom. 'Might as well take the weight of me old pins first,' he says, sounding more like his old self. 'Why don't you sit yourself down, an' all?'

She pulls out the chair opposite. 'So now,' she says, 'tell me exactly what you know that I don't.'

He pulls out his empty pipe and sucks on it. 'Since what's happened here, some of us have bin goin' down to the Farriers for a pint. I'll grant you it's a bit further to go but it's a decent enough boozer and they keep the beer nearly as well as your Dennis did – God rest his soul.'

Grace wants to rush him to the point, but she can see this is hard for the old man.

'I was on me way down there the other day when Harry Bishop rushes past me in Chandler's Walk with a face like thunder on him. "What's up wi' you?" I shouts after him, and with that he turns round –' Wilf frowns. 'Let's just say the gist of what he had to say was, that he was now well an' truly up shit creek without a paddle.'

He leans in closer, pointing the wet stem of his pipe at her. 'Seems somebody in the Farriers had told poor Harry that, if he knew what was good for him, he was to inform the Old Bill that he'd caught a glimpse of Frank roughing up your husband on the night before Dennis up and disappeared.'

'But that makes no sense. Frank was clearin' up right here when Harry himself brought Dennis home.'

'Harry was told to say that Frank must have seen him comin' along and legged it; then nipped back in here to cover his tracks.'

'That's ridiculous.' Grace stands up. 'I'll tell the coppers the truth – that Frank was as shocked as I was at the state Dennis was in.'

'Trouble is, sweetheart, they've been askin' lots of questions round here about yourself and Frank and what might or might not be goin' on between the two of you.'

He raises his hand before she can say anything. 'Regardless of the truth of that particular matter, I shouldn't wonder that they'll argue you're coverin' for him.'

'What, against my own husband?' Grace tightens her fists then sees the old man flinch like he's expecting her to start laying into him.

Straightening out her hands, she takes a deep breath and lets it out slowly. 'So what's Thin Harry planning on doing?'

'That's what I asked him straight out and he said that he wasn't gonna put a noose round an innocent man's neck for any bugger. Knowin' the nature of the crooks involved, he said he was of a mind to bugger off on his holidays – and stay away for the foreseeable future. Haven't seen hide nor hair of him since – so I 'spect true to his word he's gone an' scarpered. Who can blame him?'

'But who are these men – the crooks who want to set Frank up?'

'Harry said he wasn't certain but the fella who spoke to him is known to hang around with them Dawson brothers. It seems the Farriers is now part of their patch. Seems for some reason they've got it in for Frank – want to make damned sure he swings for Dennis's murder.'

'But that makes no sense – the coppers don't even know for certain Dennis was murdered. If they had got proof of it, I should have thought, as his wife, I'd be the first one to be told.'

'I can't answer all your questions, sweetheart. All I know is that every bugger's scared of them Dawsons.' The old man leans on the side of the table and takes his time getting to his feet. 'I thought you deserved to know why no one's likely to come in here. Right now, there's so many rumours flyin' around. Then there's more ruddy rumours about them rumours; an' most of 'em boils down to the Dawsons not wanting this place to reopen.'

Wilf straightens up to look her in the eyes. 'Every bugger round here is now too scared to cross that threshold. I'm an old man with nothin' more to me name than the clothes I stand up in, but I still looked left an' right half a dozen times before I crossed the street an' walked through that door just now. I'll do the same ruddy thing when I leave.'

He puts his empty pipe into the corner of his mouth. 'Breaks me heart to have to say such things to you, sweetheart, but not one of us is brave enough to put our head above the parapet an' I'm afraid that's the way it's likely to stay.'

CHAPTER THIRTY-THREE

Friday 4th July

Braving the driving rain, Frank walks from the bus stop to the Westons' house. Though it's not yet eight in the morning, he rings and then knocks several times but no one comes to the door. Rainwater dripping down his collar, he shouts her name through the letterbox. After a while it's clear she either won't come to the door or she's out.

Round the corner and along the street he takes in the sorry sight of the closed-up Eight Bells. He tries all the doors but they're locked. Someone's removed the signs he'd taped up announcing Dennis's death leaving just the faintest outline where the strips of plaster had been. Peering in through the clear parts of the glass, he puts his face to each door and window in turn. There's no sign of life, not one light on inside.

He hasn't the foggiest where Grace might have gone off to so early in the day.

Before he left Whitechapel yesterday, Arthur had made a good start on the documents he'd asked for. With a number of other things to see to, Frank had agreed to return the next day with the woman he'd described as his "travelling company".

Looking around, the streets are almost deserted. When he pictures Grace, she's in this place – the association is so strong he keeps expecting her to appear in front of him. Truth is she could have gone anywhere; finding her in this warren of back streets would be as likely as stumbling over a four-leaf clover.

He holds up both hands in defeat, lets them fall to slap his sides. Damn and blast it – if only he'd made time to see her yesterday, he might have persuaded her to meet him this morning.

Outside the ironmongers, he catches sight of a bloke in a green cap hanging around underneath the awning and looking aimless. A roll-up is dangling from the side of his mouth though it doesn't appear to be lit. The chap's particularly short – no more than five-four at most; brown jacket, dark green shirt and trousers; Frank could almost swear he'd seen that same bloke yesterday only he was waiting at the bus stop opposite Robbie's shop.

For a moment he's caught off guard and then, thinking through all the possibilities, he heads towards the nearest tube station; with its many entrances and exits, it's an easy place to lose someone in a crowd.

Halfway there, he stops to look in a grocer's window. By tilting his head, he hopes to catch a glimpse of the man if he's trailing behind him. Nothing. If the bloke in the green cap is following him, he's making a decent job of it – a professional job.

Frank's so busy looking behind, it takes him a moment to notice the black car coasting alongside him. Adjusting his hat to shade his eyes, he keeps up a steady pace while the car accelerates away only to pull into the kerb thirty yards up ahead. A man gets out. It's no one he's seen before. This bloke's wearing a grey hat and gabardine coat while carrying a rolled-up umbrella. Despite the rain, he doesn't put it up. Then again, he might be using it like a walking stick.

The man begins to stride out in Frank's direction – no sign of a limp. Amongst the small handful of people now standing between the two of them, Frank spots Edwina Jones – a regular who's particularly fond of a glass of stout on a Saturday night.

Frank raises his hat to her and, recognising him, she gives him back a tentative smile. 'Such terrible news about Dennis.' He draws her off to one side of the pavement. The flowers on her hat are drooping in the rain. 'I can hardly believe he could have gone an' drowned like that.'

'Yes, it was a shock all round,' he says. 'Poor Grace is beside herself – who wouldn't be?'

The approaching man steps around them still swinging his umbrella as he continues on his way. Over the old woman's shoulder, Frank observes him as he climbs a short flight of steps and extends his arm to ring a house bell. Half a minute later the door opens to admit him.

'Well, mustn't keep you nattering out here in this dreadful weather,' he tells Mrs Jones. 'I'll let you get in out of this ruddy rain.'

'You too,' she says. 'Or you'll catch your death.'

Frank takes a tube to Victoria and from there the circle line to Tower Hill. From there it's just a five-minute walk to Fenchurch Street where he catches the overground to Tilbury town. As the train takes him further east, the rain eases off. Arriving at his destination, he alights with the crowd into bright sunshine.

There's a tobacconist kiosk a few yards on with a rack of postcards outside. He buys a couple and then leans up against the wall to write his messages.

Before leaving the station, Frank pauses to watch four blokes piling up a lorry with assorted suitcases. Once they've stacked the luggage up as high as it'll go, they throw several long straps over the top and then set about securing them on the other side, much as you would a hay-wagon. The porters shout their farewells to a man wearing overalls who turns out to be the driver. The bloke's in no hurry; before he climbs up into his cab, he stops to roll a cigarette.

'You'd have a job to get any more on there,' Frank says, nodding towards the man's load. The driver looks directly at him. Frank starts kicking a stone around as casually as he can. He surveys the piled high cases with their destination labels and thinks about his own battered case – how it bears no traces of any of the places it's been.

The driver runs his tongue along the paper to seal the tobacco inside. He nods at his load. 'Most of this lot's bound for the SS Salvation.' Frank notices his slight Irish accent. 'She's in the docks right now taking on her cargo and that.'

The man blows a stream of smoke out through his nose. 'Come the morning she'll be on her way down river to the landin' stage where she'll pick up another twelve hundred or so brave souls makin' that one-way trip to Melbourne.'

'Sooner them than me,' Frank says. 'I'm only down here looking for an old mate of mine. Not sure where his digs are. He's a bit of an argumentative sod – tends to fall out with people faster than he should do. I heard he likes to drink in the Mermaid so I was planning to start there.'

'That's a sailor's watering hole.' The driver takes a long drag of his cigarette before pinching out the burning tip and sticking it behind his ear for later. 'Sure, the place is normally wall to wall with all them Tars.'

'Me and my mate were in the Royal Navy together. Needless to say, he took to the life on board far better than I did.'

The Irish bloke nods towards the lorry. 'If you're determined to stick your nose in that place, I'm going right past it. Hop in and I'll give you a lift down there.'

'Thanks, pal,' Frank says. 'That'll save me a bit of shoe leather.'

It doesn't take him long to conclude his business in the Mermaid. On the walk back to the station, he pops into a post office to buy stamps and then posts his cards in a postbox a bit further up the road.

By the middle of the afternoon, Frank's back in the Smoke and heading west again towards Victoria. The city air's been freshened by all that rain. From there he strides out past the Palace. The royal flag is flapping in the breeze as he heads up the Mall towards the theatre district in search of the business premises of Mr Irving Reynard.

He'd seen the place advertised in the small ads; it's meant to be just off the Strand. Dodging some sizable puddles, Frank walks past a number of turnings with no luck. In the end, he's forced to retrace his footsteps and start over again. One thing's for certain – he's not going to be asking passersby for directions.

CHAPTER THIRTY-FOUR

Grace had spent most of last evening wondering where she might find Frank. In desperation, she finally plucks up courage to go back to his lodging house.

It's a strange sensation to be retracing the steps the two of them had taken together on that Sunday night. She passes the alleyway they'd snuck into in search of a bit of privacy. In daylight, the place is squalid and strewn with rubbish. How could she have been so distracted that she didn't notice?

Grace has to walk a further mile or more, doubling back looking for a landmark. Finally, she remembers the police box on the corner and turns to be faced with two rows of soot-blackened identical houses. Their small front gardens are unkempt, used only as somewhere to put the bins. Such a street would have been for the well-to-do in the past; she can see the stubs of the railings that must have been removed – melted down for the war effort. Frank had reached up to pick a blossom for her from a tree near the front door. In daylight she can see it's a poor stunted thing springing from the gap between two frontages. She remembers the two iron handrails and these lead her up the worn smooth steps to the front door of number eleven.

Ten-thirty in the morning and yet the smell of cooking cabbage is escaping from an open basement window. An age after she pushes the old-fashioned bell, a middle-aged woman sticks her head round the side of the front door. Her salt and pepper hair looks like it hasn't seen a comb in a while.

'Good mornin'. You must be Mrs Harris,' Grace says, in her pleasantest voice. It's odd speaking to the woman face to face like this when she'd snuck out of this same house at dawn. She can hear music – possibly an operetta – coming from somewhere. 'I'm really sorry to bother you, but I'm looking for Frank – Frank Danby.'

The landlady folds her arms across the front of her sagging chest. ''Fraid he's not 'ere.'

'D'you have any idea when he'll be back? I really need to speak to him.'

A door must have opened, the violins have become strident – the same grating notes over and over. Behind Mrs Harris, a man's voice. 'Who is it, Mum?'

'No one important.' Blocking his view with her body, the woman's head swivels round like an owl's. 'Nothin' for you to worry about, Malc. Go back to your music, love.'

He retreats and the music becomes muffled; she has the landlady's full attention again. 'I need to see him about some-thin',' she says, 'somethin' really urgent.'

'I'm sorry, dear.' The woman's face softens at her obvious distress. 'He's gone an' cleared off for good. Shame really – he was a decent sort; always passed the time of day and you could have a laugh with him at times – not like some we get 'ere. My Malcolm's already got someone interested in his old room.'

'I see.' When she turns to go, the landlady touches her arm: 'Didn't catch your name, love?'

'It's Grace.'

'Ah yes – such a pretty name.' She bends closer. 'He left somethin' for you. Stay right there, darlin' – I'll be back in two ticks.'

A minute later she reappears with an envelope in her hand. 'Frank made me promise I'd put this into your hands and your hands only.' She chuckles to herself. 'You young people, you do make me laugh sometimes. Cheer up, duck. Remember what they say about the course of true love, eh – how it don't have an habit of runnin' smooth?'

She forces a smile to her face and thanks the woman, stuffing the letter into the bottom of her handbag away from any prying eyes. She doesn't dare to read it until she's back inside the Wetsons' house.

Grace has been over those same damn words a dozen times or more but still can't decide what to do. If only there was more time.

The ringing doorbell shakes her out of her reverie. She opens it to Inspector Collingwood. Behind him, Sergeant Bradley's burly figure is blocking the light. Looking over his shoulder, to the street behind, two women dawdle, don't even bother to disguise their piqued interest.

'Good day to you, Mrs Stevenson.' The inspector raises his hat. 'You remember Sergeant Bradley?' His thin moustache seems to quiver like an animal's whiskers. 'May we come in?'

'Of course.' Grace steps aside to let them through. She shows them into the front room, aware that their dark outlines are probably still visible from outside through the net curtains. 'Won't you please take a seat.'

Moving aside some knitting, Collingwood puts down his hat and perches in Lottie's chair. Grace chooses the sofa directly opposite.

Cradling his helmet like a rugby ball, the sergeant remains standing by the door as if poised to catch her should she try to make a run for it. 'Can I get either of you a cup of tea?' Her voice sounds like someone else's – some actress she's heard on the wireless.

'No, but thank you.' The sergeant shakes his head.

Collingwood leans forward then clears his throat to show

he's getting down to it. 'As you're aware, we've been trying to ascertain exactly how your husband's body may have gotten into the river. To be quite certain of our conclusions, my super arranged for a second pathologist – a Doctor Kilburn – to examine Mr Stevenson's body. Doctor Kilburn's subsequent report is clear even to a comparative layman like myself.'

He stares straight at her, his brown eyes unblinking. 'He concurs with the first pathologist, Doctor Sibley that, prior to his entry into the water, Mr Stevenson was rendered unconscious by a considerable blow to the head. Forgive me, but for your clarity, I need to go into more detail.'

He turns his head to the side and waits.

'Go on,' she says, hardly trusting her own voice.

'From the size of the indentation in your husband's skull and the minute fragments of wood embedded in that wound, both pathologists concur that the implement most likely would have been a wooden cosh of some kind.'

'Was he hit deliberate though? Couldn't he have slipped and hit his head on something wooden?'

The way he's peering at her now, she could be a specimen under a microscope. 'Quite so,' he eventually says. 'I believe we've arrived at the crux of the matter.'

It's a relief when he looks away to fish his notebook out of his pocket. He flips through the pages until he finds what he's looking for. 'You see, there were marks on your husband's ankles and lower back, which Doctor Sibley agrees were more recent than his other injuries and *consistent with the unconscious man being carried or dragged into the river by his assailant.*'

He snaps the notebook shut. Her head is spinning like she's got up too quickly. She watches his mouth moving but finds it hard to piece together what he's saying. 'Just to be clear, Mrs Stevenson.' She forces herself to concentrate. 'We're now in no doubt your husband was unlawfully killed – murdered.'

The room and everything in it turns black. When she opens her eyes, the other copper, the sergeant, is handing her a cup of water and telling her she should drink it.

She takes a sip.

'I have no wish to cause you further distress, Mrs Stevenson, but now that you've recovered a little, I'm afraid we must turn to the pressing matter of your late husband's possible assailant.'

The cold liquid seems to be lodged in her throat. She pulls herself upright – this is important.

'So far, Mrs Stevenson, our foremost – you could say our *prime* suspect – is your erstwhile barman; the man currently calling himself Frank *Danby*.'

'Calling himself?' She peers at him. 'I don't understand.'

'We believe Danby is the alias he's been using for quite some time.'

'So, if his name's not that, what is it?'

'It would seem that, in actual fact, there are a number of options to choose from.' A twitch of his mouth – the beginning and end of a smile. 'In the past, the man you know as Frank Danby went by the name of Frank *Walton*. There could have been others. However, we now know his real name is Francis John *Whitby*.' He waits for that to sink in. 'I'm sorry to have to tell you that, far from being the solid citizen you described to us, Mr Whitby is a deserter from the armed services – the Royal Air Force to be precise. He was finally and officially declared absent without leave in October of 1942.'

'I know nothin' about that,' she tells him straight. 'I was down in Brighton when my husband took him on. At the time I was looking after my mother who was gravely ill. Dennis must have checked Frank's papers an' satisfied himself the man was honest – you have to be very careful when you're running a pub.'

She makes herself take another sip of water and it helps steady her. 'In any case,' she says, 'all that can't matter now – war's been over nearly seven years, after all.'

That gets him going. 'These things certainly do *still matter*. The fellow deserted his country in her very hour of need.'

His face has reddened to boiling point. 'And I can assure you, desertion is still punishable by imprisonment.'

'Well then, it's quite a bit of luck you finding all this out about Frank – and *so quickly*.' She's in no doubt they've been tipped off by somebody; it's not hard to guess who might be behind it.

Collingwood picks up on that straight away. 'We pride ourselves on being thorough in our enquiries, Mrs Stevenson.' He frowns. In his dark eyes she sees exactly what he thinks – how her and Frank have been tarred with the same brush.

The inspector sits up a little straighter. 'I gather the two of you have become rather *close*.' Oh yes, he's enjoying himself now. 'You may seek to defend the man's character, but let me assure you he's nothing but a cowardly deserter – a man who stooped so low as to abandon his own motherless son.'

Grace is shocked to the core. 'Frank has a son?' She guesses Collingwood caught her reaction alright. 'What happened to the boy's mother?'

'A sad business. Poor woman was killed in an air raid up in Sunderland. Stray bomb meant for elsewhere, so I believe. The child was found in the rubble – a rather miraculous survival by all accounts. Later that autumn Whitby finally went AWOL. Without a backward glance, the man completely abandoned the care of his infant son to others.'

Grace stands up. 'I won't deny I'm taken aback by what you've just told me. Obviously, this puts Frank in a new light, but it doesn't mean he had anything to do with my Dennis's death.'

The inspector jumps to his feet to tower above her. 'I beg to differ. Mrs Stevenson – I believe we can easily guess at his motives. With your husband well and truly out of the picture, Whitby would be in a position to take full advantage of the situation. An attractive young woman with a Free House establishment to her name and plenty of money besides – these would be powerful attractions to a penniless drifter. Let me speak freely – the blighter had already got himself into the ideal position to comfort a widow who had already taken a shine to him, so to speak.'

Collingwood interrupts her protests. 'You may wish to deny it, Mrs Stevenson, but let me tell you, given that Whitby can offer no alibi for the estimated time of your husband's death, his guilt could not be more obvious. We intend to arrest the wretched man on suspicion of murder. If he hadn't already cleared out of his lodgings, he would be behind bars as we speak.'

The inspector's eyes are full of scorn when he looks at her. 'I want you to think hard before answering my next question.' He steps a bit closer; she can smell onion on his breath. 'Do you have any idea of his current whereabouts?'

In the note just inside her skirt pocket, Frank's written the time and place he'll be waiting for her this afternoon. Collingwood would only have to move his hand a few inches and he'd have everything he needs to arrest him.

'No, I'm afraid I don't,' she says. 'I have no idea whatsoever where Frank might be. Dennis and I were both deceived about his character. I sincerely hope you catch up with him.'

'Let me assure you, Mrs Stevenson, we most certainly will; and very soon.'

He turns on his heels. 'Please don't trouble yourself – we can see ourselves out.'

CHAPTER THIRTY-FIVE

Frank's quick to pay Irving Reynard for his trouble and leave the emporium. True to say he walks out a new man. It's a short distance to the bus stop on the Strand where the evening crowds have already begun to build up. As he walks along, he practices using the stick – careful to transfer some of his weight onto it each time. Already, his hips and back feel a little out of kilter.

He's forced to wait in a long queue before he can board the bus. It's packed to the gills upstairs and down. A smartly dressed chap of about forty gets to his feet in front of him. 'Here, you look like you need a seat more than I do. Be my guest.' Frank's delighted that Irving's handiwork can pass muster even close up.

'Thanks, mate,' he says, trying not to overdo the croakiness in his voice. He grips the rail along the top of the seat and sits down with some care.

Despite the traffic, he gets to Whitechapel earlier than he'd expected. The rain's eased off at least. He thinks it would seem less suspicious for an old man to wait inside the café he's chosen where he can take the weight of his feet. Anyone watching is likely to take Grace for his daughter.

Frank chooses a table just inside where there's got a good view of the street. A few of the added eyebrow hairs are protruding down into his vision and he has to feel to be sure they're still in the right place.

As he waits for his tea, he opens his case and takes out a small pad of writing paper and extracts the fountain pen from his jacket pocket.

London

4th July

Dear Annie,

I hope you are all well. I trust you got my last letter and the postal order I enclosed.

When I wrote to you, I was hoping that, come September, we might go hopping together down in Kent. I'm sorry to say my situation has become more complicated since then. It pains me to let you down again like this, but it's fair to say I'm in a spot of bother and I need to go away for a bit. Right now, I can't say for how long it's likely to be.

You know I will send you money when I can. Already I can hear you saying that money is scarce compensation for my absence and I would agree with that wholeheartedly.

Tell the boy Uncle Frank misses him and is really sorry we're not going to see each other for a bit.

When I get a chance, I'll write to him separately.

Oh, Annie – this is the last thing I want to be saying to you and I know what you must think of me because of it. The situation I'm in is not of my making and please don't believe it if you should hear any lies about me. I swear to you I've done nothing I'm ashamed off.

It's a comfort to me to know that, from the start, you've always loved the three of them just the same. Now your oldest is bringing in a wage it must be a help. Lord knows I'm sure it's a struggle for you at times, but you've always done a fine job as a mother and a loving home is the greatest gift anyone could wish for and I should know.

For now, I'll say cheerio.

Give my love to all and kiss the boy on the forehead for me.

Frank x

He looks up when the shop bell tinkles. Two middle-aged women come in and begin making a ruddy fuss about which table to choose, as if any of that really mattered.

The waitress brings him his tea and he sips at it as he watches the hand of the wall clock move a minute at a time. She should be here by now if she's coming. There's the crowds to think of – anything might have delayed her. It's more than likely she didn't get his note; probably a bad idea in the first place to leave it with Mrs Harris; what other choice did he have?

Frank seals Annie's letter inside its envelope and puts a stamp on it before tucking it into his pocket ready to post. He's been slipping slowly but now his teacup is well and truly empty.

Outside, he's reluctant to leave. Standing in the drizzle, he thinks over what he'd written and feels sick to the stomach at the thought of having to send her such a letter.

Ten more minutes pass and still there's no sign of Grace. At his feet, the rain's stained his small suitcase dark around the edges. In a few minutes, he's going to have to go or Arthur will shut up shop. Just five minutes more – that's all he can spare.

The young forger comes to the door. His face clouds when he sees him. 'What d'you want?'

'Can you spare an old man thruppence for a cup of tea?'

'Clear off, will ya?'

He's about to close the door when Frank grabs it. 'Hold up, Arthur, it's me.'

Arthur stops struggling with the door and peers at him over his glasses. 'Well I never.'

'Glad to see I managed to fool a man who's used to spotting fakes.'

'You fooled me good an' proper – that disguise is astonishin' – doubt your own mother would recognise you.' He looks him up and down again. 'The stick's a nice touch.' Arthur steps aside to let him in. 'Tell me, why go to all this trouble?'

'Occurred to me I might need a different string to my bow. In fact, I'll be needing a few extra papers for this new look of mine.'

'You know yourself, they only want you Down Under if you're young and fit – they aren't so keen on old gits.'

'Let me worry about that,' Frank says as they walk through. 'Right now this wig is itching me ragged. I just need you to take my ruddy photo so I can take the wretched thing off and have a good scratch.'

The man frowns. 'All in good time. First, let's get one thing straight – even if *you* want to go capering around – *I'm* not doin' any of this for fun and this'll cost you extra.'

'Don't let my disguise fool you – I'm perfectly serious.' Frank takes off his hat and coat and lays his cane over the top.

Arthur sits down at his desk and removes his glasses. He puts on a pair of half-moon specs, hooks them over his ears and bends to examine his own handiwork. Satisfied, he passes the passport over for Frank's approval. 'Think you'll agree that's indistinguishable from the real thing,' he says. The look of pride on his face makes him seem altogether more boyish. 'You were talkin' about a travelling companion on your trip – so where's this mystery woman of yours?'

'A good question,' Frank tells him. 'Right now, I've no flaming idea. She could be anywhere.'

CHAPTER THIRTY-SIX

From two hundred yards away, the sickly smell fills the air and gets stronger at every step. A stranger would know for certain they were approaching a biscuit factory. Despite the fact that it's spitting with rain, Grace is dressed up in a pale-yellow frock with an orange cardie. She's topped it off with a particularly bright scarf – all red and pink roses and is wearing her new sunglasses for good measure. Much as she's tempted, Grace is careful not to look behind her – not even a quick peek.

There it is, straight ahead. The yard outside is empty and full of puddles. Pigeons line the gutters; their pale droppings smeared halfway down the height of the blackened walls. She knows from experience that once that hooter goes, they'll come pouring outside and rush away on foot or on bikes. Some of the younger girls walk to the shops in gaggles. With it being a Friday, knocking-off time is an hour earlier.

There's only another ten minutes to go but she can't just go waltzing in there asking for Dot. Instead she paces the open yard. She knows the lie of the land – had worked here herself for a few months before taking the job in the pub. Round the back, there's a flight of metal steps that will take her up to the landing by the ladies' toilets. Every Friday, they place a massive bin up there for all the dirty uniforms. She just hopes Dot doesn't hand hers to somebody else today.

The hooter goes – a long wail not unlike an air raid warning. Grace waits for the first wave of running workers to swamp her. People come streaming out of every exit, all at a crazy pace like they can't bear another single second in the place. In all the chaos, it's easy to nip round the back and up the steps.

The landing is full of women. One or two take notice of her and give her clothes a quizzical look but they're in too much of a rush to care about an outsider being present. She spots her friend amongst the other girls. 'Dot!' She pushes through to grab the girl's arm and march her straight into one of the storerooms. 'I need your help.'

'What?' Dot frowns. 'Why? What the hell's goin' on?'

'In here.' Grace flicks on the light switch and leans against the door she's just closed. 'I'll explain later.' She keeps her voice low. 'I need you to swap clothes with me right now.'

'No, I won't do it.' Dot just stands there with her hands planted on her hips. 'Not unless you explain.'

Grace unties her headscarf and hangs it over one of the hooks on the back of the door. 'I think, in fact I'm pretty certain, the Old Bill's followin' me.' She takes off her cardie and then steps out of her frock. 'I need you to pretend to be me, so they follow you instead.'

'What the hell have you gone an' done, Grace?' Dot shakes her head and retreats to the back of the room next to the shelves of clean overalls.

'Look, I'm not askin' you to do anythin' much,' Grace tells her. 'The two of us will start walking back towards your place together and then we'll say our goodbyes, and then you – lookin' like me – will go off by yourself somewhere.'

'Where am I suppose' to go, for pity's sake?'

'I don't know.' It's so quiet out there they must have all left. 'You could go to the park or go an' do a bit of shoppin', if you'd rather. Let them follow you around for a bit, then you just go home.' She stands there in her underclothes. 'Go on, Dot – take that blouse off, will ya?'

228

'Hang on one ruddy minute – you still haven't told me why the police are followin' you.'

There's a steady drip somewhere nearby like a quiet heartbeat. 'Because they're on the lookout for Frank and they think I might lead 'em to him.'

'Why in God's name are they lookin' for Frank?' Dot undoes a few buttons then stops. 'And where the hell are *you* goin' while I'm waltzin' around pretendin' to be you?'

Feeling exposed in her smalls, Grace walks towards her. 'Never mind all that, we need to hurry – I promise I'll explain later. Please, Dot – I need you to trust me. I swear to you I haven't done anything wrong.'

Dot's brown eyes stare at her, she sees herself reflected in those dark pupils. 'Please, Dotty, I really need your help.'

The girl shrugs her shoulders. 'Never could say no when you look at me like that.'

Grace gives her a hug. 'Here – you'll need my scarf on to hide yer hair. I've brought a different one for me.'

Dot shrugs off her blouse and begins to unbutton her skirt. 'Supposin' I go off to the park, what then?'

'Then you just feed the birds or summat. After that, like I said, you can go home.'

She hands her clothes over. 'But I haven't got anythin' to feed the ruddy birds with.'

'Then just go for a bit of a stroll round. It don't matter where you go or what the 'ell you do.' Grace stands back to admire the transformation. 'That's it – now the sunglasses. Perfect.'

'Well – if you're a sight for sore eyes.' Despite her smile, Flo looks worse than the last time she'd seen her. The poor woman can't be more than thirty-five but for all her money and that bleached-blonde hair, her face could be a good ten years older. Careworn she'd describe her as, like all the fun's been sucked out of her. The woman's whole body looks pinched in – in fact she could do with putting on some weight.

'I'm not sure where he is,' Flo says through lips too red for such pale skin. 'Think he might be in the garden; come on through.'

She herself might look a bit of a sight, dressed as she is in Dot's old working clothes and a scarf tying her hair up like some washerwoman.

'You remember our Pete and little Eric.' The light catches on Flo's gold bracelet.

Their two sons have grown lanky and awkward. The older lad's hair's grown a lot darker while his little brother's almost unnaturally fair. Clearly not remembering her, the boys smile shyly at her but hardly look up from their game.

'Pete, for goodness' sake put that wretched tortoise on the floor. He's not happy on that car – you can see that for yourself.'

They walk past a formal dining room that looks so starchy you'd never feel comfortable in it; maybe that was the point. 'How's Elsie these days?' Flo asks.

'Mum was in a terrible state a few weeks back.'

'Really?'

'Turned out to be a bad case of pneumonia. I had to go down to Brighton to look after her. Don't worry, she's much better now, thank the Lord.'

It's clear no one's told Flo about Dennis. This far out, she probably doesn't get to pick up the gossip that's always flying round the East End.

Grace decides not to say anything. 'Yes,' she says. 'Mum's almost back to her old self, I'd say.'

'Well, I'm glad to hear it. Do give Elsie my love when you see 'er next.' Flo opens the glazed back door. 'Here we are.' Grace has only seen gardens this big in magazines. 'He's over there – them flamin' roses are my Jackie's pride and joy. If it's not the greenfly he's worryin' about, it's the black spot and then there's all sorts of funguses. He can't afford to leave 'em alone for a minute.'

They walk over the unnaturally green lawn towards the

flowerbed. Grace's short heels keep sinking into the damp grass. 'Can I fetch you a cup of tea?'

'Thanks,' she says. 'D'you know I'd love a cuppa right now, Flo.'

'Jackie!' Her husband turns round. 'You remember Elsie Smith's girl Grace? She says she wants to talk to you about summat.'

His secateurs are poised over the withered head of a rose. 'Grace,' he says, 'well I never, this is a surprise.'

Flo holds her ground, looks from one of them to the other.

'You bein' a man of the world, Jack, I thought you might be able to give me some business advice,' she says. ''Spect you remember the Eight Bells – our pub. We was doing very nicely until recently, but now, I have to admit, business isn't what it was. With you being such a successful businessman, I thought I'd come and ask you for some tips.'

'Well, if you're talkin' business I'll leave the both of you to it,' Flo says. 'Any sugar, Grace?'

'No thanks – girl has to watch her figure.' She smiles. 'Drop of milk would be good, if you've got it.'

Flo winks at her husband. 'I dare say she's sweet enough.'

'Yes, I dare say she is,' Jack Dawson says, chopping a withered flower head clean off.

CHAPTER THIRTY-SEVEN

With his wife well out of earshot, Jack's expression drops. 'Got to hand it to you, Grace, it must have taken some bottle for you to come here to my *home* like this; an' in broad daylight.' He snips three more flower heads off; the last one barely out of bud. The petals fall at her feet. 'If you were a bloke, I'd reckon you've got some balls.'

'Take that as a compliment, shall I?'

'Having come all this way to see me – and I do hope you're not trailin' the Old Bill behind you – you'd better say what it is you came here to say. Spit it out, gal.'

A smile tugs at the sides of his mouth. 'Oh – hold up.' His dark eyes narrow, the pupils are pinpricks in the sunlight. 'Do I detect a touch of hesitation? You haven't thought this through very well, have ya?' He shakes his head. 'I'm right, aren't I? Dearie me, little Gretchen Schmidt, have you got some lessons to learn.'

He turns away to cut at a white-headed rose. 'This one's called Queen of the Snow – lovely shaped flower and such a delicate perfume. Bouquet's the fancy word for it. As you can see, this here's the last one to flower. This whole bush has had its first flush of blooms – they're always the best.'

Dawson holds the rose right up under her nose; the sweet stench of it turns her stomach. 'If I want it to flower again,

I have to cut it back hard.' He demonstrates by snipping off some rosehips. 'You could say it's for its own good.'

Grace stands firm. 'I came to talk to you about Dennis.' She takes a deep breath – in for a penny, in for a pound. 'I want to know who it was went an' murdered 'im. I've bin told you or some of your *associates* might have bin behind it.'

'Someone's been feedin' you a load of porkers, sweetheart.' He steps closer, holds his secateurs inches from her chin. 'That husband of yours was a prize bloody prat, that's for sure, but why the hell would I want him dead? He was a good customer of ours; liked his nags, did Dennis.'

Grace wants to step back but her heels are stuck fast. 'You've got a cheek callin' him a good a customer when you lot have bin bleedin' him dry for years.'

'I'd say our Dicer was very lenient when it came to his debts. When all's said and done, no bugger forces a man to gamble. Just like nobody forces him to go peddlin' his hooch where he has no business to.'

She pulls one heel free and then the other. 'Is that what it was then – they was steppin' on your shoes with their dodgy whisky? Couldn't you have just warned Dennis – told him to stop?'

'I believe the whole lot of them had been given a warnin' already. They chose to ignore it.'

With surprising gentleness, he leans forward to lay the white rose on the wooden table next to them; almost a gesture you might make at a graveside.

'See, what you have to realise, darlin',' he says, 'is that the secret of good business is delegation. And when you delegate, stands to reason your *employees* have to be given a bit of leeway to act as they see fit.'

Grace notices how he'd glanced over her shoulder back towards the house. She can hear the rattle of a tea tray getting closer. Dawson waves to his wife. 'I can't be held responsible if individual members of my workforce occasionally overstep the mark.'

'Here we are then,' Flo says. 'I'll pop this down here, shall I?'

'Thanks, darlin'.' He picks up the rose and presents it to her. 'For you – a beauty for a beauty.' Flo's cheeks glow with pleasure.

'Just be careful of its thorns,' Grace tells her. 'Even a little prick can draw blood.'

A look of annoyance passes over Jack's face. 'I was just tellin' young Grace here, that the art of good management is delegation.'

'Hope you like digestives, Grace; they're Jack's favourites.' No one speaks as Flo pours the tea.

Jack clears his throat. 'Another golden rule of business is not to get too friendly with your employees or they're sure to take advantage. Keep 'em at arm's length an' you can't go wrong.'

Flo straightens up. 'Sit down – make yourself comfortable, Grace. I'll leave you two to carry on with your chat. The boys'll be wantin' their tea.' The chair's still a bit damp but she sits on it all the same. Jack does the same.

'You wouldn't believe how much two growin' lads can eat.' Flo hands her a delicate cup and saucer, then picks up the rose. 'Married fifteen years an' my Jackie's still an old softy.'

Jack takes a sip of his tea. 'Makes a bloody good brew, my missus.' The cup and saucer look too delicate in his hands.

Once Flo's gone back indoors, he puts his tea down. 'I'm surprised at you, Grace. I would have thought you'd enjoy playin' the merry widow. From what I hear, you've got quite a bit of insurance money comin' your way.' He picks up a biscuit, waves it in the air in front of her face. 'Some might say that *inadvertently* – now there's a big word for you – inadvertently, my man done you a bit of a favour.'

'A favour!' She's tempted to grab the teapot and throw that scalding tea right in his face.

'We all know your Dennis was a poof.' He chuckles. 'What

– you don't like the word? Well then, how about a *fairy*? Let's not beat about the bush – if you'll excuse my pun. Your dearly beloved was a *queer*. It's common knowledge he only married you to cover it up. Ask me, you're well shot of him.'

The tea things rattle as she stands up. 'No one did ask you for your ignorant – your stupid, bigoted opinions Jack Dawson.' She's shaking from head to foot. 'My Dennis was a good man and he didn't deserve to die.'

Purple in the face, he stands up. 'You need to calm yourself down, gal – we don't want Flo seein' the two of us arguin', do we? Upset her an' you upset me – got it?' He tries to plant his hands on her shoulders, but she shrugs him off.

'Listen carefully, Grace Stevenson. I'm an old army man an' I don't like insubordination in the ranks. As a rule, I don't comment on the way I run things because that's my business an' no bugger else's. Just this once I'm prepared to tell you that the fella – for the purposes of our discussion I'll call him a subcontractor – who overstepped the mark with Dennis has already been dealt with.'

He lifts both hands and holds them open to the sky. 'Like this lawn, he's pushin' up daisies. If you came here for retribution – hark at me, I swallowed a dictionary – it's already been seen to. Far as I'm concerned, whole thing's done and dusted.'

'What about Frank – you've made him carry the can, ruined his whole life and left him facin' the noose when he's an innocent man.'

'Ah – now I get the picture. I heard you'd got more than a soft spot for that fuckin' deserter.' Jack steps right up next to her, breathes down into her face. 'You know, sweetheart, you really do need to improve your taste in men. Beautiful girl like you could have her pick.' He runs the back of his hand across her cheek.

'Mean to say, first you go for a flamin' poofter who's a compulsive ruddy gambler. I'll grant you at least he *did have* a bit of money behind him with that pub. Now you're shot of him, you've gone an' set your sights even lower – on a penniless, fuckin' coward. A man who deserted his country an' abandoned his own ruddy kid.'

He picks up the secateurs, points them right at her. 'I gave you a chance once before an' you turned me down. I'm a fair-minded man an' I'm prepared to overlook your lapse of taste an' come to an arrangement with you that's mutually beneficial. I like to think of myself as a connoisseur of beautiful things an', even dressed like that, you, my darlin', are a thing of beauty.'

'Yes, I'll do a deal with you,' she says. Tethered by her sinking heels, Grace steps out of her shoes. The wet grass is soft and giving under her bare feet. 'I know you want my pub an' I'm prepared to sell it to you for a song – two hundred pounds. As you well know, that's less than a tenth of what the building alone must be worth.'

A satisfied smile is already playing on his lips.

'That's right,' she says, 'I'm practically givin' you the whole ruddy place lock, stock and barrel. A legal transfer no one could argue with. On one condition.'

'Sweetheart, I'm all ears.'

'In return, I want your solemn and lasting promise to leave me and mine alone from now on. And by mine I mean any man I choose to be with.'

He pouts, then looks her up and down.

'Fair enough, it's a deal.' Jack transfers the clippers to his left hand, spits on his right one and holds it out towards her.

When it's clear she's not prepared to shake his hand, he lets it drop. 'Here comes Flo – I 'spect she's been watchin' through the window; must have noticed we was rowing. I'm a man of my word; I'll stick by our deal, Gracie, but I'd like you to put on your best smile for her sake before you fuck off out of here.'

Jack snips away at more faded heads. 'I'll have my lawyers draw up the appropriate documents this evening an' send 'em round first thing in the mornin'.' He doesn't look at her once.

'Like I said, I don't expect you to find your way back here again. If you do, you know what to expect.'

'Keep to your end of our bargain an' I won't need to.' She'd have asked for more money but it's already too late. Grace throws away her unfinished tea and puts the cup on the tray.

Turning away, she gives Flo a wide smile.

'All done then, are we?'

'We've finished our business chat,' Jack says. 'Unfortunately, Grace has to dash off.'

'It was nice to see you again Flo,' she says. 'Thanks for the tea. Sorry I can't stay for a natter.' She picks up her shoes and walks barefoot across the lawn. 'Cheerio,' she shouts back.

'Come back anytime,' Flo calls after her. 'And don't forget to give my love to Elsie.'

CHAPTER THIRTY-EIGHT

From Whitechapel, Frank catches the tube to West Ham. He leaves the Underground station and finds the gents' lavatory where he remembered it. Once the place has emptied out, he locks himself in a cubicle.

It's easy to pull off the wig but the heavy eyebrows and moustache aren't so easy to peel away and leave his skin feeling raw. How do actors do this every night?

Still quiet out there – as far as he can tell no one else has come in. He folds the walking stick up and fits it into its case. Once he's stowed the rest of his props away, he listens at the door to be sure and then leaves the cubicle.

Frank washes his face in cold water; the carbolic soap stings his skin as he scrubs off the greasy stage makeup along with the remnants of the adhesive. Confident he's more or less a normal colour again, Frank puts on heavy specs and carefully adjusts the brim of his hat to shade his eyes.

Back at the station, he boards a crowded train to Tilbury. Staring at his reflection in the window, he's pleased to see how different he looks from the last time he made this trip. A signalling problem adds ten minutes to his journey time. Once he's left Tilbury station behind, he walks briskly along Dock Road.

After half a mile he spots a Bed & Breakfast sign – there's

no shortage of such places in this town. Inside the front window a small sign declares there are Vacancies. It's a tall, terraced house and looks a bit rundown so it ought to be cheap enough.

A woman in a wraparound apron comes to the door, cigarette dangling from the corner of her mouth. She hoists her considerable bosoms above her folded arms. Frank can't begin to guess at her age.

'Call me Pam, everybody does,' she says with a friendly enough smile. 'Once you've seen the room, I'll be wantin' payment in cash. Can't afford to be too careful in my line of business.'

They pass a cramped little room off the hallway. 'That's our dining room,' she says, with an unwarranted air of importance. 'I always lay out the breakfast things in here so guests can help themselves. They leave at all hours of the morning, you see. Some of 'em desperate to get ahead of the queue, poor things. Most seem to be headin' for Australia. Paid their ten quid for a ticket alright but most ain't got much more than the clothes they stand up in to their name. Course, once they gets you out there, you have to cough up the full fare if you changes yer mind an' want to come home again.'

She looks him up and down. 'Where you off to then, darlin'?'

'Melbourne,' he tells her.

Pam lights another cigarette from the butt of the last and stubs the old one out in a brimming glass ashtray. 'I'll show you the room – don't worry, it's clean.' She twists her mouth to blow the smoke away from his face. 'No cockroaches and no bed bugs – not like some places round here.'

They climb a steep staircase leading to a dingy landing. Pam has to stop to get her breath back – a process that includes several more drags at her fag. 'I lock that front door at ten minutes past eleven on the dot. If you're not back by then, you'd better find another establishment.

'Here we are then, room eighteen.' The room is very much what he expects. At least there's a small sink in one corner. 'Lav's along the hallway at the end – there's only half a dozen rooms that use that one. If you want a bath, it's downstairs. It'll cost you another shillin' an' you'll have to book a time with me. That's it, really. Alright, Mr, ah –'

'Frank,' he says. 'No point in us getting all formal is there, Pam?'

She knocks the ash off her cigarette and makes no attempt to catch it. 'Try not to make too much noise when you come in – there'll be plenty of kiddies sleepin'. Oh, and make sure it's just you, I don't hold with no unexpected female guests.' She gives him a quizzical look. 'Nor male ones for that matter.'

'Thanks a lot,' he says. 'This'll suit me just fine.' Once he's handed over the cash she leaves.

He sighs with relief as he turns the key in the lock. Doesn't bother to unpack. Frank inspects the bed and finds it somehow manages to be both hard and soft at the same time. Covers look clean enough.

Frank lies down with his hands behind his head and stares up at the electric light. He recalls all those nights before an op – the struggle just to get to sleep.

A tawny owl calls out. No – for pity's sake it's only a wood pigeon. Even so, his heart won't slow down. The rickety red shade is tilted at an angle, casting a fiery light onto the walls.

With no warning the trembling starts. A faint sound turns into screams that grow louder and louder filling his head. Flames are leaping everywhere – catching the curtains, the bed, engulfing the room. Searing heat on his skin; his nostrils fill with the stench of smoke and burning flesh.

Screwing his eyes shut, he blocks his ears with his hands and prays for it to stop.

Still not himself, Frank's relieved to be back outside breathing in fresh sea air. The dusk has deepened and darkness is hiding the worst of the town. Along the waterfront, all the dancing lights are conjuring up a glamour that's entirely absent in daylight. The onshore breeze carries the briny smell of the sea along with a dank earthiness from all the mudflats.

Passing the window of a shut-up shop, Frank checks his reflection again. With his thick-rimmed specs and trilby he's almost unrecognisable to himself. All the dressing up is making him feel like some bad music-hall turn.

He passes a few more side streets and then the road takes him round to the left. The pub he'd been told about – the George and Dragon – is right there on the corner in front of him.

Inside, it's packed to the gunnels with seamen, many of them still in uniform. The air is so thick with smoke he's forced to shut his mouth. His eyes are smarting. When his glasses fog up, he takes them off and stuffs them into his jacket pocket.

The stink of sweat and warm beer is overpowering. Everybody seems to be in fine spirits, arms around one another's necks or shoulders as they swap stories or belt out raucous songs. Pushing his way through, Frank hears the names of far-flung places being bandied about like anyone else might talk about the districts of London.

All too aware of his rapidly disappearing cash, he buys half a bitter and props himself against the far corner of the bar to wait. He takes a couple of sips then puts his glass down; though he's thirsty enough, he'd better make it last.

Every few minutes he looks back towards the door. The chap he's meeting hadn't specified an exact time. Someone watching him would say he had the desperate look of a man who's worried about being stood up. When he checks, he can't see a single woman in the place – even the bar staff are men. Someone nearby starts up a rendition of Wild Rover and despite the many loud groans, at the *No neigh never* bit the whole bar seems to clap three times in unison.

'Is there somethin' wrong with yer beer, mate?' The speaker is a young chap with a deep tan dressed in sailor's whites. The hat perched on the back of his fair hair is in danger of sliding off.

'No point in hurrying a good beer, is there?' He gives the bloke a wry smile.

The sailor waves a ten-bob note at the barman. 'Over here, Fred. Give me two pints of Truman's.' Once he's been served, the sailor slides one of the pints across to him. 'Get that down ya, pal.'

Frank starts to protest but the sailor plants a heavy arm across his shoulder. 'Look, mate, I can see from the way yer toyin' with that half pint you must be skint. We've all bin there and no doubt will be again, more's the flamin' pity. There's no shame in it.'

'Ta very much.' Frank's touched by this unexpected generosity. 'To your good health.'

'Cheers, mate.' Beer slops out of the sailor's glass as he knocks it against Frank's. 'Never look a gift horse in the mouth – ain't that what they reckon, Charlie, me old mate?'

The Charlie he's talking to is an older man with the name of the same ship across his hatband. Frank hadn't noticed him standing behind them clutching a part empty glass. 'So where exactly are you hiding *my* drink, young Ronnie?'

'You – you're bloody rollin' in it. You can buy yer own. Our friend here – what's yer name, pal?'

'Frank.'

'Our friend Frank here has been nursin' a ruddy half for the last twenty minutes. Now that can't be right on a Friday night, can it?'

'Is that so?' His smile reveals the teeth of a younger man. 'Well now, I'd call that a travesty. If it's work you're after, Frank, sure I happen to hear talk of a ship that's not fully crewed-up.' Charlie must be from Southern Ireland; County Kerry possibly because his accent's exactly like Liam's.

Liam – Frank hasn't thought of the lad in a while. He'd never asked their bomb aimer what he was doing in the RAF in the first place with his home country being neutral. The lad would have just turned thirty-one now, if he'd lived.

He's nudged back to the present by Charlie's elbow. 'She's a bulk carrier heading for somewhere in North America – I forget exactly where.' Leaning over, the sailor manages to knock Frank's glass, spilling a good inch of beer. 'Yer man over there – him with the bald head and pipe waving his glass around – he's the fella to speak to.'

'Thanks, mate but as it happens, I'm s'posed to be meeting a bloke in here about a job.' Frank looks up at the clock behind the bar. 'He should be here shortly.'

'Ah well, if you've a change of heart, or the other fella doesn't show up, you'd best go and have a natter with baldie there. Though I'd wait till the fella's stopped singing with such gusto or you'll be deaf for a fortnight.'

Seems it's easy to pick up work on a ship if you're not too fussy where she's heading. Charlie's right, if his man doesn't show up soon, he might as well go and have a chat with the bald bugger now attempting to demonstrate how to drink a pint backwards and getting it mostly down his front.

They all get pushed from behind when a group of lads at the back spread out to spin a bottle. While it's spinning, they chant something to the tune of Waltzing Matilda.

Frank goes cold before he hears them more clearly: '*Who'll buy the next round? Who'll buy the next round?*' they're singing – not *Ops in a Wimpey* after all. Frank sips his beer. Hadn't he learnt a long time ago how there's no ruddy point dwelling on the past? He's beginning to give up on the bloke he's waiting for when the man strolls in. Frank detaches himself from the sailors. 'Just off for a slash.' He walks on past the man into the gents'.

While he's taking a piss, the bloke comes in and stands alongside him at the urinal though he doesn't relieve himself.

Frank feels him slip something into his left pocket. 'All arranged. That's everythin' you'll need.' He turns and heads for the door. 'Best of luck, mate.'

CHAPTER THIRTY-NINE

Saturday 5th July

Grace is almost at the Eight Bells when a car draws up along-side her. As soon as it stops, Collingwood jumps out of the backseat. 'Mrs Stevenson,' he says, lifting his trilby and then planting it back down on his head. 'Might we have a word with you?'

Sergeant Bradley gets out from the driver's side and comes to stand in the gutter behind his master.

'Of course,' she says.

Collingwood nods towards the pub. 'I see the place is still closed up.'

'Yes. I've only come back to sort out some of my personal things.'

The inspector looks like the cat that's got the cream. 'Would one of those personal items include a passport, by any chance?'

'What's it got to do with you? Your men gave me all that stuff back.'

'I must say, I was more than a little surprised to learn that you and your late husband had need of passports. You don't strike me as the sort woman who regularly takes foreign holidays.'

Grace would prefer not to imagine what sort of woman

he has her down as. 'As it happens, Dennis took me to Paris for our honeymoon,' she says. 'Not that it's any of your flamin' business.'

She carries on walking with the two policemen at her side. There's movement behind several of the lace-curtained windows nearby – goodness knows what's being made of this. 'If you think I'm goin' to keep answerin' your questions out here in the street,' she says, 'you've got another think comin'.'

'Well then, why don't we continue our discussion inside?' the inspector says.

When she opens up, once again a pile of post is snagging the bottom of the door.

'Allow me.' Before she can stop him, Collingwood picks up her letters and starts sorting through them. 'Mm, I see you have a postcard here.'

'That'll be from me mum, I 'spect.' She takes off her head-scarf. It's hard to keep the tears at bay when she catches sight of Dennis's old jacket hanging there ready for him to put it on. 'She likes to send me them funny ones with the fat ladies on the beach.'

Grace watches him turn the postcard over and then back again. It's too dark in the passageway to see what's made him so curious. 'This wasn't sent from Brighton. The postmark says Tilbury, if I'm not mistaken.' Bringing it closer, he squints at it. 'It was posted only yesterday morning.'

'Yes, well, I've had so much post since Dennis died. Lot of people I've never set eyes on from all over London, never mind Essex and Middlesex, Kent even – they've all sent their con-dolences. He knew a lot of people. Still, it makes you wonder if they might be after somethin'.'

There's not much room for the three of them in the hallway. 'You'd better come through to the kitchen,' she says, looking at Collinwood. No point her addressing Sergeant Bradley when all he does is stand there stiff as a ruddy dummy.

'I thought we should have a little chat, you and I,' Collingwood says. 'Lay our cards on the table, so to speak.' He plants his hat in the centre of the table next to the salt and pepper like he's just placed his first chess piece. She thinks of her father and how he taught her to play chess when she was off school with the mumps that time.

'Mrs Stevenson, I'll come straight to the point: we know that you've been engaged in an intimate *sexual* relationship with Frank Whitby. In fact, Sergeant Bradley here found you both in a state of undress on the very morning they called round to break the news to you of your poor husband's demise.'

'And they jumped to the wrong ruddy conclusions. Dennis had just disappeared for no reason. Frank kindly offered to stay here to protect me.'

His moustache twitches: 'Really? To protect you from what exactly?'

'He wouldn't say – only that he had his reasons to be worried for my safety. He offered to sleep on the sofa and I agreed. We slept in separate rooms.'

She's careful to look directly at Sergeant Bradley now. 'Your chaps looked around the place – you must have seen where Frank had been lying. The sofa was too cramped, so he had to make do on the floor.'

The sergeant clears his throat. 'I can confirm that we did find a makeshift bed on the living room floor, sir.'

The inspector strokes his moustache. 'Be that as it may, let's move on, shall we? There's been talk that you're in the process of selling up here?'

'I'm surprised you have time to listen to gossip,' she says. 'Besides, whether I choose to sell up or not is no business for the police.'

'At the moment, we have no evidence to suggest you were Mr Whitby's accomplice in the murder of your husband. So, unless we find proof to the contrary, we have no plans to bring charges against you.'

He holds his finger up in her face like he's the headmaster and she's the naughty pupil. '*However*, now that Whitby is the chief suspect in your husband's murder, should he contact you in any way and you subsequently fail to inform us.' He cocks his head to one side. 'That would be an entirely different matter – such a failure would mean we could well bring serious charges against you for obstructing justice and so forth. Is that understood?'

She nods.

'Has Whitby contacted you since we last spoke?'

She looks down at those over-polished brogues of his. To his face she says, 'I haven't seen Frank or heard a thing from him, and that's the truth.'

'Be under no illusion, Grace, we are going to find Mr Whitby very soon and when we do, he'll be sent for trial. In my considered opinion, a jury will likely find him guilty of murder and, as a consequence, he will be hanged by the neck until he's dead.'

How the bastard relishes saying those words. Grace is in no doubt, that a swift conviction would be another feather in this vain man's cap.

Instead of leaving, Collingwood continues to stand there toying with his hat. 'You know, until he went AWOL, Whitby had had the devil's own luck. His service record states he was the only surviving crew member when the Wellington he was in crash landed on its return from Bremen.'

'So what saved him?'

'The plane broke her back on landing. Whitby was in the rear gun turret. Seems it snapped off on impact and was separated from the main fuselage. Rest of her went up in flames before anyone could rescue the poor blighters inside. They pulled Whitby out with only a few cuts and a broken arm.'

The inspector puts his hat on but shows no other sign of leaving. 'After he was discharged from hospital, he was sent back to his squadron – ruddy fool only had three more ops left and he'd have completed his tour.'

'But hadn't his wife just been killed in an air raid – wouldn't that explain it?'

He raises both eyebrows. 'That may be so, but their child survived. What about little Thomas left with no parents – just think on that, Mrs Stevenson.'

He strikes the table with his fist. 'And what about the duty Whitby owed to his squadron,' (thump) 'and to his country?' (thump) 'I'm a former RAF officer myself and I can tell you that, whichever way you care to look at the man's actions, he took the coward's way out. A path that inevitably led him into a life of crime, deception, violence – oh yes we have evidence of that too – and finally to the murder of an innocent man for his own venal motives.'

'I'd be interested to know if you found all that out about Frank's past by yourselves. You see, my guess would be you were tipped off about a lot of it.'

The man's expression remains fixed, unreadable. She takes a step towards him. 'Shouldn't you be askin' yourself, Inspector, exactly why someone would want to provide you with that information in the first place?'

Grace knows better than to say anything more. With luck, that's rattled him out of all his ruddy certainty.

As she's showing them out, Collingwood stops to pick up the same postcard as before. He turns it over several times. 'It seems strange there's no signature on this – not even an initial.'

Turning towards her, he reads aloud: *Looking forward to my trip on the high seas tomorrow. Will write again when we reach our destination. Look after yourself. All my love. xxx*

'Maybe they didn't have room to put anything else,' she says.

He passes the card to Sergeant Bradley. 'I wouldn't consider that to be a woman's hand. What do you think, Sergeant?'

'I think you're right, sir. It looks very like a man's handwriting to me.'

Grace tries not to react, but she can't help herself – she

knows her cheeks have reddened and she can feel her heart racing. 'I'm afraid I don't recognise the writing,' she says. 'An' I've no idea who might have sent it.'

CHAPTER FORTY

Frank's stomach rumbles; his breakfast had consisted of two bits of bread with a scraping of marge and Marmite – hardly enough to keep a man going for the rest of the day.

The stench of the marshes hangs in the air. He intends to join the queue nearer the ship's scheduled departure time, though that's not until the afternoon. Whatever happens he's determined to stick to his plan – he's learnt before how things can go awry if you start to deviate. Which means right now, he has plenty of time to kill.

He walks a mile or so before he finds another gents' – the smelliest yet. Once inside the narrow, fetid cubicle, he takes out all the items he needs to transform himself into an old man.

If only he had a mirror. The first thing Irving had taught him (while recounting his own days in rep) was how to smear the grey powder right into his skin – rubbing it to emphasise any natural creases but taking care to avoid the upper lip. Next, he takes out the false moustache and spreads the adhesive as evenly as he can.

When someone bangs on the door, Frank nearly drops the bloody thing down the lav. There's more thumping but this time on the other two doors.

He turns round to be sure his feet are in the appropriate

position in case they look underneath. Any minute he expects to see a police helmet over the top of the door or even below it.

There's more thumping and cursing and then someone starts rattling his door. 'Will one of yous hurry up, I need a shit somethin' awful.'

The toilet to his right is flushed. 'Hold your ruddy horses, will ya?' some bloke says before the door is unlocked.

Releasing his breath, Frank doesn't move an inch. The glue will lose its grip in a minute, but he needs to steady his nerves, or he'll drop the wretched thing.

'Halleluiah – at long bloody last,' the desperate bloke declares.

Blocking out the hideous noises that follow, Frank presses his moustache into place. He attaches both eyebrows in turn and then, desperate for fresher air, unfolds the walking stick, unbolts the door and walks out.

As luck would have it, there's a small shaving mirror above one of the basins. He washes his hands – though of course there's no soap. Satisfied that he's alone, he adjusts the angle of the wig and checks the grey face powder is reasonably even. Not bad; though possibly less convincing than before. This ought to fool most people at an arm's length – he just has to make sure no one gets much closer.

The weather is much finer than yesterday so there's a danger he'll start to sweat it off. With such calm conditions, it's a good day to be setting out on a long sea voyage.

The previous evening, he'd taken a bit of time to get the lie of the land. He knows a man of his supposed age wouldn't just walk around aimlessly, they would sit on a bench and look out at the estuary; it's not so bad, after all, to have to while away a few hours watching sea birds.

He finds an empty bench facing the sea and slowly lowers himself down onto it. Just below, a stock-still grey heron is peering down into the shallows. He's struck by the patience it shows while it waits for its prey to show itself. There's something of the dinosaur about the way the bird carries itself.

The place is teeming with sailors and dockers and scurrying clerks along with the hundreds of milling passengers clutching their precious possessions while trying to keep a tight grip on their children.

Everywhere he looks there are gulls of one sort or another. Their mournful cries mix with the blunt reports of metal striking metal and petrol engines. Weighed-down lorries, buses, and cars keep coming and going in an endless stream; loading and unloading in clouds of exhaust fumes and honking horns.

Some over-excited youngsters have managed to break free from their parents and are running around in between people's legs or just staring up at those big ships in wonder. And they are a hell of a sight, the sheer scale of them dwarfing the docks. With so much going on, not one single person gives an old man sitting on a bench a second glance; old age would be the perfect disguise if he planned to rob a bank.

Around midday, he catches sight of a swarm of uniformed men checking various berths along the length of the wharf. He's too far away to tell if they're regular policemen or customs officers. This could be perfectly normal – they must have to carry out a lot of spot checks for contraband and that sort of thing.

The temperature is rising and his head's getting uncomfortably hot under the wig; if he starts to sweat too much, it could streak his makeup. No wonder so many women keep a powder compact handy.

Sitting down on such a hard surface for so long has made Frank genuinely stiff; the pins-and-needles in his legs ensure he gets up slowly. Leaning on his stick, he totters down to one of the cafés he'd spotted earlier. On the way there, he puts some money in the slot and picks up a newspaper – it won't look odd that he's keeping his head down at the table if he appears to be reading.

It's lunchtime and the cafe is too busy for anyone to notice another old man buying a cup of tea and some biscuits. When a couple of blokes get up to leave, he sits down at their table and unfolds his Daily Telegraph.

From time to time Frank glances out of the window and each time he spots yet more policemen. A good many are positioned just outside the baggage hall scanning the faces of every person waiting to go inside.

Frank tries to take his time; makes himself dunk the biscuits one after the other before sipping at the rest of his tea. He has to keep checking the moustache is still in place. Underneath the table his legs are trembling, his left foot pumping the way an old man's never would.

Two o'clock. It's no good, he's done with all this waiting around – better to get it over with one way or another. Yes, now's as good a time as any to make his move.

He folds his paper and stuffs it underneath his arm before picking up his old case. Leaning on his cane a little, he walks out of the café and heads for the ship. With the bright sun beating down, it feels like some spotlight is being shone on him as he walks off towards the baggage hall.

His heart is racing, his palms slick with sweat. With so many coppers milling around, he's careful to avoid the outer queue. Instead he chooses one of the central ones, stands in line just behind a young couple holding hands. From time to time, the man gives the woman's shoulders a reassuring squeeze.

The tremors in his hands could give him away but he can't seem to still them. Along with everyone else, Frank slowly shuffles towards one of the entrances. He tries to look straight ahead most of the time, conscious of the eyes of the policemen sweeping back and forth over the crowd. Any minute he expects a shout to be aimed at him, but he's carried forward by the swell of the crowd.

Once he's inside the hall itself, the sheer scale of the building overwhelms him. Sunlight is shining down through an ornate glass dome at the centre of the high roof – it feels like he's stepped inside a cathedral. The effect is humbling. This towering construction is the very first or the very last building every traveller goes through as they depart or board the big liners.

All the people around him are heading in the same direction – on their way to a new life. The adults in the queue are surprisingly quiet, as if contemplating the enormity of what they're about to do. If some might be harbouring last-minute regrets, not one of them steps out of the line.

Toys or biscuits are being offered to worked-up children. Nearby, a baby starts to wail and it sets off dozens of others. The people around him are so young – barely a line on their faces. He's reminded of that other queue, full of over-excited young men on their way to a life of adventure, or so they thought.

He spots more coppers – some of them in plain clothes – patrolling the building; they stroll in between the lines running curious and distrustful eyes over everything and everyone. Bags, cases and toys seem to attract equal attention. Could be looking for a stowaway teddy bear – for a second the idea makes him smile.

Keeping his head bowed a fraction, Frank carries on shuffling forward; with each step he gets closer and closer to the desk where he, like the other passengers, will have to present himself and his travel documents for inspection.

Someone grips his shoulder. 'Excuse me, sir.' The hand is attached to the arm of a tall policeman.

'Is there a problem, officer?' His heart is beating out of control.

'You dropped your newspaper.' Smiling, the copper hands it to him and he's forced to look him in the eye. 'You might want to hang onto it,' he says. 'A little reminder of home.' He studies Frank's face for a moment. This could be it.

'You're not wrong,' Frank says. 'Thank you.' He tips his hat as the copper turns and walks away.

At long last, he reaches the head of the queue. 'I see you're sailing to Melbourne, sir,' the young clerk says, only glancing at him.

Frank clears his throat. 'Yes, my daughter, um, she has a place in Griffen Crescent, North Melbourne. My dear wife died last year. After that I promised myself I would go and see my grandchildren while I still can.'

The man looks him full in the face perhaps sensing his nervousness. 'Never been a great sailor,' Frank says. 'Can't say I'm looking forward to weeks at sea.'

'I'm sure you'll find your sea-legs in the end.' Smiling now, the man barely looks at Arthur's handiwork. 'Okay then,' he says. 'That's all in order. Hope you have a pleasant voyage, sir.'

Already, the clerk's hand is outstretched ready for the next person's papers.

Following the general movement, Frank finds himself back in the sunshine amongst the crowd out on the landing stage. Shielding his eyes with his hand, he cranes his neck to look up at the enormity of the ocean liner berthed alongside them. Men, women and children are streaming up the gangplank while the ones already onboard are leaning over the rails to take a long last look at their homeland, knowing that, in six weeks, they'll have travelled as far away from here as it's possible to be.

Under his feet, the platform Frank's standing on feels almost like a living thing as it writhes up and down in the swell.

CHAPTER FORTY-ONE

Saturday, 12th July

Grace has been feeling sick all morning though she hasn't actually thrown up. Remembering Lottie's advice, she tries a bit of dried toast and it helps a little.

The place she's renting isn't much but it's all hers – at least for the time being. With two small rooms and a tiny bathroom, it's cheap enough and easy to keep clean compared with the pub.

The last of the bread is gone and all the cream crackers are gone; she'd better pop round to Smithson's on the corner.

On the way back, she bumps into Wilf Barnet in the street, though she wishes she hadn't. He's a nice enough old man but every time she sees one of their old customers it jolts her back to the Eight Bells and the life she's been forced to turn her back on.

It's not long before Wilf mentions the trams. The old man takes off his cap and holds it to his chest. 'I stood there last Saturday in the Old Kent Road, with all the rest of 'em, waitin' for the very last one to go past and, d'you know, I said to the chap what was standin' alongside me – and he agreed wholehearted – that it was just like being at the funeral of a dear friend you'd known all your life.'

He doesn't even notice her reaction, doesn't for a minute think about what he's just said.

'That was a sad day for London,' he says, 'and no mistake.' When he shakes his head, his bald head catches the light at an odd angle; if she squints, he almost has a halo. Despite everything, the thought of Wilf Barnet as an angel of the Lord makes her smirk.

'Course there was all that cheerin' and flag wavin' when she did appear, but what was the point of it, eh? I got a glimpse of a fella with this gold chain of office round his neck standing there getting his photograph taken with the others like they were giving the old girl a proper send off. And some of 'em in the crowd sang Auld Lang Syne, would you believe? But what was the flamin' point of that when it was already too late to save her.'

'To be honest, Wilf, I never used 'em much,' she says. 'But still it's a shame they've gone.'

'It's not like they were going to listen to the likes of you and me,' he says. 'Always the same, en it?'

'I'd better go,' she says. 'Got things to be gettin' on with an' that.'

She's expecting Dot, so when the bell rings, Grace rushes downstairs with a smile on her face. It's a nasty shock to see Inspector Collingwood standing there – though this time without his trusty sergeant at his heels.

'Good day to you, Mrs Stevenson.' He raises his hat. 'The Westons supplied me your new address.'

'Did they now?'

'Would you mind if I step inside for a moment?'

Grace does mind, she minds very much but isn't going to give him the satisfaction of showing it. 'I'm up on the second floor,' she says, leading the way up the stairs. She can't banish the thought that he's the sort of man who might take the opportunity to look up her skirt.

The inspector's eyes flit over her living room; can tell he isn't impressed. 'Only temporary,' she tells him, though she can't think why. 'What was it you wanted? Dot's coming round in a bit – we're off to the pictures round the corner an' it starts in half an hour.'

'Be assured I won't detain you for long.' He takes off his hat but keeps hold of the brim. 'As Mr Stevenson's widow, I thought you should know that, though Frank Whitby has managed to elude us thus far, he –'

'Hang on a second,' she says, 'by *eluded* d'you you mean Frank's given you lot the slip? Is that right?'

Oh, she can see that gets him going. 'Yes, I'm afraid the man managed to *give us the slip* last week, as you put it. But I can assure you the situation is merely temporary.'

'So, are you tellin' me that with the full resources of Scotland Yard out to get him, Frank's managed to escape?'

'Yes, but Whitby clearly had considerable help. Thanks to your mystery correspondence – the unsigned postcard he sent you – we were able to trace his movements to a Tilbury bed and breakfast establishment. Unfortunately, the wretched man managed to board a vessel heading for Melbourne – that's in Australia.'

'I know where that is,' she tells him. Grace has to sit down as she tries to take this news in.

Collinwood remains on his feet in front of her. 'As I was about to explain, the situation is a temporary one. We were able to identify the vessel he boarded by examining the passenger lists. There was a particular anomaly in the paperwork.'

The smell of the Brilliantine on his hair is turning her stomach again. 'We weren't able to ascertain how this anomaly occurred in the first place. All involved are denying any irregularities have taken place and trying to claim it was simply a clerical error of no significance.'

'You're suggestin' somebody helped him, but you don't know who – is that right?'

Collingwood keeps pushing the crown of his trilby in and then turning it over and pushing it out again. 'Like I said, the situation is temporary, I assure you.'

She stands up. 'If you don't mind me sayin' so, it seems to me that a good many things are *eludin'* you at the moment, Inspector. You reckon Frank had assistance from someone but whoever it was managed to cover their own tracks.'

'I have no doubt that Whitby received considerable financial help from some *misguided* person in order to pay a corrupt administrator for their assistance.' He shoves his hat towards her face; looks like he'd very much like to hit her at this moment if he could get away with it.

Grace stands up daring the little runt to lay one finger on her. 'If you're suggesting I was the one who helped him, you're wrong. Although it's none of your business, for your information I haven't received a brass farthing from Dennis's life insurance because he'd stopped payin' the premiums more than a year ago.' She laughs in his face. 'I know what you're thinking – I'll say it for you, shall I? He must have needed the money to pay off some of his gambling debts.'

The doorbell rings again. Grace goes to the window. Dot is dancing about impatiently on the doorstep. It's hard to lift the sash but she opens it enough to stick her head out. 'Hang on – I'll be down in a sec.'

Grace turns back to her visitor. 'So, if Frank's ship is on its way Down Under, I wouldn't think there's much you can do about it. It seems he's got away scot-free.'

'Ah – but that's where you're wrong.' Collingwood looks all cocky again. 'We've already telegraphed the ship's captain to inform him of the situation. What's more we've alerted various port authorities although I am not at liberty to be more specific at this time.' Collinwood only just stops short of poking his raised finger at her nose. 'So, you see, it's all been in vain. Francis John Whitby will be arrested when the vessel next docks. As a known deserter from the armed services and now as a fugitive to be charged with a capital offence, the man *will* be brought back to this country to stand trial for murder.'

Grace grips the back of a chair for support. 'Well you never know, he might just *elude* you again.'

'Oh, not this time, Mrs Stevenson. His guard will be down. He'll be congratulating himself that he's got away from us but all the while the net will close on him just when he thinks himself a free man at last.'

From down in the street she hears Dot calling her name. 'I'll leave you to your outing,' the inspector says, turning on his heels. 'We'll need your address if you should move on from here. Have no fear, I'll stay in touch. I'll be sure to let you know about the progress we've made bringing your late husband's killer home to face the full might of the law.'

'I wish you luck catching Dennis's killer,' she tells him. 'But it isn't Frank.'

'You know, Grace, once the trial is over and the law has taken its course, you'll have an opportunity to put all this sordid business behind you.'

He takes a step towards her with a sickening smile on his face. 'You're a young, dare I say, very attractive woman; there's plenty of time for you to make another life for yourself.'

He strokes his moustache several times before he finally opens his mouth. 'As we are told in the Book of John: if we confess our sins, he is faithful and just to forgive us our sins, and to cleanse us from all unrighteousness.'

'If I'm in need of a sermon, I'll go to church,' she tells him. 'Just comin', Dot,' she shouts, before slamming the window shut. 'I'll see you out, Inspector.'

CHAPTER FORTY-TWO

Wednesday 20th August

Children are playing football in the street down below; chalked lines on the blank wall opposite mark their goalposts. There's a dispute going on between them, their small fists curled ready. The city heat doesn't help. So much passion over whether a half-inflated football struck the wall inside two arbitrary lines.

Grace shakes her head. There are things she should be doing but she's feeling lethargic. Working at the biscuit factory has one advantage – it keeps her occupied for most of the day. And of course there's the money; that four pounds, seventeen and six in her wage-packet at the end of the week isn't to be sniffed at. She won't need to break into her savings for the time being at least.

Today was a slightly better day than the one before it and the one before that. It's the hours after work that make the time drag. The nights are worst. She's used to lying there with her brain buzzing like a load of bees are flying round and round but finding no way out.

Usually she finds it cheering to witness the energy the kids in the street put into everything they do – even squabbling. Earlier, the boys were cowboys and they'd corralled several girls and told them they were Red Indians; even tied them up loosely with their own skipping rope. Quite rightly, the girls rebelled, couple of them grabbed the rope and began to skip with it.

'You kids better keep that racket down!' a man's voice shouts though she can't see them. The quarrelling boys abandon their game and start shooting at the girls with two pointing fingers. 'Pwew! Pwew!' The girls stop their skipping to retaliate.

The commotion escalates and now the whole lot are joining in; making such a din she expects their various mothers to start the chorus of yells that will send them indoors.

She's about to close the window on their noise when she sees Dot coming round the corner looking red-faced and clutching something like her life might depend on it.

'Grace!' she cries out above the uproar. She holds her hand up. 'You've got a telegram.' Her urgency makes the kids stop what they're doing to see what the fuss might be about.

She runs downstairs to meet her on the doorstep. 'It was sent to our house,' Dot says, breathing hard. 'Look.' She thrusts a flimsy piece of paper into her hands.

With shaking fingers, Grace opens it right there in the street.

GRACE STOP. ARRIVED IN MELBOURNE STOP. SORRY FOR EVERYTHING STOP. WILL WRITE LOVE FRANK STOP

'Frank's made it to Australia,' she says, holding the flimsy piece of paper to her chest. 'Oh, my good Lord! I can't believe he's managed to escape the lot of them.'

Dot stares at her. 'So you're pleased?'

'Course I am.' She reads the words again. 'If they'd caught him, they would have strung him up for certain.' She folds the telegram carefully then stuffs it into her pocket. 'Out there he can start a new life in a new country. No lookin' back. You don't look too happy about it?'

She can't hold back the tears. Dot puts her arms around her and she sobs into her chest. 'It's just because –'

'Because what?'

She takes a deep breath. 'Now I know for certain Frank's never goin' to be comin' back. I'm goin' to have to do everythin' on my own.'

Dot pushes her away, holds her at arm's length. 'Listen to me, Grace Stevenson, you're not by yourself. Whether you like it or not, you've got me an' you got our mum an' dad for starters. I won't say anythin' about your mam because we all know she's utterly bloody useless.'

The children have crept up behind Dot. 'Bugger off,' Grace shouts, and for a moment she sees Dot thinking she's talking to her. They both turn on the kids and try to shoo them away. They only take a few steps back. For them, this is just a game like grandma's footsteps.

'Let's go inside,' she says.

Once they're up in her sitting room, Grace puts the telegram down on the table next to the wedding photo of her and Dennis and goes over to get her hanky from her handbag.

'It's not really her fault, you know,' she says, before blowing her nose again. 'I don't think Elsie was ready to be a mother.'

Dot folds her arms across her chest. 'Well, whatever excuse you want to make for your mam, if you ask me, she could have tried a lot bloody harder.'

'What is it they say in the bible? It's something like: *judge not, lest ye be judged.*'

Frowning at her, Dot says: 'I know you're a widow an' things have bin a bit awful for you lately, but you're not goin' to come over all religious, are ya?'

Grace folds her hanky and puts it up her sleeve. 'Would it be so terrible if I did?'

Dot shrugs. 'I'd still be your friend – as long as you didn't keep bangin' on about God every couple of minutes.'

'Grace pulls a stray hair back from her face and clips it in place. 'D'you know what I'm going to do first thing tomorrow?'

Dot raises an eyebrow at her. 'Go down to St John's and throw yourself at that Reverend Sawyer's feet?'

She can't help but smile. 'As it happens, I'm going to lose half a day's pay so I can go down to that police station and have a word with Inspector Collingwood.'

'What was that other saying from the bible: *vengeance is mine, sayeth the Lord.*'

Grace shrugs. 'Since when did anybody take any notice of that?'

Thursday 21st August

The station is busy. She's directed to a long bench and told to wait. The people already sitting on it are reluctant to budge up, so she stays standing.

A scruffy looking bloke is led out past them. 'You need to sort yourself out.' The copper at his side makes no effort to speak quietly. The stench of booze and stale urine spreads out into the room and she wonders if she's going to be sick. 'I don't want to see you in here again, d'you hear me?' The bloke meekly nods his head at the copper, his hair a tangled mess that can't have seen a brush for months.

The woman next to her gathers herself up like whatever the poor man's got might be catching.

It's well past nine when Collingwood deigns to see her. A young, lanky constable ushers her along a corridor to a door with the inspector's name across it. His knock is so quiet she wonders whether Collinwood can have heard.

'Come,' he says – like it wastes his precious time to add an *in*.

The inspector gets to his feet. 'Thank you, PC Baines.' The

constable shuts the door behind her sealing them in together. The room smells of furniture polish and tobacco smoke. The lights are on due to the fact that there's only one small window. His desk is stacked high with files – police business must be booming.

Collingwood sits back down in his padded leather chair behind his posh desk. On the leather-bound writing pad in front of him there are lots of black ink doodles –all of them are spirals. 'Won't you take a seat, Mrs Stevenson? I must say I'm surprised to see you here.' There's only a hard chair to choose from. Knitting his hands together on the table in front of her, the inspector says, 'How can I help you?'

'I've got something to show you.' Her hands are shaking as she unclips her handbag and takes out the telegram. 'This was sent to the Westons' house addressed to me.' She offers it up to his pincer-like grasp.

Collingwood's face shows no emotion though his neck reddens and he starts rubbing at his temple with his free hand. She's seen Frank make that same gesture when he's thinking. Banishing that train of thought, she watches the man in front of her read the telegram over again just to take it in, even turns it over to be certain it's not a fake.

The next minute, he's on his feet and walking towards the window. 'I have to admit it looks genuine enough.'

'It seems Frank's gone an' *eluded* you all over again,' Grace says.

He turns on her, a thick vein like a worm standing out in the middle of his forehead. 'You seem delighted, triumphant even, yet this is the same wretched man who murdered your own husband.'

'I don't believe that – not for one single second.' She stands up. 'Frank had nothing to do with Dennis's death. Trouble is, you lot can't see further than the end of yer own ruddy noses.'

She walks over to him daring his dark eyes to turn that fury on her. 'You know,' she says. 'In your case, if you didn't keep your ruddy nose of yours so far up in the air, you might find out a bit more about what's goin' on right underneath it.'

Not breaking her gaze, she waits for a response. When it doesn't come, she turns and walks towards the door.

'I really thought there might be hope for you, Grace Stevenson,' he says, from behind her back. 'But now I can see that charming face of yours is a mere mask to hide how morally corrupt you really are.'

She makes no reply. Instead she opens the door, walks through it and slams it shut behind her.

CHAPTER FORTY-THREE

Saturday 6th September

The Underground is a little less stifling now the weather's on the turn. At Victoria, Grace has to hurry to catch the Brighton train. Being a Saturday, it's busy and she's dead lucky to get a seat in one of the carriages next to the window. A cheerful chap insists on putting her case into the overhead rack for her.

It takes her a while to catch her breath. Sitting opposite her, there's a young boy sandwiched between his parents. Before the guard's whistle blows, he's already squirming around. After that he starts to jiggle one leg so his foot keeps knocking his mother's shoe. Not content with that, he's soon sending his yo-yo up and down, up and down, on and on until Grace is forced to look away from all the boy's spinning and wriggling.

She hasn't seen her own mother since the funeral and that wasn't for long. Elsie – she finds herself using her mother's first name more often these days – had stayed less than an hour at the sad get-together they'd had afterwards in an upstairs room at the King's Head. She'd been fretting about the trains. 'Must get back,' she'd said more than once despite the offer of a bed for the night. Their little gathering hadn't done the man justice – not by a longshot.

Ralf and Lottie had suggested they hold the wake in the

Eight Bells, but Grace had soon put a stop to that idea. She didn't imagine many locals would have the courage to show their face considering its new management. Who could blame them? She heard a few days later that the likes of Wilf, Bert, Charlie and Harry Jones had nonetheless gone there that same evening and raised a few glasses to Dennis. She was pleased to hear it even if it did put more money into the coffers of the very man responsible for his death.

Grace's thoughts are all over the place today. There's a warm breeze coming through the open window. It's no use dwelling on the past. Instead she tries to concentrate on the beauty of the open countryside as it slips past. All that space out there is hard to take in when you've spent your life in a crowded borough in a swarming city.

The little boy's father lights up his pipe and she watches the curls of smoke float up to the ceiling. For a change, the smell of tobacco doesn't set her stomach off.

Grace's mother had at least written to her – a surprisingly nice letter in which she'd tried to say all the right things. How could Elsie have known they were all the wrong things?

The movement of the train feels less soothing now and Grace opens her handbag and takes out the small tin she's filled with Jacob's Crackers. She's learnt that nibbling on one usually does the trick.

It's so odd to be heading down to Brighton again. Hard to fathom how much has happened since she'd arrived there back in May half expecting she'd be burying Elsie before long. Who would have thought the person she'd be burying would be Dennis?

At last she can see the South Downs. Despite the way the train is swaying, she goes to stand in the corridor to get a better view of those hills. Steam is pouring the length of the carriages and settling like mist over the landscape being left behind. Grace can taste the smoke in the air but at least it doesn't make her retch. She glimpses a tractor ploughing a field; a cloud of flapping birds following on behind. It looks like some giant brush is busy painting the landscape, turning it from sun-bleached yellow to various shades of brown. Way up in the deep blueness of the sky, seagulls turn in the air. How wonderful must it feel to be so utterly free like that?

Her thoughts turn to journey's end. Although her mother had invited her down, Grace is unsure what kind of reception she'll get. That's the thing with Elsie – you never could tell where you were with her. Her mother couldn't stay the same, was always changing to better suit the man she happened to be with. She ought to feel sorry for her in a way, for the fact that she can't abide to be by herself without a chap to validate her existence. As Elsie ages the more trouble she has attracting a man in the first place – never mind hanging onto him.

Brighton will be quieter now than it was in the summer and some of its gaudy attractions will have packed up and gone off wherever they disappear to until the following spring. Being a sunny Saturday, the beach is likely to be crowded still. At least the water will have warmed up a bit over the summer months. Perhaps this time she can persuade Elsie not to worry about her perm or how the pebbles hurt her feet to come in for a dip with her.

Grace's hand goes down to her belly. There's one thing, at least, that she's certain about – she'll learn by her mother's example and make sure she makes a better job of being someone's mother.

CHAPTER FORTY-FOUR

Monday 8th September

There's a stiff breeze coming off the sea; when she steps outside it threatens to tear her headscarf right off her head. Her mother's raincoat already seems a tighter fit than it used to, and she can feel the wind sneaking in between the buttons.

It's only a few minutes' walk to the bus stop. When the bus finally arrives, she chooses a seat on the upper deck for the view and so she can see everyone that's getting on and off.

The conductor's head appears and then the rest of him. Just climbing the stairs has made him unnaturally red in the face. 'Fares please,' he calls, breathless. While buying a ticket to Lewes, she asks him about the various connecting buses and it's worse than she'd thought – she'll have to change three times before she gets anywhere near the place.

By the time Grace steps down into the centre of the little village it's approaching midday. Away from the coast, that biting wind has dropped and it's turned into a warm day. What a sight it is to see all those old black and white houses, their front gardens crowded with late flowers – she's only ever seen such places on biscuit tins or jigsaw puzzles.

She walks into the only pub. Its small leaded windows mean the room is darker and far cooler than outside; there's even a log fire crackling in the huge stone fireplace. When she asks for orange pop, the young barman frowns. He looks her up and down as he hands her the bottle with a straw sticking out of it like you might give a little kid. She doesn't bother to ask for a glass.

The place is empty apart from a couple of old boys smoking long-stemmed pipes, staring into the fire and hardly saying a word to each other. Maybe there's not much to talk about in such a sleepy place. Noticing her, the old men turn to eye her with suspicion. It takes a while before they turn their attention back to the flames.

Grace takes her drink over to one of the window seats. She stares out into the road and studies every car driving by. In the space of half an hour one or two people walk past the window but no one else comes in.

She finishes her drink and walks through to the ladies' out the back. Once inside the cubicle, she opens her shopping bag, takes out a different coloured scarf and ties it over her hair. Finally, she turns Elsie's raincoat inside out. (Look, you get two macs for the price of one, her mother had once demonstrated as if it was a magic trick.)

Grace leaves by the back gate taking the footpath running alongside a stubble field to the village graveyard at the top. The church looks a bit isolated from the community it serves – perhaps they felt more comfortable keeping the C of E at a distance. There's an old bench out front that's facing the way she's just come; it offers her a good view of anything or anybody coming up the hill.

The day goes on around her. Two, then three rabbits emerge from under the hedge and start nibbling the grassy mound of a grave. It's hard to think about how some poor soul was laid to rest underneath there. Big black birds that could be crows or rooks are squawking and squabbling in the trees above her head.

Her stomach rumbles then growls like an angry bear. She nibbles on a cream cracker, leaves it a few more minutes until she feels confident enough to leave the churchyard and takes the narrow lane to her right. From there it's supposed to be no more than a mile of easy walking.

They're all too hard at it to notice her arrival. Working in a pub, she's used to the smell of hops, though freshly picked like these, there's nothing stale about them. The bitter-sweet scent of them overwhelms the air. Being a weekday, the workers are mostly women with their older children, all of them chatting away in broad Cockney. Youngsters are rushing around being scolded from time to time for getting under people's feet. A tractor arrives, its cart brimming over with long strings of green flowers.

She's heard it said they call these hop *gardens* – for some reason you should never ever call it a field. Behind the group of women, there are lines and lines of upright wooden poles stretching on up to the horizon. Plants are growing up these poles and along the strings across the top making shady patches underneath. From a distance they look more like grapevines.

The women are sweating in the heat, their hands flying as they strip the hops off each stem into the enormous sacks below. The flowers themselves look a bit like pale green raspberries. Every so often, one or two flower heads go astray but they're working too fast to pick them up.

Seeing how her sack is now full to overflowing, one woman bawls out: 'Eh, Jack!' Next thing, a bare-chested young bloke comes along with an empty sack and carries the full one off to be weighed from a big metal hook.

A middle-aged man in shirtsleeves is walking towards her. 'You here looking for work, darlin'?' He's wearing a red spotted scarf round his neck but the front of his shirt is open and she can see the sweat running between the greying hairs on his chest.

Grace frowns. 'Not exactly, no.' She clears her throat. 'I'm looking for –'

'She's looking for me.'

Frank is standing not two feet away with his arms folded and a smile playing on his lips. He looks quite different from what she'd expected – he's wearing thick-rimmed glasses and his shorn hair has lost all the blonde bits on the ends. A couple of hop flowers are still clinging to the back of his head and, across his upper lip, there's a moustache she instantly has the urge to shave off.

They stare at each other. Opening his mouth at last, he says, 'Pete – d'you mind if I take a bit of a break to talk to my friend here?'

The man looks Grace up and down before giving him a yellow-toothed smile. 'I'll allow you an early dinner break, Johnny.' He claps Frank on the shoulder. 'If this young lady was my *friend*, I'd certainly want to take me time about it.'

'Thanks, mate.' Frank grabs her by the arm. 'Let's go over here, shall we?'

She's tempted to shrug him off but doesn't. He leads her on past all the frantic activity to a large grassy area that's surrounded on three sides by rows of brick-built huts with corrugated iron roofs. Numbers and names are crudely white-washed on each of the doors.

'Thank you for coming, Grace,' he says. 'It means the world to me.'

She's thrown off by where they are; it feels like they're standing inside an arena. 'Is this where you all sleep? They're no bigger than lavatories.'

Frank's still smiling at her; that same crooked smile she'd so easily fallen for. 'You get used to it – mine's that one over there.'

Grace has no idea which one he's nodding towards. The doors of one or two of the huts are open and she can see they've managed to squeeze single bunks inside them but not much else.

Does he imagine this is going to be easy – that she's going to be putty in his hands? She can feel her anger rising. 'When you sent me that telegram from Melbourne, I thought that was it,' she says, 'the end of whatever there'd bin between us. Can't tell you what a terrible shock it was when Dot gave me your letter last week. I'm living in a little flat of me own now; if you hadn't sent it to the Westons', it would never have found me. So you see I'm only here by chance.'

Grace looks down at her hands; her fingers toy with her wedding ring, twisting it around and around. Though she's close to tears, she's determined not to give in. 'I knew they couldn't have caught you or I'd have heard – Collingwood would have made sure of that. After that telegram arrived, I assumed you must be thousands of miles away livin' a new life an' I'd never see or hear from you again.'

'You must have worked out it wasn't me who sent that telegram – I paid a sailor to send it once he got over there. I'm really sorry I had to send such a thing to you, Grace but I had to – to make sure we were both in the clear.' He hangs his head. 'My plan was always to go through all the checks, so it looked like I'd officially boarded the ship. I disembarked before she sailed using the crew's gangplank.'

When she doesn't say anything, his hand comes under her chin, raising her head so he can look her straight in the eyes. She can smell the sweet stench of hops about him. 'This time I owe you the whole truth Grace,' he says.

'Oh – and what would that be?' She's tempted to add more but doesn't.

'Once I was finally standing there on the deck of the ship, for the first five minutes or so I was sorely tempted to change my mind and do a bunk. The port was teeming with police; you've no idea how chuffed I felt outwitting the lot of them despite the odds being so stacked against me. For the last ten years it's felt like I was jinxed but I'd finally beaten it and I'd got this chance to begin again in a new country – one where I didn't have to keep looking over my shoulder.'

It's hard for her to see his true expression behind those glasses. 'Can't you take those damned things off,' she says.

'As it turns out, I need them,' he tells her. 'My eyesight's not what it was.'

Neither of them speaks. In the silence she hears the distant sound of children playing and the fut-fut of the tractor doing its work.

'You look tired,' he says. 'You must have had quite a journey to get here. Why don't we go and sit down?'

He's right – she feels exhausted by all this. They go across to sit side by side on a wooden bench that looks like it might collapse at any minute.

'Go on,' she says. 'I want to know exactly what happened on that ship.'

'Well, as I was standing there on the deck amongst all the other passengers, I noticed how they were surrounded by their families and friends. Some were throwing ribbons over the side to their loved ones on the quayside, while I was entirely on my own. It dawned on me this was no escape – not really; I was just running away like I'd been for too ruddy long and I knew this time I had to stay.' He squeezes her shoulder. 'Mainly because of you, Grace.'

'I showed that telegram from Melbourne to Inspector Collingwood,' she says, 'pushed it right in front of his eyes. You should have seen the expression on his face when he read it! He'd bin so cocksure all along they were goin' to catch you.'

Her smile soon fades. 'Did you know somebody was tipping the Old Bill off? They knew all about you. Collingwood took great pains to tell me you were a deserter and your real name is Francis John Whitby. He called you a coward.'

She sees him flinch at the word. 'He told me how you'd left your baby son behind though his poor mother had only just been killed. Is that true, Frank?' He looks away, off to his right where wood smoke is rising from an outdoor oven. The smell begins to turn her stomach. A big black pot is suspended there over glowing logs like some witch's cauldron.

'I could tell you it's a lie,' he says at last, 'but I'm ashamed to say that part of it is true.'

She stands up full of fury; half wishing she had something hard to hand. 'How could you go an' do that to your own flesh and blood?'

He stays seated, seems to be studying his feet. Finally, he looks up at her. 'I've got no excuses. I can only tell you that, at the time, I thought it was the best thing for him – that the poor little bugger would be better off without me. I left him with Clara's sister Annie; she already had two boys and I knew he'd be raised in a good family, that she and her husband would treat him like one of their own.'

'But to abandon your own flesh and blood and then just run away from your responsibilities –'

He stands up. 'Aye, I'm not proud of it but I couldn't take him with me, could I? Couldn't condemn the lad to a life on the run like me. It might not count for much, but I've always sent them money when I've got it. I even managed to see the lad from time to time.' Frank hangs his head like a penitent asking for forgiveness. 'He calls me Uncle Frank – thinks I'm a friend of his parents – a sort of godfather.'

She gasps. 'But don't you see how awful it is that the poor boy doesn't know his own father. And what about you having to keep pretending he's not yours?'

Frank takes off his glasses and throws them down on the bench so hard she wonders if they'll have broken. 'Don't for one minute go feeling sorry for me or owt like that – it's the price I should and ought to pay. The lad's happy in his ignorance – he's a credit to Annie and her husband. Clara would be so proud of how he's turned out.' He covers his eyes with his hands. 'It was me that decided to go AWOL and it's me that's forced to take the consequences.'

'You haven't explained why you went and deserted in the first place.'

'It's a hard thing to put it into words.' He starts pacing,

rubbing at that scar of his like he's trying to rub the thing out. 'Before Clara was killed, I was a rear gunner in a Wellington. One night we got shot up badly over the Dutch coast; I was stuck inside the rear turret. The rest had the chance to bale out but the silly buggers wouldn't leave me. She broke her back as we came into land and then burst into flames.' He turns to her. 'How can it be right that I walked away with hardly a scratch and they all died? The whole thing was back to front.'

'None of that's your fault.' She reaches out to squeeze his hand.

'Once I was declared officially fit for active service, I got ordered back to my old squadron.' He gives a grim smile. 'Trouble was, I couldn't find it in me to go back to doing what I'd been doing. My Clara was killed by a stray German bomb. Made me think about all the women and little kiddies and all the old grannies and that we must have been killing down below us each and every time we went on an op. In bed of a night, I started to picture it – could see them all lying there dead in the rubble.'

Staring at the sky, he says, 'It's fair enough if you get in a tussle with enemy planes but if you're bombing a target it's not like fighting an enemy you can see – kill or be killed – or owt like that. We tried to hit the aiming point, but I know for a fact a lot of the time we weren't that accurate. You had to try not to think about it. Before, I didn't really picture the consequences of what we were doing. But once you've seen with your own eyes what a stray bomb does to your loved ones, it really brings it home. I just couldn't keep on wi' it.'

'So why not give yourself up and take the punishment?'

Frank grabs her arm. 'I should have done, but at the time, I wasn't thinking straight. Head was all messed up and I couldn't face the thought of being caged up like a ruddy animal.' She can feel how much his hand is shaking.

'Once I started down that road, there was no turning back. I've done a good many things I'm not proud of to get false papers, to earn money, some sort of living any way I could.' Tears are running down his cheeks, but he brushes them off with the back of his hand. 'I'd think about my Clara. Couldn't block it out – the sight of our house with nowt left standing but the back wall; a pile of ruddy bricks where once there'd been our home. A place I thought our baby would be safe.' He wipes at his face again. 'Just because they were Germans, it couldn't make it right that we were doing the same to them.'

Grace thinks of her father – how he'd left Germany because he hated the Nazis, but the British government had interned him anyway. Somewhere she must have German relatives who might have survived the war – unknown uncles, aunties; even cousins of her own age. Her grandmother – her namesake Gretchen – could still be alive.

Where Frank's been wiping his eyes with the heel of his dirty hand, he's left dark streaks under his eyes like war paint.

She'd spent the beginning of the war down in Brighton. In '43 a squadron of bombers had targeted the town and set the gasworks on fire. She remembers looking up at the viaduct and seeing the railway line hanging there in mid-air. Thankfully, no one she knew was killed. She can picture that huge pile of rubble he came back to. What must it have been like to stand and stare at the ruins of his home – the very spot where his wife died?

Someone strikes a gong. Any minute she expects them all to rush over to eat the soup or whatever it is that's bubbling away over in that blackened pot.

Chasing a man as usual, her mother had taken them back to London and then finally deposited her with her aunty. She remembers playing around in the bombies, looking up and seeing flowered wallpaper or sometimes a picture or a mirror unbroken and hanging up in its place but unsupported in mid-air; somebody's living room half blown away; what was left exposed to other people's stares along with the wind and the rain.

Overcome by pity, she threads her arms under his and hugs him to her. 'Oh, Frank,' she says, 'what a sorry mess. What on earth are we going to do?' The sound of voices is growing louder – laughing and squealing and singing like a carnival is approaching. Frank looks down at her. Without those glasses, he's more like the man she fell in love with.

'This has been a new start for me – after all the law thinks I'm on the other side of the world. I've been thinking about going back up Yorkshire and settling down, seeing a bit more of my lad.' His red-rimmed eyes appeal to her. 'You could come with me.'

He reaches to untie her headscarf and it feels good to shake her hair free. When he brushes a few stray hairs back from her face she's tempted to kiss him for the tenderness of the gesture.

'Could I now?' She rolls her head at the thought. 'Thing is, I've got a job and me own flat. It's not much but it's mine. Then there's me friends. Not sure I'm prepared to give all that up.' Her mother is an ample illustration of what happens when you blindly follow a man.

'At least consider it,' he says. 'Will you do that, Grace?'

The hot sun on her back persuades her to take off her raincoat. 'I will,' she says.

Although his face is still strained, he tries a smile. 'Eh – some of the women here have got themselves a hop husband – for the picking season at least. You could say it's a hopping tradition.' He nudges her. 'They even give 'em a wedding ceremony where they both jump over a hop bine holding hands. Course, if you're stopping for a bit, you'll have to learn to call me Johnny. What d'you say, Grace – couldn't we give it a go, just for starters?'

Did he think she could just leap up into his arms as if all the time in between had never occurred? 'This is happening too fast,' she tells him. 'I'm really not sure what I feel right at this minute.'

The crowd is nearly upon them and she can see one or two peering at them with curious eyes. Frank looks so crestfallen; this time it stirs more than her pity. And then there's the growing child in her belly to think of.

'I might just consider this hopper's wedding malarkey,' she says, 'after all, there'd be nothin' that's bindin' in it.'

He goes to kiss her but she stops him with a raised hand. 'There's one thing you have to promise me first though, Johnny who-ever-you-flamin'-well-are-now.'

'Anything – just you name it.'

'I want you to shave that ruddy moustache off. Over the last few months I've grown to detest any man sportin' one of them.' She waves a finger in his face. 'Ahh – no you don't, mister. You're not coming anywhere near me, and I'm certainly not goin' to let you kiss me, until that ruddy thing under your nose has disappeared for good.'

APPENDIX

It is currently estimated that, in the British armed forces as a whole, the number of deserters during WW2 was between 100,000 and 150,000.

Various estimates of the total number of wartime desertions from the R.A.F. suggest a figure between 5,850 and 10,000.

Extract from Hansard
House of Commons sitting – 15 July 1952

Mr Hector Hughes asked the Secretary of State for War how many of Her Majesty's Forces were, on 31st December 1945, and on each succeeding 31st December, absent from their units; how many of these, though not proved to be dead, were then and are now unaccounted for; and how many have, and how many have not, been traced to civil life.

The Secretary of State for War, Mr Antony Head: 'On 31st December 1945, there were 17,317 men still unaccounted for who had deserted from the Army during the late war and 1,043 who had deserted since 31st August 1945. On 31st December 1951, the corresponding figures were 10,432 and 3,556. I will, with permission, circulate the figures for the remaining years in the OFFICIAL REPORT.'

Mr Hughes: 'Does the Minister agree that the fact that so many men for so many years have remained unaccounted for is contrary to good order, and cannot he devise some means whereby these men can return as good citizens?'

Mr Head: 'I have given this matter a good deal of consideration. The vast majority of the numbers referred to as deserters in the last war are either in Ireland or elsewhere overseas. The remainder have now settled down in civilian life, possibly under assumed names, and the fact that crime may be attributable to them is not borne out by the evidence available to me.'

Extract from Hansard
House of Commons – 23rd February 1953
Mr Winston Churchill – Woodford: 'Her Majesty's Government have decided that, in the circumstances referred to by the Hon. and gallant Member for Ayr and as a special measure which will not be regarded as a precedent for the future, there will be no further prosecutions of members of the Armed Forces who deserted from the Services between 3rd September 1939, and 15th August 1945.

'Men who wish to take advantage of the amnesty will be required to report themselves in writing to a Service authority. They will then receive a protection certificate and will be transferred to the appropriate Reserve to which men were transferred on demobilisation.

'Men who claim the benefit of the amnesty will not be prosecuted for certain offences consequential upon desertion, such as subsequent fraudulent enlistment, or the possession of identity documents in a false name, but the amnesty will not cover other offences against the criminal law.

'Full details will be announced in due course of the steps which men will be required to take and of the consequential measures which will be applied to men who have been convicted of desertion and are still serving, but any men who are awaiting trial or serving sentences for desertion during the 1939–45 war will be released from custody.'

Lieut-Colonel Sir Thomas Moore, Ayr: 'Does my right Hon. friend appreciate that though this generous decision will, I suppose, be welcomed with mixed feelings throughout the country, it will, at the same time, restore thousands of men once again to family and community life and thereby, perhaps, give them an opportunity to justify this clemency?'

It is estimated that by the time of the amnesty in 1953, the number of deserters still at large was between 5,000 – 13,000.

By March 25th 1953 only some 1,900 official applications for amnesty had been received.

Dear reader.

I really hope you've enjoyed reading 'Too Many Heroes.' Thank you so much for buying or borrowing it.

This book means a lot to me. If you would like to help more readers discover it, please think about leaving a review on Amazon, Goodreads, or anywhere else readers visit.

Any book's success depends a lot on how many positive reviews it gains. If you could spare a few minutes to write one, I would be very grateful. Many thanks in advance to anyone who does.

If you would like to find out more about this book, or are interested in discovering my other novels, the link to my Amazon page is:

https://www.amazon.com/author/janturkpetrie

Or go to my website: www.janturkpetrie.com

Contact Pintail Press at: www.pintailpress.com

ACKNOWLEDGEMENTS

I have to begin by thanking John Petrie, my wonderful husband, for reading and commenting in detail on the various drafts of 'Too Many Heroes' and also for sharing some of his knowledge of WW2 aeroplanes and many other technical matters. Without his encouragement this book might never have been finished.

Thanks also go to the rest of my family – in particular my lovely daughters Laila and Natalie – for their continued love and support. Special thanks also go to my delightful son-in-law, Ed, for his advice on some of the medical details. I shall always be grateful to my parents Pearl Turk and the late Sidney Turk for sharing their experiences of wartime as well as the immediate post-war period with us children.

As always, the feedback and encouragement from my fellow *Catchword* writers in Cirencester proved invaluable to this project. Early feedback from Lise Leroux and other members of the *Cheltenham Novel Writing Group* spurred me on as did the ladies of the highly talented *Wild Women Writers*. I'd also like to thank Debbie Young and everyone in the Alliance of Independent Authors (Alli) group in Cheltenham for their impressive knowledge and collective advice.

Lastly, I'm very grateful to my editor and proofreader Johnny Hudspith, and to my cover designer, Jane Dixon-Smith, for their consistently excellent work.

CPSIA information can be obtained
at www.ICGtesting.com
Printed in the USA
LVHW011634020220
645576LV00004B/849